*This special signed edition is
limited to 750 numbered copies.*

This is copy 244.

GLEN HIRSHBERG

The Janus Tree

and Other Stories

The Janus Tree
and Other Stories

Glen Hirshberg

Subterranean Press 2011

East Baton Rouge Parish Library
Baton Rouge, Louisiana

The Janus Tree and Other Stories
Copyright © 2011 by Glen Hirshberg. All rights reserved.

Dust jacket illustration Copyright © 2011 by Jonas Yip.
All rights reserved.

Interior design Copyright © 2011 by Desert Isle Design, LLC.
All rights reserved.

First Edition

ISBN
978-1-59606-408-9

Subterranean Press
PO Box 190106
Burton, MI 48519

www.subterraneanpress.com

*For Algy: hellraiser, wishmaster, dark
companion, nicest guy in horror.
No one I'd rather die (repeatedly) with.*

*And for Kate, Sid and Kim: bright lights,
rockhounds, storytellers, joy-makers.
No one I'd rather live with.*

Table of Contents

Part One
Longer Stories

The Janus Tree	11
I Am Coming To Live In Your Mouth	47
You Become the Neighborhood	69
The Pikesville Buffalo	91

Part Two
Tales from the Rolling Dark

Shomer	115
Miss Ill-Kept Runt	133
Millwell	147
Like Lick Em Sticks, Like Tina Fey	161
The Nimble Men	175

Part Three
Book Depository Stories

Esmerelda	189
After-Words	209

Part One
Longer Stories

The Janus Tree

> *"Go to it, boys and gals, fierce, fierce, up and down, swing your partner round an' round, to the beats of your heart, the drums of your hearts under your leathery skin. Go to it now while the night is still young…young… young…young."*
> —Myron Brinig, *Wide Open Town*

So much about your life depends on when you fight. And whom. I learned this growing up in Silver City, Montana, which someone proclaimed the richest ruined mountain on earth half a century ago, and where the ghosts are still waiting two generations later for the last, dazed living to leave so they can set up permanent shop in the abandoned mansions and collapsing mine shafts.

You do have a choice. You can take on the Company grinding you into debt, or the Chinese next door trying to lowball you out of your job. Take your stand against the Communists coming for your freedom, or the copper barons coming for your last unclaimed dime. You can fight for the town you hate, or the earth that dried up underneath you. For mining safety regulations, or the Apex Law that lets you follow a vein off your underground claim right into the tunnels of someone else's, and you can fight that one in court with lawyers or underground with dynamite and high-powered hoses. Up to you.

At the moment it happened, I really believed I was fighting Matt Janus for Robert Wysocki, whom I couldn't help anymore, and Mr. Valway, who may not have cared, and Jill Redround, who didn't love me. But I was doing it for myself. In a way, I guess I won.

What I remember is walking with Robert one night during the summer after sixth grade, all the way across Aluminum Street past the hunched, dark taverns with their decades-old, hand-lettered signs proclaiming NO MINERS still posted in the windows. Just in case Company employees from some other town with enough miners left to matter decided to come by on a road trip, we guessed. We walked under a ridiculous, blazing moon, down rows of tightly packed, boxy Company houses, their yards full of rusting bikes and truck parts and swingless swingsets, into a wind that pummeled our faces or horse-kicked us in the back, depending on whether we were coming or going. We were bouncing a red rubber ball we'd found somewhere. Robert had his black cloak billowing around his peach polo shirt and yellow shorts. And he had his backpack, of course.

"The Dark Lord appeared at my window at dawn," he said.

"Again?" I asked.

"He's never been at my window."

We cleared the houses, and the wind half lifted us off our feet, but we punched forward. To our right, the gouged mountains loomed black and treeless. The moonlight pooling in the biggest of the abandoned blast pits up there made it look more like an eye than a wound. To the east and below us, the plains stretched out, running free of the mountains. Robert took a cigarillo from his shorts pocket and pretended to snap an imaginary match to life on his thumb. He made puffing motions with his mouth, and the cigarillo popped out. Robert picked it off the pavement and plugged it back in his lips.

"Where'd you get that?" I asked.

"Elven Trading Post."

This meant the 7-11 the Welsh women owned on Magnesium Street, in Robert-speak. It also meant he'd been shoplifting again. At age eleven,

The Janus Tree

he'd already been caught three times. The last time, his parents had avoided reform school for him by agreeing to a weekly 110-mile trip to Missoula for a kid-shrink Robert called the Delphic.

We came to the place where the sidewalk gave out like a tapped ore vein and just kept walking, past the last houses to the rocky overlook over Snake Lake. Robert pointed down the slaggy hillside to the surface, which reflected the moon, alright, but in the hard, flat way tin roofs do.

"New ones," he said.

He was right. A whole family, it seemed. Every year, some hopeless set of ducks who'd somehow missed the memo alighted to fish and nest down there. Calling the place a lake was a local in-joke. Once, it had been the biggest open-pit mine in North America. Lately, it had started filling with a red-streaked, metallic liquid that almost *looked* like water. At least to the dumbest ducks. We usually found the ones that hadn't sunk bill-down on what passed for a beach, dead-necked, like unfolded paper boats.

Dropping to his knees, Robert scooped up a fistful of pebble-sized slag, whispered one of his spells over it, and pitched his first toss of the night toward the lake. One pebble actually dropped close enough to a dead duck to splash muck onto it. A rare occurrence, as most of Robert's throws never got near the water.

"One night," he said happily, "when the moon is full, and my aim is true…ducks will rise from the dead."

I threw some pebbles of my own, pegged one bird right on its flappy foot, and barely moved it. Then I bent down to scoop more rocks.

"What'd the Dark Lord want?"

"He summoned me to the Janus Tree."

Halting mid-throw, I turned and looked at Robert. He just stood there, toeing the backpack at his feet.

"Matt Janus came to your window?"

"He said to come tonight. At the stroke of twelve."

"Your parents will never let you out."

"My parents are offering libations."

It was the first I'd known that Robert's mother had started drinking again, too. "I'm coming," I told him.

"The Dark Lord said to come alone."

13

"Don't go, Robert. I mean it, don't go."

"Young Ted, don't be a jackanapes. It's Matt."

"He's…" But I stopped, having no idea what to say. I hadn't actually spoken to Matt Janus in close to a year. Not since his partyfreak Dad bolted for South America or somewhere, and Matt had stopped hanging around the basketball courts with me or climbing into the old quarries to have miniatures battles with Robert. I only saw him at school, where he mostly lurked by his locker or hunched over his desk in the black leather jacket his dad had given him as a going away present while his legs just kept sprouting underneath him, longer and longer. The way he always seemed to be leaning forward made him look like a praying mantis. "He's not the same kid," I finally mumbled.

"Nor am I," Robert said. Turning my way, he squared his shoulders and huffed out his practically concave chest at me.

I snorted. "Yeah, okay, Warlock."

"Sorcerer."

"I don't think you should go. I mean it. Didn't his dad just come home? I hear he's super-sick, and he never…" *Liked you*, I was going to say, and didn't.

Robert wasn't listening anyway. He stared up the butte overlooking Silver City, squinting at The Virgin of the Great Divide, all lit and glowing white in the moonlight. For the thousandth time, I wondered who had decided to build a giant statue of Mary up there, right as everyone who had the means was fleeing town. It was as though all those soon-to-be former inhabitants from all those faraway places, sharing virtually nothing except their devastating plunge into poverty, had built themselves a collective mom to wave goodbye to.

Eventually, Robert said, "I'll take the backpack."

Did Robert Wysocki really believe his backpack was magic? He never once let on either way, even to me, which is probably why kids liked him or left him alone. It also may be why I let him go. Robert just seemed to have this bubble around him. Aura, he might have called it. Or level three shield or something. Whatever it was, I think I believed in that.

Two evenings later—moon gone, thunderheads looming way out on the prairie but riding the wind clear of town—Robert and I biked

The Janus Tree

to a Silver City Copper Barons game at Anaconda Stadium, recently proclaimed the worst facility in minor league baseball by some magazine or other. We sat in the backless, splintering bleachers out past third base, several rows closer than we used to sit to the high school girls in their short skirts and pink lipstick, all of them whispering together and catching the eye of every uniformed player jogging back to the dugout.

In the fourth inning, Robert stood up, knocking my half-eaten hot dog out of my hands, lifted his backpack, unzipped it, and turned it upside down. A roll of cherry Chapstick and a single, black Darth Vader mini-figure spilled onto the cement at our feet. Before I could even react, Robert threw the backpack onto the field, where no one paid any attention to it, climbed over the three-foot wall separating the stands from the parking lot, made his way to the heap of slag beyond the left-field fence where little kids chase home run balls, and started climbing it. No one except me even looked at him until he started taking off his clothes. The cloak went last. Then he sat down stark naked on the rocks, put his face in his bone-white hands, and started weeping.

It took maybe ninety seconds for paramedics to show up and scoop him off there. The Wysocki family fled town that night for Missoula, then Seattle, and then they disappeared into Canada somewhere. I left the backpack where Robert had dropped it, which I've always regretted. And I never saw him again.

I didn't see Matt Janus either, or anyone else much for a while after that. That fall, in my first month of seventh grade, I started yelling at teachers in the middle of class for any reason I could think of or sometimes no reason. On my fourth or fifth trip to the Principal's office, I shoved her, and that was that.

My parents came to get me, but when I saw their car pull into the lot, I bolted off campus, through the neighborhoods, hopping fences, dodging broken bikes and yapping little black dogs I desperately wanted to kick and would have if I'd had time, and lost everybody on my weaving way back to Snake Lake. I think my plan was to dive in there, take a giant swallow, fill my mouth and lungs with metal. But the humped, furry dead thing splayed on the rocks nearby—could have been a crow, a baby coyote, or even a cat—stopped me. In the hard September sun, it looked gray-red, oxidized, more like a discarded mining tool than anything formerly living. Even at twelve, I understood that that's what all the residents of Silver City were, even with the Company long gone: discarded mining tools. I sat down in the slag and thought about Robert and kicked stones in the lake and stared up the mountains at the Virgin and then to the left, where the easternmost roofs of the Janus mansion could just be seen, tucked among the ledges, red and complicated, like an aerie. At some point, I broke down. After that, I just sat for more than twenty-four hours, until I was good and sick. Then I went back to my house.

My parents decided to home-school me, and somewhere in that first month I must have made some kind of decision, because I stopped battling them. All morning, I forced myself through the math and geology I hated (although I liked the bits about exactly what the Anaconda Company had done to my hometown). It was fun explaining to my parents exactly why we had to drink bottled water, and why our sheets came out of the laundry pocked with permanent orange spots that looked like bloodstains and terrified the two motels' occasional out-of-town guests, most of whom had only come to examine the business prospects in the malls my dad spent his working life developing.

Afternoons, I went to the library. There, for my English and history work, I started rooting through the dust-caked shelves full of decades-old books and periodicals. I taught myself to research. On the Friday of each week, I came home with a paper I'd written—annotated in proper footnote format—about fights my parents had never heard of despite living in Silver City all their lives, like the 1889 boxing match at a roadhouse outside the town limits, where some miner named Groeninger broke his left arm and hand in the 48th round against some carpenter named Broad and went on fighting until he knocked Broad out in the 105th. Broad died the next day, and Groeninger disappeared out of the newspapers, off the registry, completely out of history.

As surprised as my parents were by the way I hurled myself into my schoolwork, I think they were more surprised by the sheer number of kids I somehow surrounded myself with. This wasn't so much through any conscious plan as the discovery of the one thing Robert had missed, or didn't care to know: that just plain smiling, acting interested, and not expecting much can earn you a whole lot of friends.

The Janus Tree

So I came out of the library and rode skateboards (badly) down the banister-rails on the front steps and got chased out of the lot with the buzz-haired skateboys and girls. From one of the infamous picked-over junkshops in Uptown, stocked half a century ago with the belongings the mining families and their bosses could no longer afford to own or carry, I bought a set of congas. One drum-head was complete, though the other had a jagged rip down the center, like a mouth with teeth. I took my new congas to Kenny Tripton's house when he and his fledgling cowpunk band had their Thursday night rehearsals in the basement, and if I never exactly became a band member, they did get me a stool and a microphone after awhile, and I got to beat my one good conga and scream *"Hey F Off!"* when the choruses called for it, which they generally did. One of the conditions of rehearsing at the Tripton's was that we were only allowed to say "F." It became a band trademark.

I didn't join the junior high chess class at the library on Tuesday afternoons, but I lurked in the doorway, and there were seven class members, so they needed an eighth come game time, and eventually I became friends with most of those people, too. I snuck onto Anaconda Stadium field with the football team one sleety night and came home soaked and bloody-mouthed. In May, my parents applied to Mrs. Morbey, the Principal, for my reinstatement, and were welcomed enthusiastically.

"We've taken note of Teddy's progress," Mrs. Morbey bubbled as we squirmed in her cracked, green vinyl chairs across her desk from her. "It's a hard thing to lose a pal like that. We all understand."

Lose a pal. I wanted to jump on her desk. Kick the lamps over. But I didn't really want to shove her anymore. The truth was, Robert already felt like years ago. That weirdo with the backpack I'd hung around with in grade school. And anyway, as soon as that meeting was over, I was going walking with Jill Redround.

I honestly don't remember exactly how that started. At the Spring Powwow, probably. Watching Matt Janus, come to think of it. His dad and Mr. Redround, the local Blackfeet chief, had been business partners for years on casino and nightclub projects on the reservation and off, and Matt had known Jill since birth and also had the softest outside jumpshot in Butte, which is why he'd been the only white kid welcomed to play in the reservation games. Seeing him now, it was like his spine had just popped up on him like an expanding tent-pole. His blond, spiky head loomed too far over his absurdly elongated body, and his legs had stretched even taller and thinner. Also, weird muscles bulged out the sides of his shoulders, all knobby and asymmetrical, as though he'd stuffed his skin with slag. He'd always been pale enough to verge on albino, but now his cheeks had ugly, blotchy patches, and little pits, too, as though he'd been mined.

He dominated the basketball game. Not only could he still shoot from outside, but everyone just ducked out of his way as though fleeing a bear when he barged through the paint for rebounds. Twice, he caught Jill's eyes and waved. Once, near the end, he saw me, stopped in mid-dribble, and got called for traveling. Shrugging, he tossed the ball to the ref and retreated to the other end of the gravel court.

At some point, Jill wound up next to me. She had on some open-sleeved, beaded dress with fringes everywhere for the Powwow, I remember that, and she wasn't wearing shoes—she rarely did, except when forced—and her boundless black hair streamed over her strong shoulder blades and back.

"You're the only person everyone I know knows," she said. "Know that?"

I smiled—the smile I'd practiced all year long—and earned myself an answering grin. "You, too," I told her.

"And Matt, of course."

Glancing toward the court, I saw him sink a jumpshot, flash an unreadable look our way. Or maybe just our direction.

"And Matt," I agreed.

That night, at her invitation, I watched her dance the dance to Old Napi, and then we took our first boulder-scramble up the buttes. After that, we did it at least once a weekend and usually more for the rest of the summer.

I got my first shock on the morning I returned to regular school before I even left my house. "Listen, Teddy," my dad told me, over the warmed Grape Nuts he ate every morning, their smell rolling through our bright, window-jeweled, hardwood house like new soil imported from somewhere cleaner. "Mom and I put you in Valway's English class."

Tomato juice halfway to my mouth, I froze, staring at my father. Until that moment, I'd been thinking how different school was about to feel. Friends in every class. Basketball at recess without Robert darting onto the court to bless the ball. Boulder-scramble with Jill as soon as the bell rang, we'd arranged to meet by the Copper Miner fountain in the front hallway.

My dad had some blueprints half-unrolled at the table and was studying them self-consciously. This was his traditional method whenever he lost whatever straws he drew with my mother and so had to break news to me: casual, as though it were nothing.

"You know about him," I said slowly. "Right?"

"I know exactly as much as you do. Which is a few stories. Nothing."

"He keeps rat traps in his waste basket. Makes kids reach in there and get pens he's dropped on purpose. Just to see what happens."

"You ever actually see anyone with a broken finger?"

"He wears a gas mask."

"He has emphysema."

"Dad, he's supposed to be the worst teacher in Silver City, why would you do that?"

"He saw you researching at the library this summer, apparently. Went to Mrs. Morbey and begged her to let him have you. And we believe in second chances around here, don't we?" He gave me what passed, on my tanned, health-crazed father's permanently smiling face, as a severe look. "In case you failed to notice, Ted, he wrote half the articles and at least a few of the books in that Silver City history corner you spent most of last school year buried in."

Had I noticed that? I must have, but it had never occurred to me that I'd one day have to deal with him personally. I'd never actually met him, barely even seen him. He'd written *Bloody Fisted Dublin Gulch*, come to think of it; my favorite. And the one about the prostitutes the copper barons used to send to single mining men some Saturday nights, when the employees hadn't been spending enough at the Company stores or their wives were starting to get active about new labor laws or something. I'd kept that article to myself, never written about it for my parents.

"Okay," I murmured.

"Just an experiment. You don't like it, you're out of there, that's the deal we made with Mrs. Morbey. No questions, no delay. "

The second shock came ten minutes later, as I was strapping on the bike helmet I would shed as soon as I got out of sight of our front door.

"Don't make plans for Saturday," my father said. "Matt Janus Senior has invited all of us to some giant game-barbecue up at his place."

This time, I actually fumbled the bike helmet and dropped it. It landed hard-side down. Staring into it was like looking into the hollowed out rind of a melon, or a skull. I thought of Robert naked and howling on the slag heap, and I missed him, hard, for the first time in months. Last I'd heard, Matt Janus' father was all but dead.

"Not that you'd be able to make plans." My father's voice was jokey, chipper. "Sounds like everyone you've ever met, and me, too, for that matter, is going to be there. Invitation was weird, for Janus Senior, anyway. No booze bottles, no half-naked women. Just this gold-embossed card with balloons and a pick-shovel on it, I'll show it to you. *WELCOME BACK MATT PARTY. COME CELEBRATE MY RESURRECTION.* That's what it said. Odd duck, Mr. Janus. Should be something."

The third and final shock came as I stood in a tightly packed row of fellow eighth-graders before the skinny standing lockers we'd just been assigned. The lockers were dull green, the combination locks clunky and rusted. Every now and then, there'd be a snick and a laugh as another student got his lock popped open, hopped into his locker and hopped out, just to prove you really could fit a whole kid inside. Every now and then came a clang as someone banged the metal door with his head or a backpack in gleeful frustration. We'd been waiting years for this moment, after all. The lockers in the back hallway with the windows facing directly onto the hill that had once been the black, beating heart of Silver City were the great prizes Lower Magnesium Middle School had to offer for getting to the final year before high school. Our rewards.

I'd finally found the sweet spot on my own lock, clicked it open, and swung my door wide when it slammed shut almost right on my elbow. I fell back, startled, and stared up at Matt Janus breaking into his own locker with a single twist-and-yank. Opened all the way, his door completely blocked access to my locker.

But I'd learned about people, that year I'd been gone. I truly believed I had. I stepped forward, left his door where it was, and waited for him to dump the entire contents of his blue backpack into his locker. The

The Janus Tree

backpack sat ridiculously high on his immense shoulders because the straps were way too small. It looked like a beetle climbing the scaly trunk of an oak.

"Hey, Matt," I said. "Long time."

His whole torso swayed to the left, as though a wind had blown through him. Then he turned on me. His pupils looked weirdly wide in his eyes, which were shot through with red. That blotchiness I had noticed this summer was all over his forehead now, creeping down his neck into the tight collar of his black shirt like moss.

"Don't talk to me," he said, kicked his door shut, and left.

That afternoon, I followed the instructions on my schedule card all the way back past the green lockers, down a staircase I hadn't known was there, along a windowless, tiled corridor that reeked of chlorine and reminded me of the bottom of an emptied pool, and arrived for the first time at Mr. Valway's room. The door was green, thick, and closed. I was about to knock when it flew open, and a startlingly tan girl I'd never seen before stuck her poodle-nose right in mine and said, "Boo."

The girl's grin was too wide, her plaid skirt disconcertingly short, her curly brown hair bouncing around her ears as though she were hopping on a trampoline instead of standing in front of me. She didn't move back far enough as I slid into the room, and my chest grazed her elbow and then the tip of one of her breasts. My first feel.

"Whitney," she said, and did a drum roll on her thighs, her hands hitting half skirt, half skin. "Drum. New here."

I'd noticed her eyes by then. Very brown, pretty enough. Also very red around the irises. Stoned enough. I gave her my practiced people-smile, anyway. "Teddy. Ted."

"Teddy-ted?"

I blushed, started to protest, saw Jill Redround grinning at the back table, and hurried toward her.

"Hi, Teddy-ted," Jill said.

"Shut up." I dropped my books. The sound echoed off the bare cement walls.

"Teddy and Reddy," said Jill, gesturing to herself, then glancing around, pulling her black hair back into a pony tail and shivering a little. "Ready, Teddy? Not sure I am."

21

Sitting, I took in the room. Once, clearly, it had been a science lab. Instead of desks, we sat at long, black tables, each of which had a chemical sink with one of those pointy nozzles on the faucets. The school had newer science labs now, thanks to a grant from the Janus family. Judging by the rust on the pointy nozzles and the rotting, rubber hoses dangling from a few of them like dried skin from some unimaginable mine-reptile, this particular lab was probably from two grants ago.

"Surprised to see you here," I murmured to Jill as Whitney Drum flung open the door to greet two ghost-pale, glassy-eyed blond girls I'd never seen before. "Your dad can place you pretty much anywhere, right?"

"Matt Janus got dumped here. His dad asked my dad if I'd keep him company."

"Mr. Janus—" I started, and Matt strode into the room. He caught sight of Jill, then me.

Something flittered over his lips. Possibly a smile. Jill started to wave him toward the stool on the other side of her and stopped when Whitney said, "Ooh, my favorite boy at LMMS." I think Jill realized at the same moment I did where Whitney must have scored her weed. Matt followed her toward the row in front of ours, and sat down fast in her stool when she started to settle, so that she wound up on his lap. I found my eyes flicking toward the hem of her skirt against his hip. She wriggled once against him before slapping his jeans and sliding off.

In the front of the room, where the fluorescents had either burned out or been turned off, something stirred. Finally, as a group, the nine of us in Mr. Valway's last English class turned toward his desk.

The whole of it was occupied by one of those gigantic blue jugs of water that usually sit upside down in dispensers. This one rested on its rounded bottom, top open to the stale air. When Mr. Valway, grunting through his green oxygen mask, somehow shoved the thing sideways far enough to lean around the side of it and face us, the water in the jug sloshed, and some of it flew out the top and slapped across Mr. Valway's cheeks and onto the desktop. Even Whitney Drum stopped talking.

Most of Mr. Valway's face was green mask and dirt-gray eyebrow. With the wetness dripping down it, it looked like cave-wall. To speak, he lifted only the bottom of the mask, so that I never got a good look at his nose or mouth. We sat for what seemed minutes and listened to him wheeze. What we could see of his body looked lumpy, immense.

Then he grunted again. *Was that a laugh?* "Well," he said, his voice surprisingly strong, not exactly friendly but clearer than expected. "We still supply the water. Course…no bathroom within a hundred yards. So you bring your own bottles to piss in." More grunting, after that. A lot of it.

Very slowly, over the next forty-five minutes, Mr. Valway explained procedure. No lessons; those involved too much useless talking. We'd read what he told us to read. We'd write papers on topics he and we agreed upon. When the papers were finished, we'd bring them individually to his desk. He'd tell us what he thought. We'd do what he instructed. If we tried hard, we'd learn more about writing than any other students in Silver City. If we didn't, we wouldn't. If we bothered him, he'd invite us to go fishing in his trash can. Questions?

There were none. We still had ten minutes left of class. Two minutes before the bell, when I think every one of us had figured out that Mr. Valway really had closed his eyes and that his breathing through the mask had gone even and slow, Matt Janus climbed carefully onto a table and knelt next to one of the sinks.

Mr. Valway didn't move. So Matt took the rotten rubber hose hanging from the nozzle next to him and pointed it at the teacher's desk and made a soft, shooting sound. Mr. Valway didn't move. So Matt stood all the way up, his spiky blond head brushing the ceiling. He offered Whitney Drum a hand, and she hopped up beside him, laughing. I watched Jill's frowning face, and every now and then glanced toward the roundness at the top of Whitney's tanned, swaying legs. The bell rang, and we all fled.

It was already getting dark by the time Jill and I made it to the foot of the butte, and we only climbed half an hour or so before turning back. I realized we'd be doing this more rarely, now. If ever. Jill had tribal duties on weekends, and basketball, and a thousand friends, and I had a thousand friends, too, these days. And both of us worked hard. And within a month it would be winter.

She was turning up the hill toward her father's when I asked if she wanted to grab a snack at the Elven Trading Post.

"The where?"

Grinning, I said, "7-11. Sorry."

"Can't. Promised Matt I'd help him get started with bio. He's really bad at bio."

"Matt," I mumbled.

I don't know what she saw in my face, but she snapped at me for the first time in our lives. "That a problem for you? He's probably my oldest friend."

"He's..." I was waving my hands. Of all the people I now knew, Jill was the last I wanted mad at me. "He used to be my friend, too."

We didn't say anything for a few minutes. But she didn't leave. Eventually, she said, "He's really mixed up, Teddy. He really needs me."

With that, she went to him.

That Saturday, along with half the town, I got my first look at what was left of Matt Janus' father. In the morning, as though to remind anyone who'd somehow forgotten that we lived in Montana, a freak storm blew over the top of the buttes and dumped six inches of snow. By noon, the temperature had soared back up to fifty-five, and the new gray drifts came sliding off the rocks and rooftops. My family arrived spot on time, but well after most of the other guests. As we got out, my father told my mother, "Apparently, he caught whatever it is that's made him so sick while he was in Chile. Guess he finally found a party even *he* couldn't handle."

After that, my parents grabbed crystal champagne-flutes off one of the dozens of circulating trays and disappeared amongst the grown-ups, and I floated into the terraced yards. The Janus estate was laid out like a layer cake, with descending sculpted meadows interspersed with layers of wrecked, red rock that looked almost earthy, close to beautiful with the snow melting on it and the sun shooting everywhere and the giant stone house with its red roofs looming overhead. Armies of serving girls circled among us, passing out skewers of barbecued white meat that tasted peppery and wild. I couldn't get enough of it. Neither could anyone else.

I spent part of the time among some skateboys trying to negotiate the drainage ditch that dove from the easternmost corner of the house down the terraces of rock and lawn to empty against a cyclone fence, but I didn't skate. I was looking for Jill, but spotted only Chief Redround, in jeans and a black Grateful Dead sweatshirt, holding court with some business people in shirtsleeves and ties, one of whom I recognized vaguely as the mayor.

Finally, a good couple hours after we'd come, I spotted Jill and Matt way up the hillside above the house, sitting together in the mouth of the old mining shaft, right at the foot of the Janus Tree. I felt the expected stab of jealousy and then—unexpectedly—a little gush of nostalgia. In third grade, Matt and Robert and I had had our greatest-ever miniatures battle right there. It had ended with Matt's evil dwarves trying to storm their way out of the mine behind a balrog, and Robert and I bringing the balrog down with arrows made of pine sticks. For dramatic effect, Matt had spun when his balrog got hit, swept up the little metallic monster, and tossed him over the sheer edge of the cliff behind him, where it tumbled from our lives in absolute silence.

Either Jill and Matt had been watching me, or they'd sensed me watching them, because Jill stuck up her hand and beckoned. I started to obey, and Matt lifted his hand, too. *To stop me, or invite me?* I couldn't tell. Didn't care. I was passing the patio and the murmuring adults clustered among the scatter of lounge chairs there when I stopped. Slowly, my head swung around.

I did recognize him. By his teeth. Despite whatever had happened, his smile still radiated a blinding whiteness that no snow in Silver City ever did. His skin—what there was of it—hung more tan and taut then ever on his cheeks. But where once Matt Janus Senior had looked round-cheeked, wide-eyed, and relentlessly cheerful—the self-proclaimed "party-pumpkin" of western Montana—he now looked like a Tinkertoy with hide barely stretched across it. Bones poked every which way from him, instead of the startling muscles I remembered. His massive chest had deflated completely. He had no hair on his head. No brows. Nothing.

All the murmuring, I realized, had been coming from him; no one else was talking at all. He went right on murmuring as his eyes alighted on mine. "That's the great myth," he was saying. "The story everybody likes to tell. The Incas, well, they just…" he snapped his fingers, the bones clacking together like drumsticks. "Vanished. You're telling me we can find full skeletons of 350 million year-old trilobites—probably right here on this hillside—but we can't locate a single dead Indian in the ruins of his own village? You know that's what they call the town where

Anaconda relocated down there, don't you? Indio Muerto." This last he said slowly, rounding his lips around the *o's* as though blowing a smoke ring. "Dead Indian."

Abruptly, he blinked, and recognition flared in his face. "Hey, now. Young Ted. Long time. You ever hear from that poor boy? That Robert?" Then his head jerked up the hill, and he saw Jill and Matt. The white teeth flashed. I hadn't liked his smile even when there'd been flesh attached to it. "*Matt,*" he called, and a hundred feet above, his son twitched, looked at Jill, and stood. Around Matt Senior, the adults huddled closer, some of them starting to talk amongst themselves, most just glancing about like squirrels storing gossip-nuggets for later.

Matt arrived at his father's side, towering over him. His ever-present leather jacket hung open, revealing a black button-down shirt with polished buttons. "That beautiful native's monopolizing a bit too much of your time," Mr. Janus told him. "You've got fun to spread. To all your guests."

That's when I understood where Matt got the weed he was selling all over school. It shouldn't have surprised me. Mr. Janus had given Robert, Matt and me big bottles of Moose Drool beer in the basement when we were nine.

Jill stayed by the tree, and she didn't come down for a long time. I slid to the side of the house and watched her.

That tree. Long before, when I'd been a regular guest at the Janus house, I'd asked my father about it, and he said it was an alligator juniper. So I looked that up, but the book in the library said it couldn't grow where we lived. Whatever it was, it stuck almost sideways out of the rock, a stumpy pine with a scaly, black trunk that looked like an arrow buried in the side of the mountain. The only tree on that entire butte. On the uphill side of it, the branches had curled in on each other, gnarled together, and died. But on the downhill side, the same branches sprouted clusters of brilliant, green leaves whose shadows slid over the rock and Jill's crossed arms and bare feet.

When she finally came down, I moved toward her, but her father steered her away to say hello to the town dignitaries. Eventually, Matt Senior drew her down beside him in his lounge chair. He made her take sips of champagne from his own glass, and slid one skeletal arm around her shoulders to caress her skin where it poured out of her dress and play with her hair while her father stood over them, laughing. For one moment, glancing up, I caught Matt Junior's eyes across the patio. The fact that I probably wore the same expression he did unnerved me badly.

That night, over chicken that seemed utterly tasteless and flaccid compared to the meat at the Janus house, I asked why Mr. Janus had gone to South America in the first place. My mother just shrugged.

"It happens to people when they don't have to work and their wives die," she said, as if she had all kinds of acquaintances in similar situations. "I think he wanted to see who his grandparents and parents raped to make all their money. So he traveled halfway down the world to find another ruined mountain and more big, poison holes in the ground."

"Then there was that whole Ponce de Leon thing, that was funky," my dad said, pushing away his chicken barely eaten.

"Ponce de Leon went to Chile?" I asked. "I thought he was in Florida or somewhere."

My mother shook her head. "The things some people will try, just to avoid growing up."

"He seemed a little…" My father paused, considering. "Wiser, maybe? More resigned? Something."

My mother stretched her lips into a smile that looked exactly like Mr. Janus'. "*You have to get old,*" she hissed, imitating his new, shredded voice a little too perfectly. "*Everyone has to get old.*"

"Christ, you're a little too good at that," my father said. "Funky guy."

"He was funky when he was just a cokehead," I said.

"That's not nice," my mother snapped.

"'Went to see who his parents…*raped?*' Was that the nice word your mother used, Ted?"

Even my mother laughed.

I thought about Jill and Matt up the hill, under the juniper shadows in the mouth of the balrog cave, then of Matt Senior's shrinking body. "So he's better now?" I asked. "Mr. Janus, I mean?"

Now my mother sounded tired. Sad and tired. "He's dying," she said. "Couldn't you tell?"

The weather got cold, and school days dropped into their school-day rhythm. Most often, I got to my locker long before Matt, and didn't see him until Valway's class at the end of the afternoon. But every time he did arrive at his locker while I was still at mine, he threw open his door right in my face, dumped his books, and stood a few extra seconds as though daring me to say something. Then he slammed his locker and sauntered off. He never so much as glanced at me, and we never spoke.

School really had gotten better, though. Without Robert to take care of, and with the range of friends I'd made, I had people to laugh with in every class, and every class was easy. I ate lunch at a different table each day, and was welcomed at all of them. The person I most wanted to eat with was Jill, but as Student Council President, she ran meetings every day but Friday, when she mostly stayed in the library and did work.

The first kid Matt Janus brutalized was a hulking, stupid linebacker who strolled up to him on the athletic fields at the end of P.E. one day as all of us shivered in our shorts and the nearly-winter wind roared down off the rocks. He said, "Think you're tough, Mr. All-in-Black Fagboy?" The linebacker wound up in the emergency room with three broken ribs and a shattered jaw, and Matt got suspended for a week.

The second kid might have been an accident. It happened in the middle of a lunch-break basketball game. The kid had been pouring in jump shots, but Matt's team was still winning, and as far as I knew, the kid—little seventh grader, big glasses, elephant ears that seemed to flap when the wind caught them—had never even spoken to Matt. But he pump-faked the shit out of his defender late in the game, drove the lane, and went hard to the hoop. Matt's elbow caught him under the adam's apple and seemed to drive it all the way up into the back of his mouth. The kid hurtled into the basket pole and collapsed, face smashed, mouth gulping as though trying to work the adam's apple back down so he could swallow some air.

Matt was the first one on his knees at the kid's side, and he was kind of crying as the paramedics carried the kid off. No one claimed it had been anything but unintentional. But no one played basketball with Matt anymore, or anything else, either. He ate alone, and then he went out to the court, rain or snow or whatever, and stood underneath the rim in his open leather jacket, tossing a ball up and through, up and through, until someone came to buy from him. Then he'd go back to shooting baskets by himself until the bell rang and the rest of us went inside.

In Valway's class, I sat in the hissing, echoing half-light and worked alternately on papers for Valway and notes for Jill. The notes I passed had jokes in them, and funny things I'd heard other kids say, and random Butte facts I pulled off my library notecards from the year before, and invitations to go walking. Jill smiled occasionally at the jokes, topped my amusing quotations with better ones from the girls she knew, parried my Montana facts with Blackfeet lore (her personal medicine, she revealed, was an eagle-bone whistle that she carried around her neck in a beaded pouch), and rejected every one of my invitations by writing "*Can't*," then drawing a frowny-face next to the word. Occasionally, passing the paper back, she'd brush or even squeeze my hand.

While Matt snoozed at his desk or thumb-wrestled with Whitney, and the other kids did the rest of their homework or threw spitwads at each other, Jill and I raced one another to finish papers. In late October, I got into a long one about the lynching of Wobblies on the railroad bridge out the east end of town. When I finally finished a draft and took it to Mr. Valway's desk, he twitched in his chair as though I'd woken him—which I very well might have—and half turned his bulbous, veiny face toward me so that I could see the perpetual dampness reflecting the fluorescent light. Without lifting his oxygen mask, and with no audible shift in his slow, measured breathing, he started reading.

With every previous paper I'd shown him, he'd reached the end, spat out three or four concise, disinterested suggestions, and told me to try again. But this time, a couple paragraphs in, he abruptly tilted forward in his chair. His breathing didn't alter, but he looked up after a bit, and then he lifted his mask. Horrible, stupid thoughts flashed across my brain—I think I actually believed he might shoot out a tongue and lick me—and then he said, "Get me a pen."

From the flick of his hand, I thought he meant in the trash can, glanced toward it, and shuddered slightly. The thing was just a metal canister, but it had an oversized green bag stuffed in it, so that there was no way to see what your hand might be reaching for. But he thumped the desktop with his fist, and I realized he meant the drawer. I opened it and gave him a fine-tipped black marker.

For the next half an hour, he bent over my paper, scratching relentlessly at it with the pen. By the time he'd finished, the bell had rung, and everyone but Jill had gone. Eventually, he dropped the marker to the desktop, shoved the paper across at me, lifted the mask one more time, and said, "Well, now."

In the hallway outside, I thanked Jill for waiting for me, and she poked me in the ribs with her finger, kicked her tennis shoes off because no one cared after the last bell, and gave me the brightest smile I'd had from her in ages. "The score after two months," she said. "Teddy: one '*well now.*' Redround, nothing. The crowd goes wild." I asked her to go walking, she said, "Let's go to the Elven Trading Post," and once there, she bought us a bag of Funyuns and we stood in the doorway while yet another late-fall thundercloud crawled over the Virgin of the Great Divide.

On the Wednesday before Thanksgiving, my mom stopped me on my way out the door and told me I should seek out Matt and check on him. When I told her I never spoke to Matt anymore, she shrugged and said, "His father's gotten worse. He's about to die."

Walking through a slanting, stinging rain, I thought maybe I *would* check on Matt. I passed the corner where I used to meet Robert, and I thought of his cloak and backpack, and Matt's leather jacket and scowl. Not so much difference, really.

But he wasn't at his locker when I got there, and he wasn't on the basketball court at lunch, and he wasn't in Valway's room when the bell rang. Almost no one was in Valway's room that day. Jill's family had gone north to Alberta to see cousins, and three of the other six students had been rescheduled by furious parents into other classes, leaving only the blond girls, Whitney Drum, Valway, and me.

Valway looked particularly ghastly, leaning sideways in his chair with his head tipped so far back it seemed halfway chopped off, eyes closed, green mask clamped to his face like a feeding spider. Every few seconds, the mask seemed to lift slightly, and it hissed.

For the first fifteen minutes, I forced my way through some of Valway's latest suggestions on my Wobblies paper, which had ballooned to more than twenty pages. But with Jill gone and the whole school sagging toward the holiday, what little work energy I had bled away. The only consistent movement in the room came from the blondes, who kept passing

The Janus Tree

tired notes back and forth. Whitney Drum had her head down on the table, her arms—still miraculously tan, darker even than Jill's—stretched out straight, once-bouncy curls flat against her scalp. Her white sweater was too short, unraveling some, and I watched strands from the hem of it trailing down the small of her bare back where it curved into her jeans.

The first bombardment of fists-on-door shook us like bombs dropping, and set the blondes crumpling notes and scurrying off their seats. Whitney dragged her head up, turning more toward me than the door, and I saw the redness in her irises and knew Matt Janus must have been at school that day after all. Valway never even stirred.

Another flurry, longer, louder. We all knew who it was. By now, Whitney was grinning, the other girls gawping, and even Valway opened his eyes, squinting under that massive brow. Then he lifted his mask. As always, the clarity and off-hand *loudness* he could still generate startled me. "You. Ted. Better let him in. Or else I'm going to castrate him."

Whitney giggled. I got up and let Matt in. I started to say something to him, "Hello" or "Sorry about your dad," but before I'd formed a single word he was past me, sliding into place next to Whitney and dropping his huge white hand on her thigh and leaving it there.

The room reasserted itself. Valway went back to sleep. The blondes crept back to their stools and, after a few seconds of staring—along with me—at Matt's hand high on Whitney's leg, returned to note-writing. I tapped my paper with my pencil and tried revising a little more. And Whitney, after a few seconds, snuggled in against Matt and put her head down on his leather-jacketed arm.

We all stayed like that a while. Every sixty seconds, the clock on the wall lurched another drunken step toward 3:30.

I didn't see it happen. I think I might have been asleep. For a few indefinite moments—the thought disturbs me even now, for reasons I will never be able to explain—Matt Janus may have been the only person awake in that room. Then the reek flooded my nostrils, and I jerked my head up to find Whitney bolt upright in her chair, eyes hurtling back and forth between Valway slumped at his desk and Matt with the bong lit and bubbling in his cupped palms.

"Sssh," he said—to all of us, maybe—and grinned. The thing looked grimy, hideous, very possibly assembled out of a stolen chemistry beaker and some rotten rubber tubing from this room. Sucking in a huge drag, Matt held the smoke in his teeth, then blew it in a rush toward Valway's desk. The girls in the corner had gone completely still. Matt glanced that way, held up the bong, and offered it to them. They swept their notepads into their backpacks in a single collective rush and fled the room.

Shrugging, Matt lifted the bong toward Whitney, and she took it and Matt's long, white finger into her mouth at the same time. He stiffened in his chair. She was laughing so hard she could barely get the smoke to her lips.

Almost as an afterthought, Matt turned to me. His eyes had no redness in them, were almost frighteningly clear, and I saw, or for just one second thought I saw...

Both of us looked away at the same moment, Matt toward the floor, me toward Jill's seat. Eventually, Matt noticed the direction of my gaze and snorted.

"What?" he said, waving the tube of the bong. "You think she never has?"

More because of the way he said that than anything else—casual, right on the edge of cruel—I passed on his offer with a wave of my hand. Whitney snatched the tube from him and took another hit. The clock lurched, the bell rang, we all stood, and Valway opened his eyes.

"Mr. Janus," he said quietly. "I seem to have dropped my tie-clip in my trash can. Could you come get it for me?"

Whitney and I had frozen the second Valway started speaking. Now we just stood, transfixed, as Matt lifted the bong away from Whitney, dragged on it while staring right back at Mr. Valway, and then moved slowly around the table toward the front of the room.

"What is it you dropped?" he said. "Old man." His legs, I noticed, no longer looked stick-thin. The muscles that had bulged out of proportion on his arms early in the year had spread through his body now. From the back, he looked twice his age, powerful as hell.

"Tie clip," Valway told him. "Little metal heart."

Matt never took his eyes off him. Bending at the waist, he placed the bong gently on the corner of Valway's desk, as though it were an apple he was offering, then slid his hand into the green folds of the trash bag, which folded around it like an anemone's mouth. Whitney and I

The Janus Tree

strained forward, watching Matt's hand disappear up to the wrist, past it. Valway leaned back again, closed his eyes. There was a soft *smack*.

Matt's legs straightened, and then he held still for a long moment. Finally, he stood. Clamped on his middle and ring fingers was a small, rubber-guarded mouse trap attached to a blocky wooden base. With the rubber sheathing on its jaws, the snap of that trap probably wouldn't have killed a housefly, let alone hurt Matt. In slow motion, almost thoughtfully, Matt pried the trap off his fingers and dropped it in Valway's lap. Valway barely glanced at him. Matt was grinning as we left the room.

Mr. Janus' funeral was held that Sunday. The rain had stirred the dredged earth and set it sliding in filthy glaciers down the hillsides. Caked, coppery clods checkered the lawn of the First Saints Cemetery, where the preceding generation of Januses, Clarks, Heinzes, and other copper lords had been returned to the ground they'd ravaged. Jill's father gave the eulogy. At the end, he held up a fringed hide bag filled, he said, with "magic dust. Good medicine." They buried the bag with Mr. Janus. On the way home, my parents had a big fight trying to decide whether he'd been joking. Neither of them had any doubt what the bag contained.

Jill came back on Tuesday, but she barely spoke to me. On Wednesday, I wrote her a note asking what was up, and she scowled at Matt's back and then gave it the finger. But when I started to laugh, she gave me the finger, too, and moved several stools away to the next table. On my way out of the schoolyard that afternoon, I saw Matt Janus pass an elementary school kid and shove him down in the mud, then rip off the kid's shoes and hurl them forty feet onto the puddle-soaked grass.

The Monday before winter vacation, I lurked at the top of the stairs leading down to Valway's room until Jill came, then stopped her. She had her black hair tied in a tight braid and tucked into her heavy gray sweater, and her eyes looked so empty that I found myself thinking about Matt on the day of the bong. *You think she never has?*

"Let's go walking," I told her.

I half-expected her to ignore me completely, slip right past into the classroom and to her new seat a table removed from all of us. Then she sighed. "It's going to snow."

"So we'll get wet."

"I was thinking more about rocks being slippery."

"So we'll fall down."

Abruptly, she smiled. Tight-lipped, fleeting, but a smile all the same. "Soon, okay? Please?"

As in, please, let's go walking? Please leave it alone? I left it alone. But when I followed her downstairs and inside the classroom a minute or so later, I found her papers piled at her old seat next to mine, and Jill back on her accustomed stool. Five minutes into the period, she passed me a note. It had a gallows with a noose drawn on it, and a row of twelve dashes underneath. Immediately, I wrote 'S' and passed the paper back, and she sketched a head into the noose. No S. I tried other letters, began filling in the word. I'd just figured it out, gotten to $m\ o\ t\ \_\ e\ \_ f\ \_ \_ k\ e\ \_$, and Jill had a neck and trunk and one arm on the stick figure she meant to hang before I got the other blanks, when the classroom door swung open. Glancing over, we were astonished to see Mrs. Morbey, in pink business suit, framed in the grim light creeping down that hall from the stairwell.

My gaze slipped toward Matt, who tapped his closed notebook and played with Whitney's fingers, and then toward Valway, who made no move to straighten in his chair but did open his eyes.

"Albert, could I see you outside a minute?" Mrs. Morbey said.

Obviously, we knew Valway could move. He got to the classroom every day, didn't he? Nevertheless, the sight stunned us, the way he just hopped to his feet and shambled around the desk, tugging the green oxygen tank on its wheels as though pulling grandkids in a wagon. Passing our tables, he caught Matt's eye—or maybe mine—and winked. We watched his huge gut sway under his yellow-check leisure suit jacket as he left the room.

Had Matt been planning for such a moment? Was it impulse? I've always wondered. Never known.

All at once, he was on his feet and hoisting Whitney Drum by her hips onto the table in front of him. She giggled in her stoned, happy way, swatted his shoulders, and then kicked her legs around him. Her knee-length, plaid skirt had slid all the way up her thighs when Matt spun her to face him. Now he kissed her so hard her head snapped back, and I swear the crack of their teeth colliding rattled the legs of my stool.

The Janus Tree

I had my mouth open, and one of the girls in the corner started laughing—in sheer panic, I think—and then came a ripping sound, and a shred of Whitney's heart-dotted panties appeared in Matt Janus' fist as he dropped it behind him. On Jill's backpack.

Most of the rest of the time, I watched Jill. But she never took her eyes off what was happening in front of her: Matt's pants dropping to his knees; Whitney's navy-blue Espadrilles curled around his waist. She'd stopped laughing now. I could hear Jill's breathing, hard and hitched between her clenched teeth, could see her shoulders stiffen with each thrust of Matt's body. Whitney gave a single, strangled gurgle, then started crying. When I let myself look at her, I found her eyes locked on Jill's.

When he'd finished, Matt pulled his pants up, picked another ripped shred of Whitney's panties off the table, and mopped some of the blood off her legs. Then he kissed her cheek, eased her gently down onto her stool, and held tight to her hand. Valway never came back, and when the bell rang, Whitney shook free of Matt's grip and fled. Jill raced after her, and I ducked out fast and slipped through a back door of the school building and walked all the way to Snake Lake with no books except my English notebook and no jacket—everything else was in my locker—and sat where I had when I'd broken down eighteen months before. Just as before, I stayed there rocking on my heels and ducking my face against the cat-o'-nine-tail whips of the barbed winter wind.

That night, I tried calling the Redround house for the first time in my life. Why had I never done so before? I'd just had this sense that I wouldn't be welcome. And Jill had never asked me to. When the Chief himself answered, I almost hung up. But in my ears, I heard the hard hitch in Jill's breathing as she'd watched Matt and Whitney—*what Matt had done to Whitney?*—and also her voice.

Soon. Please?

"Chief Redround, this is Jill's friend Ted. From—"

"Gone to Albuquerque," he said. I recognized the slur instantly, from years of incoherent phone conversations with Robert's parents.

Gone. "When…do you know when she'll be back?"

"Mother says never," Chief Redround said.

"Will you tell her…" But I let the sentence trail off and hung up and went to my room and locked the door.

Fifteen minutes before the bell for winter break—Whitney had not returned to school either, and it was only the blond girls, Matt Janus, and me in the classroom—Matt stood up and took a single sheet of paper to Valway's desk. Even Valway opened his eyes and sat forward in his chair. Unless I'd missed it, this was the first time the entire semester that Matt had given Valway anything to read.

Valway glanced at the paper, breathed through his mask. He handed the paper back without looking up. "Go back to your desk," he said, at half his usual volume. "Matter of fact, Matt, get out of my room."

Sometime that afternoon, in the hours between the moment the school emptied for vacation and the moment the janitors finally made it downstairs to that hidden hallway for the year's final mopping of the floors, Mr. Valway died at his desk.

The Tuesday after New Year's dawned freezing, snowless and gray. I sat in the silence I'd cocooned myself in the entire vacation, poking a bowl of Kix with my spoon, watching the pebble-sized bits bump against each other and thinking of the slag outside, the empty streets of Uptown with the wind walking where once Welsh miners and local senators and German-born copper kings and Chinese dancing girls and whole armies of mixed-blood kids had whirled from bar to keno parlor to restaurant to dance hall, shouting and shopping and kissing and fighting. Once, wandering around there—Robert liked to sneak up the hill, even though his parents forbade it; he treated the whole place like one giant Dungeons and Dragons set—we'd followed this faint ringing sound all the way through the maze of streets before finding ourselves at the foot of a flagpole. We'd found no flag, just the rope, which was pinging against the pole and making the sound. On the way back, we'd passed a homeless woman staggering from one sidewalk to the other, muttering, "Somebody slapped me. Somebody slapped me."

Those were the thoughts I was having when my mother brought me the phone. As she held it out, she touched my hair gently. They hadn't asked, even once, where all my new friends had gone during this vacation. For that, I was profoundly grateful.

The Janus Tree

"Hello?" I said.

"My dad said you called," said Jill, and I dropped the spoon and glanced up at my mother. The hopefulness in her answering smile almost set me crying.

"Jill? It's great to hear your voice, where are you?"

"Home."

"Here?"

"Here, yeah, home, what'd I just say?"

I stood, spun from my mother toward the hall for my winter boots and heavy jacket. "Let's go walking. Right after school, I'll meet you by the Copper Miner fountain. We'll get good and frost-bitten."

"Tomorrow, okay?" Her voice, suddenly, was the one she'd used when I'd seen her last. And her breathing had that hitch again. "I think I'm coming back tomorrow."

"You heard about Valway, right? What English class did they put you in?"

Silence, except for her clipped, hiccoughing breath. Then, "Hey. Teddy?"

I waited, listening to her breath, holding my own.

"Thanks for calling," she said, and hung up.

Walking to school, I replayed the whole conversation in my head, sifting it. The day had proved strangely windless for Silver City, and lead-colored clouds hung over everything, smothering the mountains and suffocating the whole town. I was running late, saw almost no cars or kids until I hustled through the front doors. The bell had just rung, and the hallways filled with banging and chatter as locker doors shut and kids dragged themselves toward their first classes of the new year.

I made it to my own spot and fumbled the door open just as Matt Janus emerged from the restroom. He came up beside me, flung open his locker directly in my path as usual, and started riffling through his books. Impossibly, he looked even bigger. His black jeans barely contained him, and when he swung off the leather jacket and hung it on its hook, his arms looked positively cartoonish, almost childlike despite their size, like clubs from a "Flintstones" cartoon. They were also covered in purple-red blotches. *Bruises*?

Elbowing me even farther back without so much as turning his head, he slammed his door and started off. To either side, kids ducked away and then closed behind him. He never looked around or back, and so never noticed that one of his jacket sleeves had caught in the locker door, and that the door had not shut.

Later—much later, when I talked about it at all—I told people the decision wasn't conscious. But that was a lie. It was immediate, but I thought about it every step of the way.

I stared at the locker. At Matt's retreating back. I pulled his locker door the rest of the way open. I wasn't seeing Robert's weeping face, or hearing Jill's breathing. I was thinking of that basketball kid's shoes tipped sideways in the puddle where Matt had hurled them, half-sunk, like the dead ducks beside Snake Lake. And also Mr. Valway's damp, dour smirk.

Matt's jacket felt heavy and huge as I pulled it off the hook, more like a dog-carcass than clothing. It smelled bad, too, like caked lineament oil. Turning, I dropped my backpack and started with the jacket down the hall toward the front of the school. Toward the Copper Miner fountain.

The most immediate effect was the spreading silence. Every step I took, another group of kids glanced over, saw what I had in my hands, and stopped talking.

I didn't rush. I looked around. Saw three of the skateboys I knew, and nodded. Saw the bass-player from Kenny Tripton's band, held the coat out to him. He recoiled as though I'd offered him a dripping wolf hide. If the leather had been any less heavy or smelled better, I might have slipped the thing on, like Hercules donning the skin of the lion of Nemea. That's what I felt like. Giddy. Almost invincible.

I walked straight to the fountain, gurgling stupidly in its toilet-shaped porcelain pool. In the center of the pool stood a bronzed, bearded miner, copper shovel poised over the water. Folding Matt's coat neatly—sleeves first, zipper up—I held it outstretched in my arms a few more seconds. Then I plunged it into the lukewarm water, laying it right under that copper shovel, and held it hard on the bottom as though drowning puppies in a sack.

Without drying my own arms and without looking back, I left the jacket where it was, walked back up the row of dead-quiet kids, collected my books, and went to math.

The Janus Tree

The news that I would soon be dead reached me during milk break. Whitney Drum, of all people, came scurrying up as I emerged from second period bio and dragged me around a corner into an empty chem lab. Her eyes, for the first time since I'd known her, were all the way clear, and her skin glowed a little paler than I remembered. She looked hosed clean, and somehow more frail.

"He's going to fucking kill you," she said.

The weird thing was that until right then, I'd felt no fear whatsoever. In fact, I'd half-forgotten what I'd done, wandered through the morning in a daze. The fountain felt like months ago, and the only thing echoing in my head was that homeless woman's voice. *Somebody slapped me.*

"Beat me, maybe," I told Whitney, and tried to smile. "Break my fingers."

"End your life," Whitney said. "Stop your breathing. That's what he told me."

Just like that, my legs went, as though the bones had been pulled from them. I sat on the floor, staring at my knees.

"Get out of here," Whitney murmured. "Go home, Teddy. Jesus Christ, go home." She was sobbing as she darted from the room.

The whole rest of the snack break, I was thinking I would do exactly that, wait until the next class bell and then slip out amidst the bustle. I'd have gone right away, except I had no idea where Matt Janus went on his break. In fact, now that Valway was dead, I had no idea where his schedule took him at any point in his day.

So I waited. Once, four minutes before time, I heard heavy boots clump down the hall toward the room where Whitney had steered me. I glanced around the lab, thought about breaking a beaker and wielding it in front of me. But if Matt came, and I cut him, I'd only enrage him more. There wasn't anywhere to hide. I ducked to the side of the window carved into the door, so at least no one could see me through that. Whoever it was went past without slowing. The bell rang.

It was all I could do, the whole way down the hall, to keep from running. I kept jerking my head to both sides, waiting for that tell-tale parting in the crowd, that towering figure bearing down. The double doors of the gym stood half open, and as I passed one of them banged back and a giant roared out, but it was only Mr. Kellaway, the basketball coach, chasing a ball. He saw me leap back, knocking over two girls behind me, stared at me a few seconds, and started to laugh. Ignoring the girls—who'd realized who I was, and crab-walked away before getting to their feet—I kept moving.

Thirty feet ahead, I saw the stony gray light through the front doors. Behind me, sounds were thinning as students split off into classes, all of them watching me, most of them whispering. I could hear individual footsteps, now. Some of them heavy. I didn't look back. I kept walking. Fifteen feet. I thought of the crawl-space in our empty house. I'd take a salami sandwich and a flashlight down there, stay until Mom got back from work or Dad from whatever construction site he was on. I had my hand outstretched for the door when I thought of Jill, wondered what crawl space she'd slipped into in her house. Without thinking about it, I veered right, half-sprinted down the front hallway, and went to Spanish after all.

I don't remember any of the next two periods. I'm not sure I even got my name on the pop World Civ quiz. No one spoke to me. No one even looked at me, though they all glanced in my general direction periodically, as though I were already a ghost, something they could feel but no longer see. When I came out of Spanish, Matt Janus was standing by the fountain, and he was looking straight down the hall toward me. He waited until he was sure I was looking. Then he lifted out his folded coat from under the copper shovel, held it up, and wordlessly, expressionlessly, slid it on. He stood there dripping and staring. I ducked down a side hall and went all the way around the school to reach the cafeteria.

Once there, I hurried to get a place in the middle of the line, surrounded by as many other people as possible, but I'd been too long arriving and wound up at the end. Frantically, I scanned the huge, echoing hall, the students huddled around the squat, rectangular wooden tables, their chairs screeching horribly in the ruts in the scarred and cracked linoleum floor.

No Matt.

I scanned again. The line inched forward. The room echoed, and chairs screeched. I'd reached the edge of the actual food displays, picked a pudding and placed it on my tray, when the silence bloomed behind me.

The Janus Tree

It came like a wave of radiation, spreading from the door of the hall outward in all directions. Matt didn't waste any time. If I'd made any calculations at all, I realized right then they were wrong. Whatever Matt was doing, it wasn't for effect, or for sending a message. He didn't wait for the silence to become total. He didn't stroll in slow motion. He just came for me.

Don't turn, I was murmuring inside my head. Stupid, really. A completely inappropriate climber's thought. As if not looking, in this particular case, was going to help.

Would he do it with his hands?

It was that thought, mostly, that triggered my reaction. My hands were already gripping the food tray so hard it seemed I could feel my fingertips touching through the plastic. When I whipped it off the countertop, sending the pudding goblet flying to the side to shatter, the tray felt light, so pathetically light. Whirling, swinging wildly, I caught Matt Janus on the point of his chin and dropped him to his knees like a felled tree.

Around us, the silence exploded. Everyone was shouting, though I couldn't make out a single word over the buzz in my ears. I also couldn't blink, couldn't even look away from Matt where he knelt, chin split and bleeding, gorilla-hands at his sides. After a few seconds, he glanced up. The look on his face wasn't quelled-bully, and it wasn't amazement, and it sure as hell wasn't fear. I bolted, hurtling to the side as his hands shot out for me, and this time I kept going, through the school's front door, down the hill, off the street into the trees, and home.

From the garage, I grabbed one of the ceremonial silver shovels bankers always gave my father when he broke ground on some new project. Instead of going into the crawl space, I crouched on the couch by the front window, then later went outside so I could breathe better and hid in the pine tree in our yard, watching the road. Of course, the air out there was Silver City air, probably had less oxygen in it than what was in our house, and as the gray light turned darker gray, then black, the cold got inside my jacket, then my skin, then my organs, so that each new pump of my heart sent a fresh shock of iciness down my veins. Finally, I went back indoors.

I'd had the whole afternoon to think of something to say to my parents. In the end, I told them I felt sick, might not be able to go in tomorrow. I didn't specify what kind of sick, and they didn't ask. They turned the heat up high, though—my mother's habitual response to anyone's illness—and in the sweating small hours I lurched awake, believing I'd heard a scratch at my window. *What time had Robert said the Dark Lord had come?*

Dawn. He'd come for Robert at dawn.

The only thing that came for me was the light. I curled deep into my sheets, rolled around, twisted them up, tried a practice moan or two. I didn't usually play sick, and didn't think my parents would ask, but I wanted them to believe it. Somehow, I tricked myself back to sleep, and awoke with my mother placing the phone at my ear.

"How're you feeling?" she asked.

"Not so—" I started, and Jill's voice poured through the receiver.

"Teddy?"

"Hey." I sat up.

"Walk today?"

"You're coming in today?"

"Meet you by your locker right after last class? Wherever I have that now?"

"Okay."

Dazed, wordless, I handed the phone to my mother, ignored her questioning look, and got dressed.

I considered taking the ceremonial shovel. During breakfast, I actually pocketed the knife my mom always laid on the margarine container. So that if Matt maybe brought some toast, we could butter it before he dismembered me. I'd left my books, my backpack, even my winter coat on the school cafeteria floor. Maybe someone had collected them.

In the end, I just put on a second sweatshirt, kissed my baffled parents, and set off into a surprising, dazzling winter sun. The light carried no heat, but it caught the shards of uncollected copper and useless ore refuse in the rocks, turned the buttes blue and maroon and orange like stained glass. Shattered stained glass, but still. I came through the front door of LMMS right on time, moved steadily through my classmates, who parted before me and went quiet yet again. I glanced around for Jill, didn't see her.

Matt Janus was leaning against my locker in his leather jacket.

The Janus Tree

I could have run. I could have gone to Mrs. Morbey's and gotten myself suspended for vandalizing Matt's locker and also decking him with the food tray. I could have demanded that the police come and search Matt's locker and his pockets for the drugs he almost certainly had stashed there.

I walked straight up to him instead. *It's going to hurt*, I thought. *And then, one way or another, it's going to be over.* I thought of Robert weeping. And, yet again, of Valway's masked face. And his, *"Well, now."*

I reached Matt and stood before him. There were probably 200 kids watching. I couldn't hear them, could barely make myself believe they were there.

"I don't suppose sorry's going to do it," I said, staring at his collarbone, the masses of muscle crowding in on his neck. Then, finally, I made myself look at his face.

His expression was utterly unreadable. But his eyes...

I couldn't make sense of it. Not quite yet. I can only say what I thought: The only thing in Matt's eyes, right that moment, was Matt.

He didn't move for a while. At no point did he grin. What he did do, finally, was step back and tap my locker with his long, white fingers.

"What?" I whispered, barely breathing. "Open it?"

Matt tapped again. I twirled the combination, fumbled it twice, finally got the door unlatched. Inside, my backpack and coat and books lay neatly re-stowed. Elbowing me—not hard—to one side, Matt ducked in, pulled everything out in a single pile, and dropped it on the floor beside him. Then he stuck out his hand in a slow, graceful movement—if not for his coat, and his muscles, and the fact that he was Matt Janus, he could have passed for a butler—and gestured me inside.

For a long moment, we just looked at each other. Me, and the balrog of the abandoned mineshaft. My friend from years ago.

I stepped into the locker. Matt shut the door, shoved it until it the click told him it was locked. The bell rang, and a buzz roared through the halls. From the breathing just outside, and the weight I could sense when I pushed my hands against the inside of the door, I could feel that Matt was still out there. Soon, there was silence.

At one point, ten minutes or so into first period, with Matt still leaning on my locker, it occurred to me that nothing was over. That he was going to rip the door open now that we were alone and tear me to pieces.

Except that he didn't know the combination. Had put me—intentionally, or otherwise—in the one place in Silver City where he really couldn't get at me.

Somewhere in that whirl of thoughts, I realized I couldn't hear his breathing anymore. That there was no one outside. I waited another few minutes, heard footsteps, shouted out. It took Mr. Kellaway four tries, with me repeating that he had to bump it after the '38,' to get the door open. When I stepped out, blinking, he exploded into laughter, shook his head, and walked away.

There were terrified, stunned stares when I walked into bio a few minutes later. But there were cheers when I got to Spanish. I was shuttled to the front of the lunch line. I kept waiting for that blooming silence, the heavy footfall that would tell me the real consequences had come. But they didn't come. If Matt was in the cafeteria, I never saw him.

Somehow, slowly, P.E. and English crawled by. Fifteen minutes from the bell, I realized I was about to go walking, for the first time in two months, with Jill Redround. When we were good and high on the buttes, I was going to kiss her.

The second the bell rang, I sprinted for my locker. I knew Matt might be waiting for me there. I no longer cared. I just wanted to be waiting when Jill showed up. I didn't even notice the note taped to my door at first, because I was too busy scanning every passing face.

The note was handwritten, on the yellow legal paper Jill always used.

Gone to the Janus Tree. Matt begged me. I told him it was the last time. Call me tonight? Can't wait to see you, Teddy. RoundRed.

Dawn, I thought, my hands shaking so hard I tore the note in half. *'The Dark Lord summoned me to the Janus Tree.'* That's what Robert had said. Pretty much the last thing he'd said, when he was my friend. The night he'd gone up the hill. Seen what he'd seen.

Then I was hurling students aside, flying for the front door and out, cutting through the yards toward uptown and the road up the rocks to the Janus house.

The sun still shone, but snow was flurrying in gray, gust-driven balls like tumbleweeds. Overhead, I could see the Virgin of the Great Divide

The Janus Tree

through the drifts, blank and mysterious as a Sphinx, some other culture's monument. I was thinking of the vanished Incas, the village Mr. Janus had told us about. Indio Muerto. I could hear his voice. *You're telling me we can't locate a single dead Indian, in their own village?* Most of all, I was thinking of his crooked, decaying fingers stroking Jill Redround's upper arm, inches from the swell of her breast.

Everyone has to get old, he'd said. *Everyone has to get old*.

Vanished. Where had they gone?

When Robert had received his summons, Mr. Janus had barely got back from Chile. He must have hardly begun testing out what he'd learned in the village of dead Indians. He might not even have been positive it was working. Or what anyone else would make of the changes, if there'd even been any. Had he picked Robert because he was wacky, vulnerable, the kind of kid bullies always chose? Or because he thought—hoped—Robert was sensitive, and might confirm that something was indeed happening. To himself. To his son…

I understood long before I got there.

Inside the Janus house, nothing moved. Nothing would, of course. *Why had NO ONE asked whom Matt would be staying with, now that his father and mother were both gone? Because somehow, subconsciously, everyone else already knew, too. Not that anyone would say. And it was too much even to admit.*

Through the snow, in the red-yellow sun, I could see them on the hillside. Matt right under the tree, so that it seemed an extension of his spine, the dead branches to the right and the live ones on the left fanning open on either side of him like wings, the scaly bark so closely resembling his own blotchy, shedding skin. And Jill on her knees in front of him. Screaming.

I'd gotten within ten feet before I realized even Matt hadn't gotten *that* tall, couldn't have, and finally noticed the wheelbarrow he was standing in.

"What the *fuck*?" I screamed. And then, *"Jill!"*

Matt kicked the wheelbarrow out from under himself so hard that it swung up and smacked Jill in the forehead. She fell back flat, still screaming, hands at her face and blood spurting into her eyes. So only I saw.

I saw legs kicking. Not dancing, kicking. Not at the air, but at each other. I saw Matt's right hand yanking at the noose, his left hand wrenching at the right, all but pulling it off its wrist. Then something in the rope slipped, Matt dropped another six inches, and the snap of his neck exploded off the rocks like gunshot.

The ambulance and the hearse arrived together. I knew, even as I kissed her bloody forehead, that Jill was gone from me, too. Her mother moved her to Albuquerque for good three days later. I wrote her there. Sometimes, she wrote back. She never returned, and she never invited me down, and I've never gone.

I can't. Because every time I think of her or see her face, I see Matt's face. In the noose, kicking and fighting for his life with his father, who'd slipped inside him. Or by my locker, at the moment he directed me into it, when he was just Matt, who'd flung a balrog off a cliff, having lost a battle to a boy who stored magic in a plastic light-saber in his backpack.

I Am Coming To Live In Your Mouth

> *"This must be the very pinnacle of good fortune, he thought. To have every moment of his death observed by those beautiful eyes—it was like being borne to death on a gentle, fragrant breeze."*
> —Yukio Mishima, "Patriotism"

It happened the first time during the 4 a.m. feeding, and Kagome believed she was dreaming. This was not unusual; she almost never slept anymore, and most of her life felt like dreaming, now. She'd already flushed out Joe's catheter, sponged gently at the pus that dripped incessantly from the tumor that had devoured his upper lip, and replaced the nutrient bag on the i.v. stand. Now she was sitting quietly, holding his skeletal, freezing fingers in her own. Briney, Joe's Burmese, lay curled in the permanent indentation he'd made for himself across Joe's thighs. Once or twice, the cat half-raised one nictitating lid, flicked its stub of a tail back and forth as though sweeping the room with radar, and went back to sleep. Out on the deck, the shadows of the oaks swayed in the winter wind spooling silently down the San Gabriels, and the Nuttal's woodpecker that never left, even in the snow, knocked once against whichever pine or telephone pole it had lodged in this night.

I am coming, she heard, half-heard, rolling the bones of Joe's fingers with her thumb.

It was like the interferon year all over again. In a way, despite the realities of the current situation, watching him then had been worse. He'd slept even more, for one thing, sometimes as many as thirty hours in a row, and never less than twenty. But his sleep had been more disturbed, riddled with tremors that wracked him for minutes on end, haunted by dream-demons Joe clearly remembered afterward but rarely described to her. *Tall things,* he'd murmur. *Whisperers.*

Sometimes, that year, the moments when he wasn't shuddering or dreaming were more frightening still. His face had been less drastically scarred, then, but also tended to go sickeningly slack, drain of everything that identified *that* hawk-nose, *these* flippy ear-lobes, *this* slightly up-turned mouth, as Joe's. Looking into it had been like staring at the drawn shades of a house that had been termite-bombed.

And yet. Back then, there'd also been that one, absurd element of hope. That the interferon regimen might just work. Kill every deadly cell inside Joe but still leave Joe.

Whereas now, hours or days from the end—not weeks, she'd been assured, not even one week—Joe rarely so much as twitched. Sometimes, as she tended to him, his eyelids fluttered, but contentedly. At least, Kagome insisted to herself that was the case. And sometimes, right at this moment, he'd actually awaken and look at her, and she'd see that formidable engine in there fire one more time, all that ferocious fight, all those useless things he somehow knew locking into place behind his retinas. Once, he'd told her he loved her, that she was the only reason he was still battling. Mostly, though, he glanced at the feedbag and said, "Kidney pie. Rock on." Or, if they had a chemo or oncologist appointment later that day, "Shotgun."

I am coming to live…

I Am Coming To Live in Your Mouth

She was moving his hand against the inside of one of her wrists, now. Feeling the paper-thin membrane against her smoothness, right where the sleeve of her robe ended. Dazed, she moved his hand to her cheek. Held it there. Stroked once, so gently, down. Back up. Down again. Then she slid Joe's hand to her neck. Down farther, into the V of her robe to brush one nipple. The other. *How long had it been now? Two years? Three? They'd had such sweet touching in the eighteen months before what they'd always known was coming—or, coming back—arrived for good. Such* patient *touching, as though they'd had all the time in the world.* Now his skin—what there was of it—just felt scratchy and hard, like a dried-out loofa.

I am coming to live in your mouth.

She jerked upright and dropped Joe's hand to the hospital bed that had taken the place of their couch and swung around.

Screaming, she thought. *I should be screaming.*

She couldn't see his face. He was standing in the corner, just where the shadow of the tallest oak spilled through the glass sliding door. His stained tan overcoat hung too low, all but brushing the tops of his galoshes, which looked shiny and wet, though there hadn't been so much as a mist out there yet this fall. He had his head bent low, the brim of his trilby completely shading his face.

"Get out of my—" she started, and his voice overrode her though it was barely a whisper, hollow as respirator breath in an oxygen mask.

I am coming to live in your mouth. Because you never have anything to say.

Then she *was* screaming, crying, too, "*Out! Get out! OUT!*"

The figure in the corner didn't even lift its head, but it was still speaking, or else those words had rung a resonant spot inside her, because she could hear them over her shouting. *Coming to live. Never have anything…*

"What in *sweet God's* name?" Mrs. Thiel snapped from the stairway, and Kagome whirled, her own voice choking to silence but that *other's* still echoing.

At least the mask was down, Kagome thought, watching Joe's mother's razor-thin eyebrows squeeze together like crayfish pincers. For a long moment, she just held Mrs. Thiel's gaze, then remembered and leapt to her feet, swinging around.

By the sliding glass door, she saw the shadow of the oak shaking slightly, as though ravens had just sprung from its branches. Bare floor. The boxes of sterile needles and spare tubing tucked neatly against the breakfront. Nothing else.

I am coming to live in your mouth.

When she turned once more, she found Joe's mother smiling. The eyebrows hung in their carefully separated spaces like precisely hung photographs. The mask, in place once more.

"Jasmine?" Mrs. Thiel said brightly. "Help us greet the new day grinning?"

Moving to the stove, ignoring Kagome's elegant tetsubin tea things arrayed on the shelf by the sink, she filled the utilitarian silver kettle she'd brought with her when she'd finally dropped the pretense and moved in a few weeks before. The kettle made an ugly, banging sound as Mrs. Thiel settled it over the burner.

"Think the newspaper's here? I'll get you your crossword. Or is it more a sudoku kind of hour?"

Instead of answering, Kagome gazed down again at what was left of her husband. Her screaming hadn't roused him. *Would today be the last day? Would the next time he opened his eyes be the final one? Good God, had she already* had *the final one? When had it been? She couldn't even remember.*

She watched Joe's chest, which just lay flat.

Lay flat.

Lay flat.

Lay flat.

And finally, fitfully, inflated, as though some small child were shoving at it from inside. Joe's mouth didn't exactly open anymore, but part of his lower lip quivered as air slipped past it. He gurgled once, and pus ran down his teeth onto his tongue. Then his chest clamped down again.

Kagome glanced toward the corner. With a brief, discreet brush of her husband's palm with her fingertips, she turned to face Mrs. Thiel. She had no smile in her, and managed one. At least, it felt like she did. "Sudoku, I think," she said. Without even slipping her fuzzy robe over her robe, she crossed to the front door and stepped out into the icy mountain air to wait for the paper she knew wouldn't come for at least another hour.

I Am Coming To Live in Your Mouth

But the cold didn't help. Nor did the shower when she came inside. Nor Mrs. Thiel's superb slow eggs and salsa. The final proof for just how unsettling her 4 a.m. encounter had been came as Mrs. Thiel was clearing the breakfast dishes, leaning over her shoulder while Kagome tapped the last unfilled boxes of the Thursday *Times* crossword with her pencil eraser.

"Mulliner," Mrs. Thiel said suddenly, and Kagome stared at the puzzle. The answer was correct, of course. *65 down: Old hat, at the Angler's.* Jobs misspelled to make Wodehouse characters, the theme of the day. *When, exactly, had Mrs. Thiel started nailing crossword clues like that? Never before, in the time Kagome had known her.*

"Get the crazy glue," Mrs. Thiel said, and Kagome grabbed her hand and almost made her drop the dishes. She could feel Mrs. Thiel's scowl on her shoulders—God forbid either of them should actually show any emotion other than radiant, resolute *hopefulness*—but Mrs. Thiel held on, too. For one second, no longer.

Get the crazy glue. It was what Joe said when he turned away from a ball he'd bowled immediately after bowling it, before the ball was halfway down the lane. When he knew he'd rolled a strike, and that the pins would be flying. In the three, maybe four times Kagome had gone bowling with Joe, she'd never seen him guess wrong. *"Cause there's no guessing involved,"* he'd say. And touch her cheek gently with one finger as he returned to his seat.

I am coming to live in your mouth...

The doorbell rang at eleven while Kagome was still combing out her long, black hair and beginning to weave it into the complicated *sakkou* fashion she'd learned from her mother, and that had always hypnotized Joe. Fascinated him. "Like a wild knot," he'd said once, slipping his long fingers in and out of the whirl of loops and crosses she'd made. Then, when she'd lain still long enough, he told her what that was, as she knew he would. A knot built out of infinite sequences, with a seemingly infinite number of edges. "In the actual universe—the physical one—" Joe told her, "there's no such thing."

Abruptly, she came out of her reverie. *Hospice.* She'd blocked that out. Forgotten they were coming. Then she heard the door opening, a single strum of out-of-tune ukulele, and her first real smile of the day spread over her pale, exhausted face. Pinning the last twist of her hair into place, she stepped into the hall and caught a fleeting glimpse, *galoshes sliding silently around the corner, into the guest room they never used, who would come?*

Sprinting for the room, she threw open the door—*closed? It was closed?*—and found the erg machine Joe had ordered to keep his muscles in shape while his skin rotted off and his lungs shriveled and his organs imploded, one by one. Beyond the bare windows, she saw the tops of trees, all but bare now, swaying.

More ukulele strum from downstairs, and Ryan's ridiculous, keening laugh, and his croak of a voice. "Going down, chum. Going down hard." And then that roaring, ripping cough—the cancer growling as it fed—that told her Joe was awake.

Kagome hurried downstairs, ignoring the urge to swing around, just once, to make sure. *She'd made sure. And already knew, anyway.*

"How long has he been awake?" she asked Mrs. Thiel, who was wiping down the kitchen counters, having already washed every dish and tucked away the supplies from last night's feeding. Only occasionally did the woman allow herself a glance toward the couch, where her son, propped up, was trying to get his fingers around the Playstation controller and his thumbs into place. Finally, Mrs. Thiel looked at Kagome. And grinned.

Kagome smiled back. They stood together and watched.

Ryan, in his usual holey black *Warped Tour* skateshirt and Vans, was alternately flipping at his mop of brown hair and fiddling with the television controllers. Eventually, the screen burst into color, and pumping techno music thudded through the room. Returning to his seat, Ryan spied Kagome, waved the ukulele he was still holding by its neck in his free hand, and settled in the chair closest to Joe. On the screen, twin rocket-propelled race cars approached a starting line as the riff in the music repeated itself, then froze as the START NEW GAME? message appeared.

It was hard to remember, watching them, that Ryan had started out as Kagome's friend. He'd been her intern at *Mountain Living*. In some ways, he fit the copy editor stereotype even more closely than she did: glasses, nervous twitch to his fingers, permanent pale-yellow cast to his

I Am Coming To Live in Your Mouth

skin. Computer tan. Except he also wore Vans and played the ukulele, told invented shaggy dog jokes that made Kagome laugh—no mean feat, in this particular era of her life—and kick-boxed.

Four months ago, out of nowhere, hunched over his computer in the midst of a particularly gnarly edit, he'd mentioned his Boggle prowess. She'd said nothing, but brought Joe's travel set the next day and set it wordlessly before Ryan at lunch. It had taken her two rounds to realize he hadn't been kidding, and seven for him to win the match. Which made him exactly the second person she'd ever met to take one from her. She hadn't so much invited him to dinner as thrown down the gauntlet. He'd shown up singing "Tiny Bubbles," Joe had skunked him at Boggle but lost every Playstation game they'd tried and also computer Jeopardy, and that had pretty much been the last time Kagome had spent with Ryan except at work.

When Ryan was at their house, which was almost every night now, he was with Joe. Once the sickness consigned Joe permanently to the couch, Ryan came more frequently, not less. She didn't think she'd ever been happier about another human being's existence except her husband's.

"You'll be wanting me to say I'm lucky," Ryan told Joe now. She watched his eyes flick to the tumor on Joe's mouth. On Joe's lap, Briney aimed an annoyed glare at Ryan, then hopped down and disappeared upstairs.

"Nnuz nuuuuhne," said Joe. He couldn't really turn his head, but Kagome saw his gaze stray in her direction.

"He says, 'Because you will be,'" Kagome told Ryan. Even Mrs. Thiel could no longer understand her son.

Ryan grinned. "Then you're admitting defeat before we begin. It's what I've always wanted from you."

He triggered the game, and on screen one of the racers launched from the start and hurtled out of sight around a curve, while the other spun immediately into a side wall and blew up.

"Nnuk," Joe said. Ryan grinned wider, and kept going.

Kagome saw the panic first, and moved immediately, silently. Mrs. Thiel was right behind her, and Ryan didn't even notice until they were already beside Joe, gently disentangling his catheter tube from underneath him and beginning the several-minute process of preparing to help him up.

"What...oh..." Ryan said, wrinkling his nose at the smell and standing. "It's okay, dude." He held out his hands.

"He knows it's okay, could you get a water bucket and the sponges?" Mrs. Thiel snapped.

"Under the sink," Kagome murmured. "Thank you, Ryan."

Somehow, once they got Joe to his feet, he managed to stay there while Kagome and Mrs. Thiel bundled up the mess in the sheets and Kagome scrubbed at the slimy, brown streaks sinking into the pillows. Those streaks seemed so devoid of mass they barely even qualified as shit. When she'd finished, she leaned back on her haunches and brushed her nose with her forearm and looked up at her husband. So thin as to be almost two-dimensional, pale as paper, like an origami approximation of himself. To her delighted surprise, he was fully alert, staring back. *And smiling?*

"Nnnay nur nuky," he said.

"I'm lucky," she whispered, and kissed the bones of his hand.

"How about Tijuana Taco?" Mrs. Thiel chirped as she returned from whatever she'd done with the sheets. *Framed them, probably,* Kagome thought, then chastised herself for thinking it. "Kagome, green chile for you, right?"

"Just soup," she murmured. A few chattery seconds later, Mrs. Thiel mercifully left the house on her errand.

Standing for so long had completely exhausted Joe, and he was swaying and shivering more violently than the trees outside as Ryan and Kagome lowered him back onto the home-care hospital bed he'd chosen to die on and settled his heap of comforters and blankets and coats around him. They weren't enough, and Joe went on shivering even as sleep swallowed him.

Stripping off her rubber gloves, Kagome stood and gazed down at her husband. Behind her, Ryan muted the t.v., though from the clicking of the controllers, she knew he was finishing Joe's race for him. Starting right where Joe's car had exploded. After a while, he took up his ukulele again, stroked that quietly. The chords he played changed so slowly, she wasn't sure they were even connected or part of a song until he started half-humming a vocal line, in his strangely sweet croak that was far too old for him.

"Because you never...because you never...have anything..."

I Am Coming To Live in Your Mouth

She didn't mean to hit him, of course she didn't, but the words he had sung didn't register right away, and when they did, she panicked, spun so fast that the fist still holding the shit-rag smacked across his cheek and her knee drove the ukulele out of his hands and across the room. Stunned, streaked with brown and red across his cheeks, Ryan stared up at her, while her free hand flew to her own mouth.

"What did you just…" Her brain was screaming back to this morning, and she was crying again, too, seeing the stick-thin, galoshes-guy in the corner. *"Ryan?"*

Even as she said it, she knew it wasn't so. She hadn't seen the trilby man's face. But he'd been considerably taller. And even though his shape had been disguised by his trench coat, it hadn't been Ryan's shape. *No. It had been…what? She couldn't remember.* Furthermore, Ryan had been downstairs, just coming inside, at the moment Kagome had seen the trilby man ducking into the guest room. *Because he had been there. She was as sure of that now as she'd been that he was imaginary a few hours ago.*

"I'm sorry," she whispered, blinking to try to stem her tears. She bent to wipe at the streaks on Ryan's cheek, and he let her. "I'm sorry," she said again.

"It's okay," he said, though she'd clearly frightened him. "You've been through so—"

"That song." Dropping the rag, she slumped into the wooden chair Mrs. Thiel always sat in, leaving the armchair for Kagome. Precisely the sort of gesture Kagome despised in her mother-in-law, even though it probably had no other motive behind it than kindness. "What made you sing that?"

Now Ryan was staring. "Sing what?"

"What you just sang."

"I wasn't singing. I was barely even—"

On the couch, Joe unleashed a cough that lifted his spine off the pillows and convulsed him with shudders but didn't waken him. Kagome dug under the blankets, found the i.v. tube, and followed it down to Joe's hand. Then she held on. After a while, she turned her gaze once more on Ryan. Her eyes had dried, her features settling into their comfortable, familiar impassivity. Mrs. Theil's wasn't the only mask, she realized.

"Kagome," Ryan murmured. "I'm sorry. I was just…strumming. *Wasn't I?*"

"Yes," Kagome lied, and her heart banged. "I think probably you were."

After that, they sat and breathed and watched for Joe's breaths. At some point, Kagome's free hand found Ryan's, and for a fleeting few minutes, she felt a peculiar, suspended stasis. Not peace, nowhere near peace. But there were people in this room who loved her.

And someone else, too, who was coming to live, and Kagome gripped Ryan's hand and closed her eyes and held still and held on.

"She driving you crazy?" Ryan said. "Joe's mom, I mean? What's she so happy about, anyway?"

For a long time, Kagome didn't answer. Didn't want to. Despite the waves of panic and loneliness and nausea and fear, she wanted to stay right where she was, propped in place, like a birdhouse with birds hopping around and into it, even though there was virtually nothing left inside.

"She's never been happy," Kagome answered. "She just…she thinks it's what Joe wants. You know, he's never liked even acknowledging that he's sick. She also thinks it's why he's still here. If you don't look at it, it can't see you. That kind of thing. I think. Maybe she's right. You know he's been told he had less than a year to live since he was seven years old."

"Does she like you?"

The question startled Kagome out of her half-trance. For the first time in who knew how long, her eyes left Joe's face. She looked not at Ryan but the mountainside folding into nightshadow as the November day drained away.

Then that voice was in her ears again, and her bones, too, and the soft tissue of her arms and chest, whispering, scratching. *I am coming to live in your mouth. Coming to live in your mouth. Coming…*

"She thinks I'm a vacuum," Kagome said, and didn't cry, or squeeze Ryan's hand. She squeezed Joe's, though. Hard. "She thinks he married me to have a *calming* presence near. Because he finally got scared."

"Does she know you can beat him at Boggle? Does she actually think that *calms* him?"

"Scrabble. Not Boggle. Not ever."

Her eyes flicked to Ryan's face. Behind his glasses, his surprisingly large green eyes seemed to swivel in their sockets like a bird's. To her

I Am Coming To Live in Your Mouth

immense relief, he was smiling, a little. Somehow, in his *Warped* t-shirt, with his long legs bunched up against the hospital bed and his hair falling over his face, he looked completely adrift on the currents in this room, bobbing like a bottle with a message in it. Whether the message was for or from her, she had no idea.

Hospice arrived a little after five, an hour or so after Mrs. Thiel came back. Rising from the wooden chair where she'd stayed all day—to her mother-in-law's visible annoyance, and not once had Mrs. Thiel taken the empty La-z-boy—Kagome watched the two nurses and one social worker fan through the room, silent and efficient as the elves in that story about the shoemaker, who come in on a moonbeam. Truly, they were marvels. Even the doorbell when they rang it seemed muffled. Even Mrs. Thiel went quieter when they were here, though her ferocious half-grin never wavered.

The two nurses sponged Joe down, changed his bedding; one combed what was left of his hair while the other washed out the tumor over his mouth with a syringe. The social worker brought Kagome tea in one of her porcelain cherry-blossom cups, and may have spoken to her, too. Kagome might even have spoken back. She couldn't be sure, knew only that the muttering in her ears and her blood had gone quiet. She could hear it, still, but barely. As though it were out on the deck in the falling dark, and just once she glanced that way, through the sliding doors, and saw only shadow.

I know you, she thought, and didn't even try to make sense of that.

"You know what hospice does?" Mrs. Thiel had halfway shrieked, when Kagome had insisted on bringing them in. "Hospice kills you. You understand that, right? You think they're coming to help? They're coming to kill Joe. They're the angels of Goddamn death."

And of course, she was right. The smothering doses of morphine and methadone that ate away at the brain, the thousand other little drugs they gave that the body couldn't really take, all meant to keep Joe comfortable, mask the pain. The words they used, to settle them all. Get them ready. Or, not ready, there was no such thing, and they would never have used so crude a term. Tranquil, maybe. Sort of. Angels of death they truly were. But why did Americans always focus on the death part? What else did they imagine angels were for?

So pervasive was the spell the hospice workers cast that Kagome only noticed the positions they'd taken and realized what they were about to do a few seconds before Joe woke up. Way back in her throat, a groan formed, and though it came out choked, barely even audible, the sound grated against everything else in the room and rattled Mrs. Thiel to wakefulness. And so Mrs. Thiel realized what was happening, too.

"Get away from him," Mrs. Thiel said, but even her voice seemed to come from under a layer of gauze, as though she'd been gagged. "Get…"

Her words sank to nothing as her son's eyes flew open. For one moment, he lay there, blinking, before rolling with surprising alacrity onto his side. His glare was like a bucket of water flung over the hospice workers. They were human after all, Kagome noted; all three flinched back on the chairs they'd arrayed around the bed so that their medical whites formed a sort of picket fence between Joe and the rest of the room. The life he'd lived. Just like that, they ceased to be angels, and their features resolved into ordinary, comprehensible, *human* ones. One of the nurses had a band-aid under the lobe of her left ear. The social worker had pretty auburn hair—*just moments ago, it had seemed gray, Kagome had assumed that was a required color for the job, like a uniform*—clumped in an unflattering working bun at the base of her neck.

It was the social worker who spoke, as a new shiver rippled down Joe's obscenely articulated bones. The woman's voice was trained, alright, lulling as a 2 a.m. smooth-jazz disc jockey's, but warmer. At once more detached and more genuine.

"Joe," the woman said.

Beside Kagome, Mrs. Thiel beat her arms against her sides like an enraged mother eagle. But she held her place. Waited.

"Joe, you've fought so hard, for so long. For thirty years, is that right?"

To Kagome's astonishment, Joe answered. And his voice came out fuller, with more of his joyful, prickly *Joe*-ness than at any time in the past two months. Also with more consonants.

"Thirty-three. Got sick when I was seven."

"Thirty-three years, when virtually anyone else would have been dead in six months. Incredible. Please know, Joe. All we want is to help you make meaningful use of every meaningful second, and also provide

I Am Coming To Live in Your Mouth

comfort. To you, and your loved ones. We've been coming here a month. I've never seen anyone fight like you do."

Was Joe smiling, now? Oh, God, was Joe crying? The tumor seemed to float across his mouth, obscuring it, like one of those black blotches television stations use to blur victim's features on true crime shows.

"So now. Joe." This time, as she spoke, the social worker slid forward on her chair. As if on cue, the others edged forward, also, and Kagome almost screamed, it was like watching hyenas dance in from the edge of a clearing.

"What is your goal now, Joe? Can you tell me that?" At this, the woman gave a practiced but mournful glance over her shoulder toward Kagome and Mrs. Thiel. Kagome watched her auburn bun shake. "What do you still want to do?"

There was no doubt anymore. Joe was crying. If there'd been a smile, too, it was gone. "Survive," he said, in his dead man's rasp. Then he rolled over and went back to sleep.

"You bitch," Mrs. Thiel murmured, and Kagome started to nod right along with her, wanted to raise both fists in the air and cheer or scream, and then realized her mother-in-law meant *her*. "I can't take this," Mrs. Thiel went on. "I'm going to the movies." Already, her voice was molding back into its chirp, as though it were pottery clay she was rounding, relentlessly rounding. "I'll be back soon. Bring you those chocolate stars you like, if they have any, Kagome. Bye, Ryan, see you tomorrow?"

Moments later, she was gone, and hospice, too, leaving a message pad full of numbers to call, *any*time, for help or advice, or just to talk. They promised to be back tomorrow afternoon. Kagome returned to her wooden chair and Ryan to the La-z-boy. Ryan left his ukulele on the floor. They stayed there in silence a long time. Full night fell.

Kagome wasn't sure when she realized Ryan was asleep. He had his arms crossed tight across his thin chest, his head twisted at an ugly angle, as though someone had slipped up behind and wrenched it halfway off. His leg, barely touching hers through her skirt, felt almost hot. So palpably *living*. Gently, she reached over, lifted his head, and leaned it in what she hoped was a more comfortable way against her shoulder. When she looked up, the trilby man was watching through the window.

For the second time in less than a day, a scream jagged up her throat, but this time Kagome managed to catch it between her teeth, and her tongue and everything inside her sizzled as though she'd bit down on electrical wire. *How did she know the trilby man was watching, she couldn't even see his face? The hat and the dark hid his features, made her wonder if there was a face under there at all, his head just looked like a blacker circle pasted on the black out there.*

Because it wasn't *out there*. She was seeing his reflection. He was right behind her.

She whirled, banging Ryan's forehead with her own. His head rocked back, stars shot across her eyes and she swept her gaze wildly through the room but saw nothing. *Wait—near the counter. By the kitchen.* But that was Briney, Joe's cat, creeping back.

Tears poured through her squeezed lashes all at once, as though she'd tipped a vase that had been stored there. She couldn't stop them, felt the shakes seize her. Then Ryan's arms were around her shoulders, enclosing her. She let herself fold forward. For long minutes, she had no idea how long, she just leaned into Ryan and shook. He held tight.

The only thing she was *absolutely* certain of, later, was that she'd started it. And that she'd been looking at Joe when she did. At the stump where Joe's right ear had been, and the black, ball-shaped scar over the hole in his jaw where the second-to-last of the twenty-three surgeries she'd been through with him had focused. The little tumors swelling all over his face, seeming to wriggle when she looked away, like pregnant spiders scurrying over her husband with their sacs of young.

Partially, it was triggered by the awkward way Ryan held her, with his hands seemingly affixed to her shoulder blades like defibrillator pads he was trying to place. For most of the time Joe had been able to hold her, he'd done so like that. He'd avoided dating, most of his life. Hadn't seen the point, he said. And so he hadn't known what to do with his hands, at first. She'd had to show him.

But partially, too, it was Ryan's heat. His pale arms, with her tears streaking them, and the surprising force of his skater's thighs pushing against hers. It was like holding Joe, but a different Joe. Joe *healthy*. Joe capable of expressing the hunger she knew he felt, that was too strong for his frail frame, that he'd been afraid would shake him to pieces every

I Am Coming To Live in Your Mouth

time they touched. She wasn't exactly thinking any of this, but she was conscious of it all as one of her hands slid down Ryan's chest into his lap, and her mouth lifted and found his.

It lasted longer than she could have hoped, certainly longer than she expected. Long enough for her to wonder if they were actually going through with it, and to understand that Ryan hadn't come here only for Joe, after all. His hands had come off her shoulders at last, and they felt so *good* gliding on her back. His eyes were closed, but hers flicked constantly between this boy's sweet, helpless face and her husband's wrecked and sleeping one. It was like touching them both, touching Ryan, yes, but also Joe through him. Their mouths had come open, and she was caressing, probing, had Ryan's belt unbuckled when she saw the *cat* staring at her and froze, just for a second.

Which was far too long. Ryan gagged, his mouth snapped shut, and he banged her head again with his own as he scrambled to his feet. "Oh, Kagome," he said, fumbling at his snap and his belt and not getting either and finally staring down at himself and then her in disbelief. "I'm so sorry," he said, and burst into tears.

"Ryan," she said, and started to stand, and then she was just too tired. She watched him and offered nothing reassuring, just leaned her head into the side of the La-z-boy and let her hair droop almost to the floor. She didn't cry, didn't even want to. Mostly, she realized, she wanted to be alone. *When was the last time she'd been alone, for any length of time? A month ago? Three?*

Ryan kept crying, kept saying, "Sorry." Not until he was at the door did he say he'd be back. She couldn't even rouse herself to nod or wave.

Then she was by herself. She closed her eyes and listened. For a moment, she panicked. Even the wind outside seemed to have stilled, and nothing anywhere near her seemed to be breathing, not even her. Then, very low, she heard the rumble of Briney's purr, and after that a sudden, rattling gasp from Joe, followed by another in no rhythm. Then silence again. She couldn't even hear the air entering or leaving her own body. *Maybe Mrs. Thiel was right, and she was more bonsai tree than wife. Decorative and silent.*

And she never had anything to say.

Kagome. Even the name was meaningless, her mother had taken it from some childhood chant.

Opening her eyes, Kagome sat up. She considered dialing her parents in Sendai. But talking to them from this house was like shouting across a mountain canyon. Her mother's health—and, maybe, her father's unexpressed sense of betrayal or just loss that she'd decided to settle here—had prevented them ever from coming. And Joe's health had prevented his going. And years had piled up, like snow in the Snow Country, so deep and so quickly. Kagome didn't have the strength to traverse them tonight.

I know you, she was thinking, nonsensically. She sat.

At some point, she considered calling Ryan. Telling him he had nothing to be sorry for, that it was her fault. If there was fault. That she loved his coming to the house, and knew his presence was at least as crucial to keeping Joe alive as her own. But then she decided she didn't need to say this. Ryan was so bright, so intuitive despite his awkwardness. Like Joe was. Had been.

To Kagome's astonishment, Mrs. Thiel came home raving drunk. She stood swaying a while over her son, glared at Kagome, and Kagome wrapped her in a blanket and took her up to bed. The woman's hands were rigid with cold, as though she'd shoved them in an ice-bucket for the past few hours. As Kagome flicked out the bedroom light, she heard Mrs. Thiel murmur, "Thank you, Kagome. You are, without question, the easiest person in the world to go through this with."

Kagome almost threw herself back across the room, shrieked in Mrs. Thiel's face. *I tried to fuck his friend*, she almost said. Wished she'd said. *Easiest?*

Instead, she shut the door and stood a few silent seconds on her balcony, in her silent house. That would soon be empty for real. Silent for good. She didn't open her eyes until she was halfway down the staircase.

The hospital bed was empty.

At first, the sight made so little sense that Kagome couldn't process it, couldn't begin to think what to do. Then she was flying downstairs, all but crashing onto her face as she leapt the last five steps into the living room and stared around at the kitchen, the deck—*Shit and God, had he thrown himself from the deck?*—and saw nothing, and no one.

"Joe?" she said. Spun back to the stairs, to the deck again, expecting the trilby man to materialize out there, *he'd said he was coming, warned them he was.*

I Am Coming To Live in Your Mouth

"Joe?"

Then she heard it. One single sob. From the bathroom. Skidding across the hardwood, she rattled the knob, which was locked, beat with her palm against the door. "Joe? It's me."

"I killed Briny."

In mid-beat, with her arm still raised, Kagome froze. "What?"

Sob. Then a sawing, rattling gasp of a breath.

"Joe, please."

"It wasn't me. I couldn't help it." His voice so clear. As though, right at the end, he'd swallowed the tumor whole, or ripped it off in one last savage spasm of defiance.

"Joe."

Sobbing.

Cautiously, squeamishly—which was hilarious, in a way, given what she'd seen and done and immersed herself in ever since she'd married her husband—Kagome glanced around for the cat. Briny was so much Joe's, she'd never developed a deep-seated attachment to it. But she'd loved the way it loved him.

God, did he have it in there with him?

Sinking to her knees, Kagome leaned her forehead into the door and closed her eyes, willing herself through the wood. "Joe. Please."

"It's like I had no control over my hands. Like they weren't my hands, anymore, I wasn't even part of it." Rasp. Rattle. Long silence. Sob.

"I think I pulled her head completely off."

Kagome stifled a sob of her own, felt her fingers curl into claws, as though she could scratch her way through, opened her eyes and saw the cat. It lay curled sleepily in the impression Joe had left in the hospital bed when he'd somehow dragged himself off it, licking a forepaw, watching her through one half-open eye.

"Joe? Joe, Briney's fine. She's right here."

Silence. So long that Kagome caught herself making loud, bellows-like sounds with her breath, as though she could blow air through the wood, around the tumor and into Joe's desperate, deflating lungs. She knew what was happening, now. It had happened so many times. One of the new drugs—who even kept track anymore—had reacted with one of the old drugs. Or had built up in his system, or triggered some unexpected reaction. And now he was having an episode. And there was nothing to do about it except talk him through.

"Kagome?" Joe said, and his voice sounded different yet again, so small, like a seven year-old's. "Kagome, I don't want to die dumb. Please, I don't want to be—"

"What? What are you talking—"

"What time is it?"

"Huh? 1:15 or some—"

"Date? What date? How long have I been like this?"

Sick? Sad? Dying? She could hear in his wheeze that he was dying. The rattle had changed, gone heavy in his throat, like a motor shutting down. She started to weep, glanced sideways. The trilby man stood at the top of the stairs.

All she could see of him, really, was his galoshes, the bottom of his coat, his legs up to his knees. *No*, she thought, shrinking back, looking frantically around for anything heavy. Something she could swing.

I am coming to live in your mouth.

"Won't," she heard Joe grunt, his breath bubbling. "Oh, God, not this way. How long? I killed the…I won't. *HOW LONG?*"

Thumping, as though Joe was pounding his own chest. Or driving his head into the wall. "Joe," Kagome said, starting to weep.

"I don't want to be dumb."

"*Dumb?*"

"I want to be me."

"Joe, You've been you since the day I—"

"Date? What date? How long have I just been lying there? I killed the—"

"Never," she hissed. "Never, for one second, my husband, have you *just been lying there.*" She blinked, and the trilby man was closer. Three steps down from the balcony, visible to the waist now. Without even moving. *I know you.* Even as Kagome thought that, he was five steps down. Absolutely still, with his long arms at his sides. Like she was watching a spliced film.

Because you never have anything to say.

Trilby. Trilllll…

She was panicking, frantic, wanting to flee the house and unable to move, rolling that word on her tongue. Over and over. *Trilby. Useless*

I Am Coming To Live in Your Mouth

name, for a hat no one wore. No one she'd ever known. Where had she even learned it?

"I killed Briney. Kagome, WHAT TIME IS IT?!"

"Constantinople," she said abruptly, heard her husband gasp and go still.

On the stairs, the trilby man winked closer. Still not moving, hands at his sides. She could see the top of the hat now, the head bent down on the chest, obscuring the face.

"Come on," Kagome muttered. *Which of them did she mean? She didn't know, wasn't sure it mattered.*

"Calcutta," Joe whispered, voice catching hard, ripping on the teeth of his cough, and Kagome threw her head back, almost smiling. Almost.

"Cheating," she said, as tears erupted down her cheeks. "Hasn't officially changed its name yet."

"Just because…" Ripping, ravaging cough. Then the rattle, low and long. "…the west hasn't acknowledged, doesn't mean…"

"Fine. Chennai." The trilby man's rubber soles reached the hardwood floor. Kagome watched him come. *I will not move,* she was chanting, deep inside herself. *I will not move.*

Trilby.

"*That's* cheating," Joe said.

Through her tears, Kagome watched the trilby man twitch closer, and gripped the doorframe to keep from collapsing. The grin that broke over her face was different than any she'd ever felt there.

"How so?" she whispered. Knowing the answer. Wanting him to tell her. To have the pleasure. To *play,* once more. *Fight,* a little longer.

"It's…the name changed. Not the name…it was."

"Madras," she said.

"Madras," said Joe. "I'm sorry, Kagome."

The trilby man was five feet away; next time he moved they'd be touching. There was nothing to swing at him. Nowhere to run, and even if there was.

Mulliner. Coming to live…

"Sorry?" Kagome said, staring at the hat tipped down, the hidden face. *I KNOW you.* "Joe, you have nothing—"

"For not staying. I can't stay."

"Joe. Let me in."

"Can't…reach the door. Sorry. Sorry. Sorry."

Weeping, glaring her defiance, Kagome turned her back on the trilby man, put her mouth to the crack between the door and the wall, and began to whisper. "I love you, Joe. I love you, Joe. I love you, Joe."

Then she remembered.

Where else would she have heard such a nothing word but from her husband? *Tall* things, he'd called them, in the year of his interferon dreams. *Whisperers, in trilby hats.*

Angels of death? Walking tumors, whispering in the blood?

Or…What had that doctor said?

From the top of the stairs, there was a new sound, now. A whimper, climbing towards keening.

In her ears, Kagome could still hear the slow song Ryan had sung. Sworn he hadn't sung. On her shoulders, she could feel his hands, the way they'd moved, and hadn't moved. And in her mouth, she could taste his tongue. The sweat on his cheek that had tasted so sweet. So sweetly *familiar*.

Mulliner. Never before, not even once…

"Kagome?" Mrs. Thiel sobbed.

'It's a myth, you know. That we can't kill cancer. We can kill anything. Just…not selectively.' That's what that doctor had said. *'Now, if your husband could oblige by stepping aside, figure a way to climb out of there, just for a month or two…'*

Had he?

Kagome whirled, heart hurtling up her chest, borne on a boil of grief and nausea and loneliness and terror and *hope?*

Joe?

Mrs. Thiel had reached the bottom of the stairs, was staring at Kagome, at the closed door behind her. The rattling in the bathroom had stopped. Had been stopped for too long now. Kagome glared back, across the empty room, past her mother-in-law toward the pine trees outside. All that empty, useless wind.

"No," Mrs. Thiel said, and Kagome felt her mouth curl once more, into a snarl she'd never known she had in her. *Because it had never been there. She'd seen it before, though. In those rare moments Joe didn't think she*

I Am Coming To Live in Your Mouth

was looking, and the pain came for him, and he somehow roused that fury *in there and fought it back one more time.*

Whatever was coming, she thought. It was here.

With special thanks to Norman Partridge for the loan of the nightmare...

You Become the Neighborhood

"How'd it *start*?" Mom asks, taking a step back toward the curb. Her long-fingered hands have curled up at her sides like smacked daddy longlegs, and her braid has come loose and swings back and forth, gray and heavy, across her back. "How'd it start? How do I know?"

She tears her eyes away from the little triplex, just for a moment, and looks at me. I flinch, start to take her hand, but I'm afraid to. For so many years, after we left here, I'd see that expression bubble up, triggered by nothing: a bus sighing on a nearby streetcorner, or the sight of a tent-*sukka* billowing off the side of someone's porch, or a flying beetle landing on her hand, or a summer wind. Then she'd start screaming at me, or whoever was near. Even then, I knew it wasn't really me, and that did help, some.

Behind her, the sunset has ignited the smog, and the evening redness rises on the horizon behind the hazy towers of Century City, barely visible less than a mile from here. The traffic on Olympic is Sunday-evening sparse, the noise and the heat of it lapping around us rather than crashing down, the way it mostly did when we lived here. Low tide.

"I'm sorry," I murmur, starting back around the corner toward the side-street where we parked. "I didn't mean to bring you here. I actually forgot this place was so near. I just thought you'd want to see the building where Danny and I are going to be liv—"

"Do you remember the turtle?" my mother asks. And then she just folds her legs under her and sits down in the square of grass in front of the triplex. The angry expression has vanished. But there are tears. "Ry? Do you remember?"

She pats the grass. My legs are bare under my skirt, and if I sit there, they're going to itch. I do it anyway. For a moment, I wonder what whoever currently lives in the front apartment will think, two women camped on their lawn with their backs to the traffic and their eyes riveted to those bay windows like *paparazzi*. But if the existing tenants are anything like we were, they'll never open those curtains—too many cars passing, too stark a reminder of the carbon monoxide seeping through every little gap in the walls and window frames—so they'll never see us.

All at once, I *do* remember. And I find myself glancing toward the hedge, then the back alley where the dumpster is, half-expecting to see that little, darker-green hump in the grass. That tiny, wrinkled head turned slightly sideways. "*So it can see the sky.*" That's what Evie used to tell me.

"A hundred years after we die," I say.

"What?" snaps my mother.

"Sorry. It's what she used to say. Evie. She said that turtle of hers could live 250 years. She'd already had it for like 20. She said we could come back here a hundred years after we die and there it would be. Just being."

"Evie," my mother says, and for the first time all night—in a long while, really, at least around me—she offers up her gentle, close-lipped smile. Her softest one, that I loved so much when I was little, and lost when we left here. "Oh, God, Ry, you should have seen her."

"Mom, you used to make me call her Adopted Grandma. Didn't she walk me home from nursery school when you were at work? I saw her all the time."

"Not this time, you didn't. Oh, wow." To my amazement, my mother starts to laugh. Right on cue, from all the way down Olympic, comes a

You Become the Neighborhood

whiff of ocean breeze, just strong enough to blow out the laughter like a candle. Her shoulders tremble, though she can't possibly be cold. My shins have begun to itch.

I put my palms in the grass and make to stand, saying, "Well, I guess we should go."

But my mother is still smiling. At least, I think she is. "You asked how it started."

"Yeah. I did."

"Maybe this is it. I mean, obviously, it's not the beginning, it had to have been in full swing by then, but this is the first one I really remember. This is as close to the beginning as I can get."

Her shoulders tremble again. "Leyton," she says. "Mr. Busby, I mean…"

"I know who you meant, Mom."

"I actually don't know why he didn't blame me. Because it was kind of my fault."

I sigh, roll my head back on my neck to watch the ribbons of orange run the rim of the sky like a brush fire along a ridge. My mother follows my eyes up, and she goes rigid. She says something, too, but I can't make it out. I sigh again. "I'm not sure this qualifies as starting at the beginning."

"Mr. Busby'd moved in…I don't know…six months before? Fall of '95. I think."

"Did Evie always hate him?"

"I don't think she ever hated him, Ry."

"What are you talking about? Why else would—"

"She hated his being here. Totally different, in this case."

"Okay. Why did she hate him being here?"

My mom looks at me, and I want to weep. I've never actually seen the expression I unleash on her every fifteen minutes or so during our Sunday-night outings. But I suspect it looks like that. If that's true, at least my mother can't be as fragile as she generally appears.

"Why do you think?" she asks.

"Yeah. Okay. I just meant that that always surprised me about Evie. She seemed so open about everything, and everyone. Always talking about the Clintons, and propositions, and Greenpeace. I'm pretty sure she taught me all those words."

My mother nods. I'm still surprised she's let us sit here this long. "I think the riots really spooked her. Remember, she was eighty-four years old. She'd lived here a long, long time. For most of that, this neighborhood was one hundred percent Jews."

"A lulav in every window," I say, and my mother laughs.

"An etrog on every plate. Where'd she even get that? I've never seen an etrog on anyone's plate. Have you?"

I laugh, too. And my surprise tilts toward amazement. I am sitting with my mother in front of our childhood home—the one we left for the last time in an ambulance, with my mother in restraints and screaming—and we're laughing.

"So anyway," my mother says. "Here's our coal-skinned new retiree neighbor Mr. Busby, walking around the yard all the time in his half-buttoned, purple satin shirts—"

"That's right, those shirts!"

"—with his barrel chest stuck out. And there's little Evie, trapped upstairs tending to Stan—that was her husband—who was pretty much just a pool to pour morphine in by then. So mostly, she just stared out the window."

"'You become the neighborhood,'" I say, gliding my hands across the tops of the blades of grass, feeling their chemically treated ends prickle like gelled hair. "Do you remember her saying that?"

My mother pauses a moment, then shakes her head. "No, actually."

I do. More than once. Though I can't remember when. And even now, I don't know what it means.

My mother shakes her head again, but harder, like a dog shedding water. "You know, I really do have no idea how the pranks started. I think he might have brought her up a cold shrimp platter the first weekend he lived here. As a new-neighbor gesture, you know, not realizing. I don't think he'd ever met a Jew before, either, let alone known anything about keeping Kosher. But not long after that, she got him the gift subscription to *Hustler*, with the note that said '*To go with your shirts.*' Then he hid a bunch of those black, rubber June bugs all over that *sukka* she put up every year around back, on strings so he could make them scuttle across her little folding picnic table. Do you remember any of that?"

You Become the Neighborhood

I shake my head. "Just the picnic table. And ears of corn? Did she hang ears of corn in there?"

"He put rubber bugs in those, too. After that, it was *on*. Seemed like one of them came up with a new torture for the other every single week."

Instead of smiling some more, my mother starts muttering again. At least now I can hear her. "She was so lonely," she says. "They both were." Then some things that I don't catch. The sky purples over our heads, and the breeze brushes past.

"So, this one time…" I finally prod.

She looks surprised, as though she thought she'd still been talking to me. Her braid swings like the tongue of a bell, and her body vibrates. "Sorry. Yes. This one time. I assume she got the clothes from Madolyn. Tell me you remember Madolyn."

"Good God, how could I forget them," I say, and my mother says *them* right with me, holding her hands a good two feet in front of her breasts, and there we are smiling again. Mother and daughter. We glance together across the street toward Madolyn's duplex. "You don't think she still lives there?" I ask.

My mother doesn't respond.

"Whose ex was she again? The *Family Affair* guy?"

"Not him. The one from the knock-off. With the beard."

"Oh my God, Mom, do you remember what she told me? When I was just sitting out here with the turtle, minding my seven year-old business? She came across the street in this tiny black dress, and she had to have been as old as Mr. Busby, right? Sixty, at least."

"Older," says my mother.

"So it's just me and the turtle, looking at the sky. And here comes Madolyn and her shadows. And she stands over us. And she puts her hands right on her boobs. And then she says…" I try for a smoker's rasp, though it doesn't quite come off. "'*Just remember, Girlie. I got these for the husband. But I kept 'em for me.*' And then she turned around and went right back home."

My mother just nods, and takes a long time doing it. Her voice comes out sad. "That would be Madolyn. She was always so nice."

Nice?

More silence. Another sudden, nervous glance up in the air from my mother, and I know this can't last long. "Sorry I interrupted. You said Evie got something from her?"

"Oh. Right. Very possibly the same little black dress you just mentioned."

"What are you talking about?"

"And some fishnets. And some red lipstick. And some stilettos. Jesus, Ry, they had to have been seven inches high."

"Wait…she borrowed that stuff *for herself?* To *wear?*"

"For Mr. Busby."

At the gurgle in my throat, my mom actually grins. "It was horrible, really. And ingenious. You wouldn't think that sweet old woman…Mr. Busby's daughter was worried about him skulking around here by himself. She got him to take out a Personals ad in the *L.A. Weekly*. I helped him write it. And then I guess, maybe when I was trying to convince Evie to let me watch her husband sleep for a couple hours so she could go out and see a movie or something some evening, I must have let it slip. And that's what gave her the idea, which is why it was kind of my fault."

"You're telling me she answered his ad?"

"Made a date, told him she'd be by to pick him up. She didn't tell him who she was, of course."

"She actually went through with it? Went to his door dressed like that? What did he do?"

"I don't know, exactly. That is, I couldn't quite see. She made Madolyn and me hide in the hedge. All I could hear over our laughter was his screaming."

"That's…" I start, and don't know how to continue. I want to keep her talking about this forever, or at least long enough for me to get the picture straight in my head. Not of Evie, but of my mother crouched in a hedge with a friend, laughing. "I can't believe you haven't told me this before."

I know it's the wrong comment even before I finish. My mom's mouth twists, and her shoulders clench inward. She folds her arms across her chest.

"What happened after that?" I keep my voice light.

"Stan died," says my mother.

You Become the Neighborhood

The sun goes, dragging all that color behind it, and around us, the apartment buildings lose their depth like false fronts on a set. Across the street is Beverly Hills. A whole other world. You can tell by the curlicues on the street signs.

Without warning, my mother starts to swell. Her arms come loose and drop to her sides, and her spine arches and her head tilts all the way back as her mouth falls open. The moan seems to surge out of the grass and up her throat, rattling her teeth as it bursts out of her.

"*Mom*," I gasp, grabbing for her hand, scrambling up on my knees to try getting an arm around her.

The moan stops. My mother holds her position, completely frozen, like a sculpture of my mother moaning. Then her eyes pop open.

"Do you remember that sound, Ry?"

"Remember it? What the hell are you—"

"You don't," she says. "I'm glad." Then she folds her arms back across her chest and lowers her chin and sits there, holding herself. "I'm so glad."

Usually, by this point on our Sunday evenings, I've dutifully offered up the most innocuous details of my work life and my grad-school plans and my relationship with Danny (since I have no intention of actually *bringing* Danny), for which my mother trades seemingly grateful nods and sometimes an anecdote about women's feet from the shoe store where she works. Most weeks, she doesn't break down, especially if I have her back in her apartment and ensconced in front of her Tivo'd "American Idol" episodes—all of which she also watched when they were first broadcast—by eight. This is the first night in years where I've lost track of the time, even for a little while. And yet, I'm all too aware we're on dangerous ground.

"Do you want to go home?" I ask gently. I even touch her shoulder, and she doesn't pull away, though she also doesn't unclench.

"It usually started around 2 a.m.," she says. "Sometimes earlier than that. Mostly not, though. You really don't remember?" There are no tears, now, just a gauntness that seems to have surfaced in her chin and cheeks.

This is what she'll look like, old, I think, for no good reason.

"The most amazing thing is that I really think she had no idea she was doing it. I think she did it in her sleep. By the third or fourth night after Stan died, *I* couldn't sleep at all for knowing it was coming.

Somehow, being woken up by that, *to* that…it was just too much world, too fast.

"There wasn't any lead up. It came like an earthquake. That sound I just made, only a lot louder. And a thousand times as heartbroken. It went on and on and on, like she didn't even need to breathe. Then it would stop for maybe an hour, and then there'd be aftershocks, these quicker, more jagged moans. Those were so loud that that suspended light in my bedroom started swinging back and forth. You couldn't drown them out. I tried the fan. I tried headphones. *Nothing* worked. It was liked they'd crawled inside my head.

"Which reminds me. This was also when the spiders came."

That, at least, triggers a memory. Up until now, it's been like watching my mother recount a completely separate life. Part of which she's made up, or at least exaggerated, because I may have only been seven, and I've always slept heavy, but surely I would have heard what she's describing. And retained it.

But those webs. Everywhere, on everything. "I remember them," I say.

Mostly, I remember the wolf spider outside our front door. We had bougainvillea climbing the iron grating on either side of our little stoop. And for months that spring and early summer—the last months we lived here—this one bulbous, pregnant wolf spider would weave a new web between them every single night. We discovered the web the first time when I raced out the door one morning, headed for the park, and wrapped most of the strands around my face. I don't think I started screaming until my mom did, and she didn't start, she later said, until she saw the spider itself dangling just under my earlobe like some outsized, nightmare earring, clawing with its hairy legs as it tried to scuttle up the air into my hair to hide. My mom whacked it into the bushes with her hand, then spent half an hour calming us both down and picking the insect carcasses and threading out of my curls.

We weren't laughing, then. Or ever, really, about the spiders. There were too many of them, attracted, the t.v. said, by the freakishly humid spring, the eruption of greenery and insects that draped the hillsides and gardens of midtown L.A. and made it look, for just that short while, like somewhere living things actually belonged.

You Become the Neighborhood

But we developed a sort of affection for our lone wolf. Or fascination, at least. The way one might for a house ghost. Some nights, before sending me to bed, my mother would bring me to the front couch, draw back those bay-window curtains, flick on the porch light. And there she'd be, gray and translucent and hairy, scuttling back and forth seemingly in mid-air between the columns of bougainvillea, floating on her milky white egg-sac as though it were a balloon. Every morning, we took a broom, said we were sorry, and brought the web down so we could get out of the apartment. But we left the spider herself alone.

"Ry?" says my mother, startling me by brushing a fallen curl out of my eyes. She's never touched me, much. Not since I was very young. "What are you thinking about?"

I catch myself leaning away and feel bad, but too late. My mother has already withdrawn her hand. I try to smile, get some nostalgia into my voice. I'm surprisingly close to feeling some. I gesture toward the front stoop. "Our furry-legged friend."

She looks at my hands. Then the front of the apartment. Then she bursts into tears.

"Sorry," she says fast. "Sorry, sorry, sorry."

I reach to comfort her. But it never did any good when I was a kid, and it doesn't now. The sobs grab her by the shoulders and shake her.

They stop sooner than usual, though. And when my mother lowers her hands from her face, there's a steeliness in her jaw I don't remember seeing. "I'm just being stupid, as usual," she says. "It wasn't really that. It wasn't real. Obviously. It was just that time, those moans. I hadn't slept in so long, and those things were crawling over the place, and I missed your fucking asshole father, and…" her voice drops into its murmur. But lo and behold, it climbs back out. She looks at me. "It wasn't real," she says. "I want you to know I know."

I have no idea what to say to that. "We should get you home," I say eventually.

"Evie came down a few times that week after Stan died. Mostly in the evening, just to sit. You and I used to steal lemons off the trees by that condo complex around the corner, and I made lemonade, and the three of us would come right out here. Right about this time. We'd watch the spiders dancing up the walls and the sun going down and that turtle nosing around in the grass. Mr. Busby was away, I think his daughter'd taken him to Bermuda or something, and it was so quiet around here.

"I kept trying to ask Evie how she was doing, but she wouldn't talk about it. She talked about maybe going to see her sister in Maine, but not like she was really planning to do it. You showed her our wolf spider. She said there were lots more up under the eaves. She claimed she could hear them on the roof at night, and that she had a resident, too, who hung out by her bedroom window. An even bigger one. She didn't like its eyes.

"One night, later than usual—I was in a robe, and I'm sure you'd already gone to bed—she knocked on the door in tears and asked me to come out. She was in a robe, too. This horrible cream thing with blue lilies all over it. She was grabbing her arms to her chest.

"'They're biting him,' she kept saying. 'They're biting him. My poor Stan.' Then she showed me her hand. It was all purple on the back, she had this *huge* spider bite. Really nasty.

"'Evie, my God, you've got to treat that. Come in,' I told her. But she wouldn't. She said she had to get back. That they kept climbing on Stan and running around on him. She wasn't making much sense. Mostly, she was sobbing.

"I do remember one thing. At some point, she just started saying the word 'Gone.' And when I'd gotten her some lemonade and held her for a while—and I swear, Ry, she was thinner than you, it was like holding a garden rake except that she was so *soft*—she stuck her fingers under her glasses and wiped her eyes and said it again. 'Gone. What do people even mean when they say that? How can someone *go*? Go where? To me, he's as here as he ever was. He's right in the next room.'

"Know the worst part, Ry? What I remember thinking was that that was true. The guy'd been gone for ages. Months and months before he died. In a way, she was right.

"And somehow, between comforting her while she cried and getting her lemonade and wrapping her poor, old, squishy hand, I missed that part about the spiders biting him. I didn't think a single thing about what that meant until later that night, when Mr. Busby came home from his trip."

The silence seems almost peaceful at first, an organic lull in the conversation. But it lasts too long. My mother's staring up toward the

You Become the Neighborhood

windows of the upstairs apartment, and her mouth has formed an 'O.' Her shadows stretches out long beside her on the grass, like a web she's spun, or gotten stuck in.

"Mom. Seriously. I don't need another moan-demonstration."

She blinks as though I've dumped water over her head. As though she has no idea what I'm talking about. Yet again, I feel horrible. But this has gone on for so many years.

"I didn't know he was back," she says. "I mean, we were friendly, he even had me bring in his mail sometimes. But it wasn't like with Evie. He kind of kept to himself.

"If I'd known he was back, I would have warned him. But I didn't, and right on time at about 2:40 a.m., Evie went off. It was particularly horrible that night. God, Ry. Lying there in the dark, I think I started doing it along with her, under my breath, just to keep from going crazy. Only then—remember, I hadn't slept through the night since Stan died, so for maybe eight days running—I started thinking maybe it *was* me making the sounds, and that really freaked me out. And then the music exploded."

And there it is again. A surprising wisp of smile floating over her face. "His choice was *inspired*, in a way. I mean, he must have put some thought into it, after the moans woke him up. All of a sudden, these fat, thudding drums boom out his windows. And this bass. *Buum, buum, buum-bumm, dugga-dugga.* Rattled that picture of you on the Griffith Park merry-go-round right off my wall.

"I could hear him yelling, too. Mr. Busby. 'Hear that?' he was shouting. ''Cause I'm sure hearing you, Old Bat.'

"You know, you slept through that, too? I swear, Ry, sleeping through the Northridge quake must have trained you, because you never even moved. I jumped up, threw on my robe, and ran around to Mr. Busby's. He was holding one of his stereo speakers out his living room window, aimed straight up at Evie's. Every time the bass hit, his whole body quivered like the windshield of a car.

"Well he saw me. I'll never forget it, he was wearing these flashy green pajamas, I'm pretty sure they were the most reflective article of clothing I've ever seen on anyone. And he was having the time of his life. Grinning ear to ear. He was kind of irresistible that way, like a big overgrown lab. In reflective green pajamas. And he shouts to me, 'Evening, Girl. Think the old woman knows I'm home?'

"'Stan died,' I told him.

"'Sorry,' he yelled. 'Lot of moaning going on. Can't hear ya.'

"I told him again. That time, he understood. 'Ah, shit,' he said, and quivered when the bass hit him. He ducked inside and shut off the music. There were lights on halfway down the block, and Madolyn was out on her lanai, yelling.

"Mr. Busby stuck his head back out, shouting, 'Yeah, yeah, go back to bed' to the whole world. Then he threw his hands up to his hair, and he started rooting around and saying 'Goddamn. Is it on me? Can you see it?'

"I helped him get rid of the rest of the web he'd stuck his face through. Then I got lemonade, and he got a box of Wheat Thins. And we just stood together at his window, all night. Him and me. He kept looking up at Evie's windows. Sometimes he'd say, 'So she's been doing that a lot? That sound? Every night?' And sometimes he'd say, 'Poor old bat.' Finally, sometime around dawn, right when I told him I had work and got up to go in, he said, 'Hey. Want to see my wheels?' And he took me around to the driveway to show me the car his daughter had bought him."

"I'll bet it was shiny," I say, though I'm entranced yet again. How is it possible that I know so little about the life my mother led here, before she became the way she is?

"You bet right. And not just shiny. *Pink* and shiny. And a Jag."

My jaw drops. "I didn't know they made pink Jags. Or that anyone on this side of Olympic had that kind of money."

"His daughter bought it for him. And this is the thing about Leyton Busby, Ry. This is what I think Evie never understood. That was all he wanted to talk about. It was all he cared about. I don't think he cared about the car itself one little bit. 'She paid half down,' he told me. He never even walked around it, he just stood there in his shiny pajamas, which his daughter also bought him, beaming away. '*Half*. To cheer me up, she says. Like I need so much cheering.'"

"But he *was* cheerier that morning. Just not about the car. I always hoped…" The sudden turn of my mother's head catches me off-guard. Headlights from a passing car sweep her face, and her eyes flare like fireflies in the gloom. Guilt blows through and past me, faint and salty.

You Become the Neighborhood

"Well," says my mother. "I just hope his daughter knew that. Somehow, I got the impression maybe she didn't." Shadows have settled back over her face, but I can still feel her eyes on me. Another one of those near-smiles flutters across her lips without landing there. "For a long time, Mr. Busby and I just looked at his car. Once, he said, 'Watch this,' and then he jumped from one side of the bumper to the other, then pointed into the paint job. 'You see that?' he said. 'There's a pink me in there.' I was about to go inside when he asked, 'You figure she's awake? The old bat?'

"I told him I didn't even know what time it was.

"'Sun's up,' he said. 'She's super-old. And I don't hear moaning, do you?' When I shook my head, he said, 'Right. Let's go see what we can do.'

"I was too surprised to do anything but follow. And…I remember the air, right then. It was so clean. Like it never is here. There were hummingbirds beating around the bougainvillea. And bees buzzing. You could actually see the outlines of all the trees and cars and people, without that haze around them, you know? Everything just seemed so *substantial*, or something. Like we were really here, for once. If that makes any sense."

"I actually know exactly what you mean," I say quietly.

This time, for one moment, that smile actually lands. Beats its wings on her lips. Lifts away again. I want to reach out, snatch it back. But it's too late already. Again.

"We got upstairs, and Mr. Busby banged on Evie's door, and he was right, she was up, dressed, had her hair out of her curlers. I think she maybe forgot herself, because she just threw the door open, then shut it halfway real fast, but not fast enough. That's when I realized Stan was still in there." Now it's my turn to stare. My mother's staring, too. But at the building, not me.

"Mom. What?"

"It'd been eight days. Maybe longer, I don't know. I just caught a glimpse. The hospital bed, the i.v. stand with the tubing wrapped around it for disposal. And Stan. He was half-curled up in the sheets. This little cocoon husk she'd been married to for 63 years."

"Wait. You mean his body? She *kept* it?"

"'Oh my God,' I remember saying. I tried to elbow Mr. Busby out of the way, but he wasn't going.

"'Is that Stan?' he kept saying. 'Mary Mother of God, woman, is that Stan?'

"She tried to slam the door on us. But Mr. Busby wedged himself in the frame and wouldn't let her. I think she hit him. He didn't budge. She looked terrible. Bloated and pale and patchy. Maybe it was the light, but even her skin had gone gray. She was practically transparent. Like a column of dust motes you could scatter with one hand.

"'Oh, Evie,' I told her. 'Come downstairs. Let me take care of this for you.'

"She didn't put up much fight. She hit Mr. Busby a few more times. Then she said she'd appreciate that. But that she'd wait up here with Stan.

"So I went down and woke you and showered and looked in the Yellow Pages and found an undertaker who said he'd come. And then I went to work. When I got home, I knocked on Evie's door, just to check on her, but no one answered.

"And then you got the mumps. And my work went crazy, and I almost lost my job because I kept having to take off to care for you. And your dad got himself thrown in jail again. And the spiders got into everything. And somehow, weeks passed…"

This time, instead of muttering, she goes completely still. Sits there in the grass. Until, with a shriek, she scuttles backwards on her hands, smacking at her legs and jabbing her hands up the sleeves of her summer blouse and raking downward with clawed fingers. Welts well up in her skin and boil over. I try to grab her wrists, but she claws me, too, then scrambles all the way to the sidewalk and stands up.

All this time, she's kept her eyes glued to the upstairs windows. My tears surprise me. I'm not even sure what they're for. It's not like this is atypical behavior.

"Mom," I whisper. "I'm sorry I brought you here. I didn't mean to."

"It wasn't real," she says again, spitting the words. "You need to know I know."

"Okay. I know you know."

"No you don't."

I close my eyes. "Okay, I don't."

"Maybe you want to know what I saw. Maybe you should. Maybe then you'd stop looking at me like that."

You Become the Neighborhood

"I'm not looking at you like anything," I sigh, standing to start negotiating her back toward my car.

"That's what I mean," she says, starting to cry. "So I'm going to tell you."

We've attracted attention, finally. A curtain has stirred in the apartment next to our old one. Mr. Busby's old place. And across the sidestreet, a stoop-backed old woman with a basket on her wrist and a long, white cane has emerged onto the sidewalk. Her hair is some crazy L.A. old-lady color, practically fuschia in the twilight. She has a hand shading her eyes, as though even the echoes of orange in the west are too bright for her.

"Hey, Mom? We should probably go. I think it's time to get you home. Simon Cowell and the gang are waiting."

"I don't know what made me call them," she says. "The undertakers." The sky has gone royal blue, and even the blue is draining away as though it's being siphoned. The breeze has developed a bite, too, and the old woman across the street has made her way to the crosswalk, and now she's inching in our direction. She's thin, all in white, her stoop so pronounced that she almost looks likes a cane herself, for the shadows to lean on.

"Mom?" I say, with even more force than I intend. "I want to go, even if you don't."

"I hadn't seen Evie in a while. I went up and knocked a few times. Mostly, there was no answer. I thought she'd finally gone away to see her sister or something. But then sometimes I'd hear her through the door. She sounded so small. I could hardly understand her.

"Mr. Busby tried a few pranks. "Going to lure her out,' he'd say. 'Get her blood going. Leyton knows what the ladies need.' He'd stop every Jehovah's Witness and Mormon missionary he saw and direct them to Evie's door. One night around midnight, he came out on the grass with a ukulele and sang 'Tiny Bubbles' at the top of his lungs, except he kept saying 'Tiny Evie' instead. But she never appeared at the window. We had this possum family that took up residence by the dumpster, and he made a trail with orange peels and lettuce right to her door and got the whole family to camp outside it. But as far as I know, she never saw them.

"And then one day...you were still so sick. I was so worried about you. I'd spent all my summer pay to bail out your dad, and my reward was having him call in a drunken stupor every night to tell me either that he was going to make it up to me, somehow, or that he was going to kill me. Depended what he'd been drinking. I think it must have been the possums that made me even think of it, because to be honest, I didn't have time or energy to worry about Evie. She'd stopped moaning. But instead, she kept prowling around up there, every single night, at any hour. I think she was barefoot, at least. I could barely hear her. Just these little scratches. Little slides. Back and forth, in little lurches. All blessed night. Just enough to keep me awake. It also made me even more sad. And tired. I'd never been so tired in my whole life. This went on and on.

"Until that one day. The last day." She takes a huge breath and holds it, as though trying to cure hiccoughs. She does that for so long that her knees start to wobble.

"Mom, come on," I say.

"I came home." Her voice shakes. "And I saw the possum family at the top of her steps. And the spider webs all up and down the stairwell, as though no one had used it for years, which was ridiculous. The mailman went up there every day, for one.

"But something about it gave me this weird feeling. And it set me thinking. I hadn't been invited to Stan's funeral. Evie hadn't said anything about it whatsoever. I was sure she would have invited me, or talked to me. I went inside and found the number of the undertakers, and I called them.

"And that's when I found out. They'd come, alright, on the day I'd summoned them, and knocked at the door. Evie had answered them through it. She said everything was taken care of. And the undertakers said okay and left.

"I hung up. I had no idea what to think. Then you started crying. And your father called. Then he called again. And you cried some more. And I started crying. I think I just switched on the t.v. and left you in the living room with a popsicle and a blanket and ignored you when you yelled for me. I locked myself in the bedroom to try to get some sleep before Evie started pacing again. I think somehow I must have got some, too. Because this time it was the screaming that woke me up."

You Become the Neighborhood

"Jesus," rasps the old woman in white, right next to us, and I jump forward and whirl around. How is it possible for something that slow to sneak up?

She's got a crooked, stumpy hand in my mother's hair. Holding on to her braid, like a child grabbing a cat's tail.

"It really is you," she rasps, her voice so honeycombed that it might be the wind talking.

Even then, several stunned seconds pass before I recognize her. And my mother ignores her completely. She just rambles on, as though the woman isn't even there.

"I hurtled out bed and came racing out the door. I thought it was you, even though it sounded nothing like you. I just felt so bad. So guilty. About so many things." Tears stream down her face. To my astonishment, she lays her head on the old woman's shoulder. The woman strokes her braid.

"*Madolyn?*" I gasp. While thinking, *where's the rest of you*? The shapeless dress drops without interruption past her waist. The sight is horrifying to me. Incomprehensible. Sad. Wrong. New York without the Trade Centers.

"It took me a minute to realize the screams were coming from outside. From the driveway." My mother burrows deeper into Madolyn's collarbone, which looks bony, now, and can't be comfortable. "I raced around the building. And there was Mr. Busby, standing by what was left of his Jag."

Madolyn still holds onto my mother's braid. I have to stifle an urge to grab her wrist, shake her loose. It's like my mother is a child's pull-toy, and as long as Madolyn keeps yanking her hair, she's got no choice but to keep talking.

"I never thought you'd come back here," the old woman rasps. "Either one of you. You look good, Ry. Like you made it. I thought you might."

"They'd broken every single window," says my mother. "Bashed the windshield to pieces. Stolen all the tires. Knifed the seats." She speaks faster and faster. One of her hands has snared itself in Madolyn's dress. "On both sides, into that beautiful pink paint, they'd keyed the words *Black Fag*."

I blink. "What? Who?"

"Leyton was just shaking, when he wasn't shouting. I felt awful. I tried to say something comforting, but he wasn't having it. I didn't even hear what he was saying at first. That he was actually accusing Evie of this. And even if I had, it was so crazy. But how could he not be crazy, after that? 'Oh, Leyton,' I told him.

"'Too far,' he was shouting. 'Too far, Old Bat. Not funny. Way too far.' And then…" My mother twitches in place, and Madolyn gives a gentle tug on her braid. "Then…" Again, the twitch and tug. Like she's stuck.

"Mom," I say. "Let's get out of here."

"He started for the stairs. He was still screaming 'Old Bat' at the top of his lungs, and—"

"Come *on*," I snarl, yanking her away from Madolyn. A shudder ripples from her neck all the way down into her feet, and she stumbles against me and then straightens up.

She's holding my hand. Standing tall. Somehow, I've forgotten that my mother is taller than me. She's blinking furiously. She reaches up and at least smears the wetness flooding her face. Only then does she seem to see Madolyn.

"Oh," she says. "Hello."

Madolyn eyes her up and down. Her skin is tanning-bed orange, her brow surgically lifted so high that it seems pinned to the crest of her head. She looks like a doll, a Madolyn action-figure, denuded of its most characteristic elements. Sanitized.

"*You*, on the other hand, don't look so different from the night you left. I'm sorry to say."

My mother tries a laugh. As if Madolyn were kidding. "I was just telling Ry the story. It seems so silly, now."

"Silly," says Madolyn.

The urge to get my mother away from here, and from this woman, has become overwhelming. I'm way past questioning it. I start to pull her toward the curb. But she digs in her feet and won't budge.

"I just thought she should know." She's practically chirping, trying so hard to sound like an ordinary, comfortable person that it breaks my heart.

"I agree," says Madolyn. "She should."

You Become the Neighborhood

"You know," my mother says, forces a laugh, waves an airy hand. "What caused me to…it seems so ridiculous, in retrospect. What I thought I saw."

"Thought?" says Madolyn, very quietly.

"It was just such a hard year for me, you know? Such a terrible time. Watching that poor old woman go completely to pieces. And Leyton stomping around his place and the yard, not knowing what to do with himself or how to go on, and you across the street—" she's talking to Madolyn, almost accusing her— "in your little mausoleum to yourself, with all those pictures of you and a guy you don't love on the cover of *People* or whatever, blown up to cover every inch of wall-space. And that moaning and pacing upstairs every single goddamn night." She turns to me. "And you. My sweet, sweet daughter. Sitting out here by yourself day after day, with no one to look after you properly. With a turtle for a playmate. We were all so lonely. So, so lonely. I guess I got lonely, too."

"You become the neighborhood," I blurt, and tear up again.

"I guess it all just boiled over. Messed up my head. And when Leyton got up the stairs and started banging on that door, screaming for Evie to come out…When he kept banging and banging and banging, while I was screaming for him to stop…

"That's right, you were there, too, Madolyn. You saw it all happen. My big breakdown." She laughs that laugh again; it's horrible, like a CD skipping. "You were there when the door opened."

Madolyn has straightened over her cane. The botox injections have made actual facial expressions impossible. But her eyes are ice-cold. "Yep," she says.

"She was there," my mother tells me, patting my hand. "She helped me when I broke down. When I started screaming. When the paramedics came. You probably called the paramedics, didn't you, Madolyn? She helped them get me in the ambulance. Made sure they knew about you. I never thanked you for that. How'd I even get that picture in my head, Madolyn? I still don't know."

"The one you saw, you mean."

"The one I thought I saw. When Evie's door opened."

"So you think you didn't see it? Is that what you're telling me?"

"Mom, please." My own voice starts to crack. *I'm too late*, I think. *One more time.*

"You mean, giant spiderlegs scuttling out onto the landing?" The skipping laugh crescendos. "Grabbing Leyton and yanking him inside?"

"That," says Madolyn. "And those sounds. Like a cat being ripped inside out while it was still alive." She nods her fuschia-haired, copper-skinned head. "Sounds about right to me. Pretty much what I saw and heard."

My mother stops laughing. Stops breathing again. Sways on her feet. "Stop it," she says.

With a shrug, Madolyn steps toward her. "I'm just saying your memory matches pretty perfectly with mine."

"Oh, you bitch." My mother's voice is a pig-squeal, now. She's shaking all over. "Stop right now."

"You better bring her inside," Madolyn says to me. "She's going to collapse."

"You cunt whore, stop," squeals my mother, throws her head back, and screams.

"*Mom!*" I try to grab her, but she jabs her elbows into my ribs, staggers away, and drops to her knees in the grass.

"Say you're joking," she hisses. "Say it right now."

If Madolyn gets any closer to my mother, I'm thinking I will bowl her over. Drive her into the ground, cane, basket and all.

"Get away," I tell her.

Instead, she plants the cane and sits. My mother folds into a little hump, then tilts sideways against the old woman, and lays her head in her lap.

"There, now," Madolyn says, and strokes my mother's braid. And there they sit.

It's insane, the stupidest sensation of this stupid evening yet. But most of what I feel right then is jealousy. And guilt, for the last fifteen years. Especially the last few. I've been old enough to treat my mother differently for a long time, now.

Abruptly, Madolyn lifts the lid of her basket, reaches inside, and pulls out the turtle. I gasp, folding down beside them. My mother lies in Madolyn's lap and shakes and coos like a baby. Madolyn lays the turtle in the grass, where it begins to nose about. Head sideways. Eying the sky.

You Become the Neighborhood

"That's him? Evie's?" I stammer.

Madolyn nods.

"You saved him?"

"Afterward. Yeah. When the police were done."

"Police…" I reach my finger in front of the turtle's nose, the way one does with a kitten. The turtle pulls its head into its shell. Noses out again. Sidles sideways to get at more grass.

Madolyn watches him, too, shaking her head. "I found him under the couch. Under all the webbing."

In her lap, my mother twitches.

"What the hell are you talking about?" I snap.

"What there was. A lot of ugly smears of God knows what, all over the walls and the floor and even the ceiling. A lot of web. A lot of mess. All the windows smashed out, and wind just whipping everything around. No bodies. Not Stan's. Not Leyton Busby's. Not Evie's. No one's."

"Are you…" I don't want to say it, or think it. Most of all, I don't want my mother to hear it. It comes out anyway. "Are you seriously saying she was…?"

Madolyn strokes a curved, clawed hand down my mother's cheek. Her face is so blank, you could project anything there. At the moment, insanely, I'm projecting grandmotherly kindness. The moon has just started to rise behind her, and there's this white nimbus floating around her fuschia head.

"Well, that's one of the possibilities, I suppose," she says. "I've thought of a few others, down the years. Mostly, I try not to think about it, to be honest. All I know for sure is that Evie wasn't in there when the cops came. No one was. And no one saw or heard from her, or from Leyton Busby, ever again. And that ever since, I've been keeping a good watch. I don't know what for, exactly. But I watch that building real close. The whole neighborhood, really. Just…seems like what I'm here for, maybe. And I keep my own house *clean*."

It's the way my mother's lying there, I think, that makes me break down and weep. The way her knees have drawn up. The shudders wracking her. "You become the neighborhood," I whisper.

"Second time you've said that," said Madolyn. "What's it mean?"

"Hell if I know. Evie used to say it."

89

Leaning back on her hands with my mother in her lap and Evie's turtle nosing around near her hip, Madolyn glances down at what's left of herself, or maybe my mother, both of them suspended in pale moonlight. Then she looks across the street toward her own home, where she's lived alone, I'm all but certain, for going on thirty years. Then she looks up at Evie's windows.

"You know what I think?" Her voice is like a rainstick, a rattlesnake's warning, a fire going out. Like she's praying and fighting and giving up all at the same time. "I think maybe if you live long enough, and you see enough…" Again, she glances down. "And you lose enough, and life gets at you enough, and does what it's going to do…"

Then she looks at me. Actually reaches out and wipes some of my tears away, while the shakes seem to sizzle out of my mother, through the grass like lightning, and up into me.

"Sooner or later, Hon. For better or worse. You become you."

The Pikesville Buffalo

"I saw, or dreamed that I saw, standing upon the extreme verge of the precipice, with neck out-stretched, with ears erect, and the whole attitude indicative of profound and melancholy inquisitiveness, one of the oldest and boldest of those identical elks which had been coupled with the red men of my vision…

A negro emerged from the thicket, putting aside the bushes with care, and treading stealthily. He bore in one hand a quantity of salt, and holding it towards the elk, gently yet steadily approached…The negro advanced; offered the salt; and spoke a few words of encouragement or conciliation. Presently, the elk bowed and stamped, and then lay quietly down and was secured with a halter.

Thus ended my romance of the elk. It was a pet of great age and very domestic habits, and belonged to an English family occupying a villa in the vicinity."
—Edgar Allen Poe, "Morning on the Wissahiccon"

Late that November, a few months after his twenty-four year-old wife was diagnosed with breast cancer, Daniel felt a sudden urge to see the Great Aunts. He tried Ethel first, calling five times over a two-hour period, but kept getting the busy signal which meant either that she was talking to one of her children or stepchildren or—more likely—that she'd taken her phone off the hook to avoid talking to them. Finally, he called Zippo and got her on the first try.

"Of course, dear," she told him, sounding muffled as ever, as though she were speaking through the orange wool shawl she always kept about her shoulders.

"Could you beam the news over to Aunt Ethel?"

"What? Oh, Daniel." It was an old joke, his father's, about the telepathic link that seemed to connect the sisters.

"How's your lovely Lisa, honey?" Zippo aked.

"Okay, I think. Still not sleeping very well. The doctors think they got it all."

"Poo-poo," said Zippo, and Daniel hung up.

The next morning, he awoke before five, kissed Lisa where she lay twisting in the blankets, and, for the first time in over a year, drove the hour and a half from his dumpy beach-neighborhood shack on the Delaware coast into Baltimore, then out Reiserstown Road toward Pikesville. The early morning gray never lifted, and the grass everywhere had already died. Something about the old neighborhoods near the Great Aunts had always unsettled Daniel, even during his childhood, when he'd visited them every weekend. The low, red-brick houses seemed to have too few windows, too many chimneys, and they were always tucked back in the shadows of the tallest trees on their lots like little warrens. Rotting, unraked leaves littered the lawns. The oaks and elms and black locusts stood midwinter-bare.

Pulling up outside Ethel's house—which was small, stone, and too long at either end for its slanted roof, as though emerging from the maples with its hands on its hips—Daniel shut off the car and was surprised to see his own hands shaking. He sat a few seconds, staring through the windshield at the gray, thinking not of Lisa but of cancer. It was true, what Zippo had told him not long after his father had died. Cancer didn't just kill people; it blurred them, left a hazy, pointillist

The Pikesville Buffalo

blotch where memories of the lives they'd lived before the disease should have been.

Abruptly, he slammed his fist down on the horn. For all they knew, Lisa really was finished with cancer. Forever. They'd caught it early, taken it out. He really needed to get the hell over it.

Which was exactly why he'd come. Popping open the door, he stepped onto the pavement, expecting Pikesville silence, winter wind. Instead, he got Xavier Cugat.

Before he even reached his Aunt Ethel's front steps, Daniel was smiling. It wasn't just the incongruity—all those congas and horns sashaying down this street of old homes and older Jews—but the volume. Daniel swore he could see the surrounding houses shuddering on their foundations, the drawn curtains in nearby windows twitching their skirts. He half-expected the police to arrive any second.

Daniel tried the front doorbell first, but of course, that was useless. Hunching against the cold, he slipped around the side. He was already past the screened-in porch when his aunt opened the side door.

"Oy-yoy-yoy," she said, nodding at his coat, one hand fluttering off the hips she could no longer shake and making mambo motions. "Is it really that cold out?"

Daniel stared. The rooster-crest springing from his aunt's scalp glowed a luminous, freshly dyed red. She was wearing blue-jean shorts, a yellow t-shirt with a Queen of Hearts playing card and the legend *Aunty Up, Baby* imprinted on it, and yellow vinyl slipper-sandals that displayed her virtually nail-less hammer toes in all their glory.

"Can't you feel it?" Daniel half-shouted, moving forward to give her a kiss.

"Skin of a crocodile." Aunt Ethel pulled demonstratively at the folds on her forearms.

"Toes of a troll."

She smacked him playfully on the cheek, kissed him in the same place, then used her thumb to smear the lipstick she'd imprinted there. "You find a troll who looks this good at eighty-two, give him my number, okay?" With an arthritic lurch Daniel realized afterward was a butt-bump, Aunt Ethel shuffled off inside, beckoning him with more of her rhythmic, slinky hand movements.

"Aren't you worried about the neighbors?" Daniel called, shutting the door.

"What?"

"The racket. What if they call the cops?"

"The music? Honey, everyone within four blocks is stone deaf."

She disappeared into her tiny kitchen to bring him the bagel, lox, and purple onion tray he knew she'd have prepared and refrigerated for him last night. The stereo shut down, and for one delicious moment, Daniel found himself alone, submerged in the familiar dimness of his Aunt Ethel's house.

The memories that assailed him centered mostly around shivas, but were no less sweet for that: there was the midnight flag football game in the sleet fourteen years ago, two days after Uncle Harry's death, when Daniel's father—frail already, and with a hacksaw cough, but still slippery as a snowflake—solved the absence-of-spare-socks problem by suggesting they use yarmulkes for the flags instead; there was the morning he'd crept upstairs with Ethel's perpetually wan, humorless thirty-four year-old son Herm after the early Mourner's Kaddish at the shiva for Zippo's second husband Ivan. He and Herm had used an entire roll of electrical tape, some torn-up egg cartons, and a box of discarded nine-volt batteries to try to get Herm's home-made, childhood train set to run just one more time. It hadn't, but the light-towers at the miniature baseball stadium flicked on a few times, and one of the crossing gates lowered and its bells rang; there was the three-hour jokefest after Rabbi Goldberg went home on the last night of Mack's funeral two years ago. It began with Daniel's recitation of Mack's favorite about the rabbi, the leather worker and the circumcised foreskins, and ended when Daniel's father—barely able to speak, and confined to a wheelchair he couldn't even sit up in—somehow gasped his way through the Fuck One Goat joke, while all the cousins and step-cousins alternately giggled and snuck glances at Aunt Ethel's half-horrified mouth, quivering as it fought the laughter welling behind it. Daniel had been laughing, too, until he saw Zippo leaning into the shadows against the hallway wall, her eyes riveted on his father, her mouth pursed and her shoulders drawn back as though she could do his breathing for him.

The Pikesville Buffalo

Or had that been at the shiva for Zippo's third husband, Uncle Joe, whom Daniel had only met twice, but who had the gorgeous lesbian granddaughter? Or for Uncle Bob, Mitchell's shyer, gentler best friend?

No. Mack's, because of the jokes. Just the way Mack would have wanted it. If he'd had his way, he'd probably have had Aunt Ethel blasting Xavier Cugat during the graveside service, too.

Standing now in Aunt Ethel's tan-carpeted living room with the tea mugs on glass shelves and the library-sale Dick Francis hardbacks lining the walls, Daniel thought of what his mother had called Aunt Zip, years and years ago: the Angel of Mercy, or else the Worst Luck in the World. Tears teased the corners of his eyes, which had adjusted to the gloom, now. He glanced toward the wall of photos, blinked, and moved closer.

"Uh…Aunt Ethel? Where'd everybody go?"

In she came, balancing not just the bagel tray but a chipped, porcelain jug of orange juice and a set of thirty year-old novelty glasses featuring stencils of Jim Palmer in his Jockey underwear on the sides.

"Eat, you look thin," she said, somehow maneuvering the tray and glasses onto the tiny coffee table. "I got your favorite. Onion, sesame, pumpernickel." She gestured toward the pile of toasted bagels.

"Just one of my favorites would have done."

"Well, I have to eat, too, don't I?"

Without waiting for him to choose, Aunt Ethel bent forward, drew half an onion bagel from the stack, and began slathering it with cream cheese and onion bits. Daniel gestured at the wall.

"Aunt Ethel, we really have to talk about you letting the buffalo herd play with the photographs."

She lifted an old, open hardback off the table out of the way of the food and held it to her chest. The phone rang.

"Ugh," she said. "I don't feel like talking."

Daniel grinned. "Okay, I'll leave."

She tsked and smacked his leg with the book, then studied him a while.

"Too thin," she said.

She reoffered the bagel, and Daniel took it, though he wasn't hungry. Almost casually, he glanced at his aunt's hands, looking for signs of shaking. There were none.

"Seriously," he said. "What happened to the boys?" He nodded toward the wall, most of which was blanketed with the same collage of framed snapshots of children and stepchildren and grandchildren Daniel had practically memorized during all those childhood visits, or more likely during the shivas, when there was so little to do but eat and stare at faces. But sometime in the past year, Aunt Ethel had apparently replaced the photos of herself and Aunt Zippo and the six husbands they'd buried between them.

"They're right there." She began pointing down the row of new photos, each of a different shaggy, horned, decrepit-looking buffalo standing atop a grassless little hill in front of a cyclone fence. Unless it was the same buffalo.

Laughing through a mouthful of bagel, Daniel said, "I meant your boys. Joe, Mack, Har—"

"There's Harry." Aunt Ethel directed his gaze toward the farthest-right buffalo. "Sleepy-eyed and slow as ever. Here's Joe. And see Mitchell, could he be any more of a cliché, do you think?"

Baffled, Daniel followed his aunt's finger. This buffalo had one of its legs off the ground and its head lifted, gazing not at the grassless ground but through the fence.

"Look at him," Aunt Ethel said. "Still busy. Somewhere in that yard, some overwhelmed, mesmerized sheep dog just agreed to purchase the complete long-term care plus annuities package."

Daniel started to laugh again, but the expression on his aunt's face stopped him. She wore the same loving smile she'd always leveled at him. But she was looking at the photographs.

"Aunt Ethel. You're naming your buffalo pictures?"

"The buffalo, not the pictures." Folding the book against her chest, Aunt Ethel gave a satisfied sigh. "And we didn't name them, what are you talking about? Did you name Lisa?"

"What?"

"How is she, by the way? Oy vay, she's been through so much. You both have. So young."

Laying the book on the couch and pinching his cheek, Aunt Ethel toddled out of the room with the empty orange juice jug. Daniel stared after her. It should have been funny. Just the latest of the thousand ways

The Pikesville Buffalo

his aunt had found to flood her days with happier thoughts than her days seemed to merit. He wondered if she'd told Zippo. Somehow, he didn't think Zippo would be amused.

Daniel looked down at the hardback on the couch and bent to pick it up. It had no cover. But a number of its pages had been dog-eared, and when Daniel flipped to the first, he found a passage highlighted in bright pink marker. *"The Holy Spark that fell when God built and destroyed the worlds, man shall raise and purify, from stone to plant, from plant to animal...purify and raise the Holy Sparks that are imprisoned in the world of shells."* Next to the word 'shells,' in the mock-parchment margins of the page, his aunt had drawn a smiley face.

Not Dick Francis, then. He flipped the book on its spine and raised an eyebrow. He'd never known his aunt to crack a Sidur in synagogue, let alone the Kabbalah in her home.

"You're going to have to come to the graves, okay?" Aunt Ethel said from the other room, and Daniel started.

"I'm sorry?"

"Thursday's cemetery day, remember? I'd be okay skipping, I mean, they're not *there* anymore, but you know your other aunt. 'A grave needs stones.' So come with us, and afterward we'll go get coddies."

"Ugh," Daniel murmured. "Is that even real fish in those things?"

"What do you think the mustard's for?"

Daniel started to smile, but stopped halfway. He was looking at the buffalo. Remembering Mitchell coming home from work, which is pretty much all anyone remembered of Mitchell. Harry with the trains. Most of all, Mack, spooling jokes through endless dinners, teaching his aunt to rumba on two replaced hips.

For the first time in his life, he wondered if it had been a good idea coming here. He leaned forward to lay the book back on the couch, came face to face with the photograph of the buffalo with its leg in the air—Mitchell—and saw the cheetah for the first time.

Had that been there a second ago? Had he really not noticed that?

There it was, anyway, its nose to the gate of the fence in the background, one paw through the chicken wire. The blotchy, irregular spots on its fur looked more like mange than coloration, and there was an ugly pink patch above its back right haunch and another at the base of its neck.

"Aunt Ethel?" he called. "About this cheetah..."

"Mack?"

"*Mack?*"

The front door burst open, and Daniel swiveled toward it. From the tiny entrance way, he heard the scuffle of heavy boot heels, started to call a hello, but stopped when he heard the tremor in Zippo's voice.

"They're out. Ethel, my God, they're loose. All of them."

Daniel arrived just in time to see Aunt Ethel stumbling for the front closet, grabbing at the long, yellow overcoat she'd worn all of his life, and starting out the front door before Aunt Zip put a crooked, age-stained hand on her wrist.

"Honey, you're going to freeze."

With an annoyed glance at her shorts and t-shirt, Ethel hurried off down the back hallway toward her bedroom. That hallway, too, had always been lined floor to ceiling with family photographs, including a random series of Daniel at various ages, some of them with his parents. From where he was standing, Daniel could only see that there were still pictures. Had the one of his father been replaced, also? With orangutans, maybe?

Was there even one of Lisa? Had he ever given Aunt Ethel one?

Then Zippo's hand was on his cheek, pulling his gaze around. Where Ethel was essentially a fire hydrant with hammer toes, Zippo loomed like a tall, bent oak. Whatever dye she used either never took or she kept washing it out, because her gauzy hair was mostly white tinged with blue.

"Hello, Aunt Zip." He leaned in to kiss her, but halted midway. "Aunt Zip? What is it?"

Both of his aunts could produce tissues from mid-air the way magicians did coins. Almost always, the tissues were for others, but now Zippo dabbed at her own eyes. The orange eye-shadow on her lids looked caked and layered and permanent, like veins in sedimentary rock.

"Nothing, sweetie," she said. "It's your silly old aunts. You look thin."

Even more unsettled, Daniel kissed her, anyway. "It's great to see you."

"Oh, Daniel. I'm so sorry you're having to deal with all this again. So soon after your dad, I mean. It's not fair."

"It's never fair," Daniel said quietly. "Isn't that what you taught my mom?"

The Pikesville Buffalo

"Yes." Aunt Zippo's face had long since begun to cave in, the nose sinking into its cavity and the mouth losing shape, and there were red, spidery blotches everywhere. She looked like a cherry pie. With whip-cream hair. She dabbed once more with the tissue. The tissue vanished. "But I meant for me." With that singular smile that always looked half-melted, almost all mouth-turned-down, Zippo touched his cheek, and Daniel felt simultaneously near tears and buoyed.

The Angel of Mercy. The Worst Luck in the World.

Ethel rumbled back into the entryway, and Aunt Zippo clucked.

"What?" Ethel snapped. "Let's go. Daniel, you're driving."

Ethel hadn't changed her top or her shorts. But she'd somehow yanked on yellow winter tights and a long-sleeved thermal undershirt beneath them. Feeling a surprising grin creep onto his lips, Daniel followed his aunts out the front door into the icy morning.

He actually had to hurry to get to the car before them and flip the locks. Before he could do it for her, Ethel had somehow bent low enough on her creaking hips to pull the passenger seat-lever and climb into the back.

"Ethel, I'll sit there," Zippo said.

"Oh, be quiet, you're too tall." Ethel yanked the seat into position in front of her. "Come on, Daniel."

"Ladies. Would either one of you like to tell me where we're going?"

For an astonishing moment, even Zippo looked exasperated with him. "The farm, Honey. Where do you think?"

"The farm. Right. Either of you want to tell me which…" But he realized that he knew. At the same moment, he also realized what had seemed so strange about the buffalo on their hill. Other than the fact that there were photographs of them on his aunt's wall.

He'd seen those buffalo. Knew that hill.

"Buddy's Farm," he said.

"Of course, Buddy's Farm," Ethel snapped, "let's—"

"Oh," said Zippo, and moved off toward the white Le Sabre parked a good five yards behind Daniel's car and another five from the curb.

"Zippo!" Ethel called.

Ignoring her sister, Zippo leaned into her front seat and returned with a white baker's box wrapped in bowed white twine. She handed

Daniel the box before circling the car and lowering herself into the passenger seat.

"That couldn't have waited until we got back?" Ethel asked as Daniel keyed the ignition.

"Daniel's here." Zippo smiled that upside down, half-melted smile and patted his leg. "Daniel gets chocolate tops."

The shudder that rippled across his shoulders startled him. At least it passed quickly. "Thank you, Aunt Zip," he said. He started to wrestle with the twine, and Zippo clucked and took the box from him and neatly unpicked the knot.

"Let's go," Ethel barked.

Mostly, Daniel knew the way, though he couldn't remember driving to Buddy's Farm himself before. In fact, he didn't even think he'd been there in at least ten years. The sun had slipped through the cloud cover, though its light served only to turn the dead grass and the bare trees whiter. He started to turn right, Ethel corrected him with a clipped, "No," and Zippo began pushing random buttons trying to tune his radio.

"What do you want to hear?" Daniel asked through a mouthful of thick, fudgy frosting from the cookie Aunt Zip had practically stuffed between his lips. "Don't know if I've got any big Xave, but—"

"The news, Honey. The update. Hurry."

The hurt in Zippo's voice—and even more, that low trill of panic—alarmed Daniel all over again. He punched the Band button and got a talk station, expecting weather, traffic, the usual babble. Instead, there it was.

"*The National Guard has been activated,*" the reporter's voice was panting. "*Once again, residents of Pikesville, Sudbrook Park, and Woodholme are asked to stay indoors and off the roads. And if you're driving on the beltway, until these animals are located and secured, please use extreme caution, and be aware that there may be substantial delays.*"

"*Even more substantial than usual,*" laughed the throaty, in-the-studio host, and Daniel stared at the dial.

"What the hell?" he said, and the first sirens screamed behind him.

He barely had time to pull to the gravel shoulder before a train of police cars rocketed past. In the window of the last, Daniel glimpsed a deputy loading a long, black rifle.

The Pikesville Buffalo

"Oh my God," he murmured, turning toward his aunts. "Did you see…"

But they had seen. He could tell by the looks on their faces. Ethel's eyes had gone steely, her mouth firm and flat. Even more disconcerting was the way Zippo dropped her head into the folds of her shawl and hugged her arms around herself.

"Maybe we should go home," he said. Neither aunt answered.

Checking the rearview mirror multiple times, Daniel edged back onto the street. A helicopter whirred past overhead. Cautiously, Daniel turned the radio lower. When neither of the aunts objected, he turned it off. They drove in silence for a while.

"Hurry up," Ethel murmured, though her tone lacked its usual barking cheerfulness.

On both sides of them, the houses vanished. The road cut through cropless farm fields now, divided only by stands of oak and elm, a few half-hearted wooden fences.

"So," Daniel finally said, if only to break the strangely pregnant silence. "I guess Buddy still lives there?"

"He still does," Zippo said.

"And he still keeps random animals, just for fun? Buffalo? Cheetahs? Remember when he had that elephant? How is he even allowed to have animals like that? Ooh, remember those hairless alpaca or whatever they were, and—"

"They're *our* animals," Ethel said, and smacked the backseat. "Goddamn him."

"Yours?"

"We're sponsoring them," Zippo said. "Ethel and I. Buddy's their caretaker."

"Some care," Ethel snapped, and Zippo shushed her.

Then, abruptly, they'd arrived. Daniel recognized the hillside with its sagging cyclone fence, and the prickly ash tree with the forked trunk and the bare branches curling in on each other like clawed fingers on an arthritic hand. The parked police cruiser with its rooftop light-bars flashing was another clue. By the time he'd brought the car to a stop on the gravel, Aunt Zippo had her door open, and Ethel was practically pushing her from the car.

"Hold on," Daniel said. "They're not just going to let you…"

But both of them were out, now, and Aunt Ethel had already lumbered to the top of the long drive that dropped through the field of dead grass to the farmhouse. A burly police kid with shoulders roughly the width of the tire axle on his cruiser had stood to block her. He wasn't really a kid, Daniel realized as he hurried forward. Just a whole lot younger than Ethel or Zippo. His black night stick and the holster of his gun bumped against his leg.

"You're going to escort me?" Aunt Ethel was saying. "They really are teaching better manners at the academy these days."

The cop—blond, probably not even thirty, cheeks flushed with the cold—just stared at the bobbing, flame-haired bird-woman in front of him. Ethel was several steps past before he recovered himself and stepped into her path again.

"Are you telling me you didn't notice the police cars?" the cop said, folding his arms. "The helicopters everywhere? Lady, you really ought to turn on your radio." He reached out, intending to steer her firmly back up the hill.

"What? Son, I don't hear so well."

Somehow, she'd got by him again. Beside Daniel, Zippo sighed and moved to follow her sister. A nervous tremor twitched in Daniel's throat, and he hurried after them.

The cop had moved to grab Aunt Ethel's arm again. Only when she glared at his hand did he think better of it. From across the fields, somewhere on the other side of the hickory forest that bordered Buddy's farm, a siren wailed. Answering wails and their echoes flooded the air, as though a wolf pack had materialized in those trees.

Which, all things considered, didn't seem so improbable.

"Look. Ma'am," said the cop. "You can't go down there."

"Why, did Buddy warn you about us?"

The cop stared again. Ethel waddled off with Zippo right behind her. By the time Daniel reached the policeman, he was staring down at his own hands. There was a chocolate top cookie in them. The policemen looked up, and Daniel shrugged, started to smile.

"They're going to get hurt. Laugh about that," said the policeman, and returned to his car.

The Pikesville Buffalo

Daniel had just reached the bottom of the drive when Buddy himself came around the side of the farmhouse with a hose and a slop-bucket. His glasses really were as outsized as Daniel remembered them, ballooning from his sockets as though his eyes were blowing bubbles. His paunch had swelled and sagged, and his still-thick hair had finished draining of color. He took one goggle-eyed look at Ethel and dropped the bucket.

"Aw, Christ, now my morning really is complete. I thought it was complete before, but now it's perfect."

"You let them out," Ethel snarled, and Daniel all but ran to reach her side. Never in his life had he heard Aunt Ethel snarl. At anyone.

They're going to get hurt.

Ethel was still snarling. "You let them go."

Flinching, Buddy lifted the hose. Daniel really thought he might blast them, started to lunge into the path of the spray. "Let them?" Buddy shouted back. "Let them?"

"How does this happen? What do you pay your fence guy for? With our money."

"It was that goddamn cat." Buddy was looking at Daniel now. Pleading, Daniel realized. He fell back a step. "That fucking cheetah."

"There's no need for that sort of talk," Zippo said quietly.

"He got the lock off, don't ask me how. Pushed open the gate. I saw him do it. But by the time I got out here…" Waving his free hand in front of his bubble eyes, Buddy the Exotic Animal Farmer seemed to sag into his skin. "Look, I'm the one in trouble. Big trouble. So just…"

But Ethel was shaking her head, staring at her feet. And smiling, now. "Oh, Mack," she said.

"Where did they go?" Aunt Zippo asked.

Buddy shrugged, seeming to sag more but also puff out, like a pillow being smacked and fluffed. He gestured with the hose toward the woods. "Mostly that way."

"Mostly?"

"That's where the cops are. They're worried about that elementary school over there. One of them broke straight off that direction, though." Buddy waved behind the house. "Toward the beltway."

"Which one?" Ethel asked.

Buddy's head rolled up out of his neck wrinkles. Behind his glasses, the magnified frog-eyes blinked.

"What?"

"Which one? Who headed for the beltway?"

"Which one? Lady. They're buffalo."

"You're thinking Mitchell," Aunt Zippo said, and Ethel nodded. "Be just like him, wouldn't it? First chance he gets, straight for the office."

Without another word, his aunts set off side by side, not back up the path but around the side of the house toward the woods. Buddy just stared after them. But when Daniel moved to follow, the farmer grabbed his wrist.

"Watch them, okay? They're going to get shot."

For a second, Daniel thought he meant the buffalo. But those eyes were trained on his aunts. And Buddy's other hand kept banging the bucket nervously against his own leg. Daniel nodded, and the farmer let go.

In the woods, sirens screamed again. His aunts had already gotten a surprising distance down the slope toward the forest, and they'd linked arms. Ethel had her head on Zippo's shoulder, so that her red hair and the wool shawl blended into a sort of mane. They moved in lurches through the winter light, the birdless, silent morning, and Daniel felt his breath catch, hard, and shook his head to fight back the black thoughts.

"Aunt Ethel," he called. "Aunt Zip. Stop."

But they didn't stop. Indeed, they seemed to gain speed, like fallen leaves the wind had caught. He started to call again, but didn't want to draw the attention of the ghost-wolves in the woods. Or the very real policemen with the shotguns. He started to run.

He caught his aunts just as they drifted through the tree line, and they looked surprised to see him.

"Daniel, what is it, Honey?" Aunt Zip said, but he couldn't answer. Aunt Ethel patted his arm.

They stepped together into a hollow, empty silence. No ground animals rustled the dead leaves here. The trees stood farther apart than they'd looked from the farmhouse—this was more an orchard than a

The Pikesville Buffalo

woods—and daylight lay between the trunks like white paper where something had been erased. Daniel watched the steam of his breath coalesce momentarily and then evaporate, leaving more blank places.

"Listen," Aunt Ethel hissed.

Sirens shattered the quiet, and Daniel ducked and threw his gloves over his ears as his aunts clinched together. This time, the answering echoes seemed much closer.

"That way," said Aunt Zippo, the moment the wailing stopped.

"Both of you, wait," Daniel said. "This isn't a joke. They've got guns."

"Joke?" said Aunt Ethel. "Got any good ones? No one's told me a good one since Mack died."

"Except my father," Daniel murmured.

"You mean the goat? Oy." She shuffled away through the leaves. Zippo followed, and again their speed surprised Daniel. He had to hurry to keep up.

"Aunt Zip," he said. "We're going to get shot."

"Honey, why would they shoot us?"

"See the hair?" Aunt Ethel was gesturing at her own head but only half-turning. "If I could grow enough of this, I could sell it as a hunting jacket. Hurry up."

"We're coming, Dear," Aunt Zip said, and they both moved ahead of him again.

Through the trees a considerable ways ahead, Daniel thought he could see chain-link fence, and he also heard voices.

Aunt Ethel somehow moved faster still. In the path, they came across a steaming pile of shit. The smell burrowed straight up Daniel's nostrils, and he gagged.

"What?" said Aunt Zippo,

He pointed at the ground. "Can't you smell that?"

"I can't smell anything anymore. I miss smells."

"Trust me. You don't miss this one."

"You wouldn't think so."

"Is it buffalo?"

Aunt Ethel should have been too far ahead to hear. But she slapped a hand to her forehead and said, "Oh, brother." In her tights, on her stick-legs, she looked like a little girl dressed as a crone. Or a clown. She couldn't really get shot, Daniel thought. Anyone who got her in his rifle sights would be too busy laughing.

"I'm worried about her," he whispered.

Beside him, Zippo sighed. Her shallow breath barely made an imprint on the air. "She's just old, Honey. The way we all get. If we're lucky."

"Yeah, but she's different. Acting different."

Without slowing, Zippo looked her sister up and down. "She looks pretty much like Ethel to me."

"Yeah, well, she's changed her reading habits."

"Her reading habits?"

"All my life, she's read Dick Francis. Pretty much only Dick Francis."

"Have a cookie, Daniel," Aunt Zippo said.

He had no idea from where she produced the chocolate top, or how she'd managed to keep the dollop of frosting from getting smashed.

"Aunt Zippo, she's naming the buffalo."

"She didn't name them." It was her voice, not her words, that prickled in Daniel's chest. She sounded dreamy, or maybe just distant, as though settling into that detachment that supposedly comes for the old at the end and makes dying easier. Except that his mother had always said that was bullshit. A bedtime story people told their children as they watched the life leave their parents. Daniel felt tickling in his tear ducts again. He thought of his father, his lost uncles, and was overcome by an urge to grab his aunts' crooked, cold hands and hug them to his chest. He took one of Zippo's, tugged her forward to where Ethel had stopped, and came out of the trees into sight of the schoolyard.

Then he dropped Zippo's hand and stared straight ahead.

It was like being at a Natural History Museum. Like looking through glass at a diorama full of stuffed, dead things.

There was the section of fence, first of all, trampled into the ground. Half a dozen police knelt in a ring around the perimeter of the schoolyard with their rifles aimed through the links in the remaining chicken wire. The lights from their cruisers flung splashes of red, like paint ball blotches, across their otherwise colorless faces and the dead grass and the hunkered, gray brick of the school building thirty yards away and the whimpering, teary-eyed children clutching each other by the swing sets. Between the children and the school, their shaggy flanks heaving as

The Pikesville Buffalo

they panted and chuffed and lowered their horny heads, four full-grown buffalo bumped around and against each other and expelled geysers of breath into the freezing air.

"Oh, no," Ethel said. "Oh, boys."

How long, Daniel wondered, had this scene been frozen like this? He could see what had happened. The recess bell ringing. The sound startling the buffalo, who'd rumbled right through the fence, smack in between this last group of straggling kids and the safety of their classroom.

On the blacktop, Daniel saw two teachers and a towering African American man in pinstripes gesturing furiously at each other, the kids, the cops. All along the fence, walkie-talkies spit static and snatches of hard, unintelligible instruction.

"Harry?" the African American man called abruptly, and both Ethel's and Zippo's heads jerked toward the buffalo. The same buffalo, Daniel noticed, the one farthest to the right with his nose in the grass and the broken tip of his horn jutting toward them like a shiv.

But the man was talking to one of the kids. And the kid was lifting his red hood off his ears. He was maybe eight, blond-haired, with chipmunk cheeks that would have amused either of Daniel's aunts for weeks on end if they could have gotten their pinching fingers on them. He wiped a hand across his tear-streaked face and waited.

"Just walk this way, son," the pinstripe man was saying. "Around the fence there. Come to us. Harry, lead them this way. All of you, now. Come on."

None of the children moved. In the center of the yard, the buffalo stamped. One of them knocked horns with its closest neighbor, though the gesture looked accidental to Daniel. More like two old men bumping into one another with walkers than rutting.

Then the kid in the hood moved. The moment he did, the buffalo with the broken horn looked up, snorted loudly, and raked its foot along the grass. Instantly, rifles leapt to shoulders as the cops locked in, and the buffalo froze, sweeping its gaze once across the whole assembled mass before him. It chuffed again, pawed more frantically and tore a huge hunk of dirt out of the lawn.

"Damn it," spat a nearby radio.

Harry—the kid, not the animal—burst into fresh tears. Half a dozen safety catches popped free on half a dozen guns. Daniel was so busy watching the police that he didn't notice Aunt Zippo moving until she was halfway across the yard.

"Jesus," a policeman yelled. "Someone grab her!"

But Aunt Zippo had already reached the herd, and as Daniel's mouth dropped open, she disappeared amongst them.

Even the children went silent. Around the old woman, the buffalo began to pant and paw nervously. One of them bumped her with its flank, and Daniel saw her stagger and get bumped by another and almost go down amidst their stamping feet. The one with the pointed half-horn had moved into the circle, now, and it was poking at Aunt Zippo with its head lowered and its front foot working furiously at the grass.

For one more moment, the unreality held. Daniel stared at the animals snorting around his aunt, alternately ignoring her and then brandishing horns and banging themselves against her. The eeriest thing wasn't their presence. It was their *physicality*. Their breath and their scraped, hairy sides and their deep-set, black-brown eyes and the way their skin seemed draped over their skulls rather than attached to it, as though they were already skeleton and hide, and there was something else, something not-buffalo, underneath there.

His aunts' faces, Daniel realized, looked the same way. Everyone's did. His father's. His wife's. Hell, even his own face. Our features little more than cloaks life shrugs on while it camps inside us.

Somewhere to his right, a walkie-talkie crackled. Rifles shifted, held. Ethel was just staring, her hands over her mouth. Daniel threw his arm around her shoulder, squeezed once.

"I'll get her," he said.

"Oh, God," said his aunt.

Then he was through the fence, flinging up his hand, screaming, "Wait. Don't shoot."

"*Hold fire!*" someone shouted.

Two guns exploded. Daniel ducked, whirled, waved a frantic hand, and broke into a run as the kids screeched and bolted for the blacktop. Over the tops of the nearest buffalo, Daniel could see his aunt's orange

The Pikesville Buffalo

shawl, the back of her head with its thinning, blue-white hair like a cloud coming apart. The head disappeared as his aunt went down.

"No!" Daniel screamed, and the buffalo broke as one into a plunging, sideways dash toward the far end of the schoolyard, away from the children and the blacktop and the mass of muzzles and threatening faces.

All of them, that is, except the one with the horn. Harry. He had slid, with surprising grace, onto his front knees. Aunt Zippo was kneeling beside him. The buffalo seemed to hover there a moment, and then slipped the rest of the way to the grass.

Aunt Zippo laid both her hands on the animal's throat, under its mane. Its great, black hooves had splayed to either side of her, and blood bubbled from the holes in its gut and over Zippo's gloves.

"Ssh," she was saying, in that hypnotic, even cadence she seemed to have been born with, or maybe just learned through too much practice. So many years of practice. "Ssh, Harry." She never looked up, not once. She just kept whispering, over and over, until the buffalo died.

It took hours, after that, for the truck to come, and for the animal wranglers to wrestle the surviving bison into it. By the time Daniel and his aunts got back to Ethel's, it was too late to drive home, and he was too shaken, anyway. Ethel ordered pineapple pizza, which Daniel barely touched but which his aunts devoured. Ethel burst into tears once, and Zippo sat beside her and said, "I know. I know."

"How many times?" Ethel sobbed, swiping at her cheeks and smearing pizza grease there.

Producing yet another of her magic tissues, Zippo wiped the grease away. "There doesn't seem to be a limit."

"You know, I still miss him the most. Harry."

"I know."

"I didn't love him the most. He pretty much slept and worked and built Herm's trains with him and wouldn't let us eat donuts enough. But I miss him the most."

"He was the first," Zippo said.

"Don't eat that last pineapple," Ethel said, and snatched the final pizza slice from the box. Abruptly, she looked up at Daniel, held the slice toward him. "Unless you want it, honey."

Daniel shook his head, closed his eyes, saw skeleton-flashes of white light, like the projected shadows of a CAT-scan. When he opened his eyes, his aunts were holding hands.

Zippo went home, and Ethel set him up in her son Herm's old room with the train bedspread still draped over the bed. Daniel read a Dick Francis novel until well after midnight because he didn't think he could sleep, nodded off with the book on his chest, and woke up weeping.

He didn't think he'd called out, but his aunt was at the door within seconds anyway, in a pink nightgown that had to have been at least thirty years old, and with what looked like a matching bonnet on her head. She didn't *ssh* him—that was Zippo's purview—but she asked several times if he wanted a bagel, and she clucked a lot, and in the end she sat on the edge of the bed and patted his hand, over and over.

"How do you do it, Aunt Ethel?" Daniel asked, through tears he couldn't seem to stop. "How do you survive the love you outlive?"

Aunt Ethel just patted his hand, glanced around the room, out toward the hallway, still lined with photos of the families she'd created or joined, the children she'd borne and the families they'd formed. The hallway was also where she'd moved the pictures of the men she and her sister had buried, after replacing them in the living room with the buffalo.

"I know what Mack would have said," she told him.

"What?"

"'Did you hear the one about the rabbi and the stripper?'"

That just made Daniel sob harder. When he'd gotten control of himself again, he looked at his aunt. "What about you, Aunt Ethel?"

"Me?" She shrugged. "Mostly, Hon, I think I just keep deciding I want to."

It was a long while before the tears stopped completely and Daniel felt ready to lie back on his pillow. Ethel brought him warm milk, and he actually drank it. And it was after two when he awoke the second time, to the sound of the porch door swinging open.

Instantly, he was bolt upright. "Aunt Ethel?" he called. Grabbing his pants off the chair, he hurried down the darkened hallway, through the

The Pikesville Buffalo

living room onto the screened-in porch. The side-yard lights were on, flooding the tiny yard.

Ethel was by the screen. Fifteen yards away, right where the grass disappeared into the stand of pines that marked the edge of her property, the cheetah crouched on its haunches, its tail whapping at the dirt. In life, even more than in its photo, the thing looked ancient, its yellow eyes rheumy, its fur discolored or missing entirely. It also had its disconcertingly tiny head cocked, its mouth open, and one front paw crossed over the other. There was something almost cocky in the pose. Composed, at the very least. Like a gentleman caller.

"Oh my God," Daniel mumbled. "How on earth did it…"

"Mack's home," his aunt said, and glanced just once over her shoulder at Daniel.

"What?" But he was thinking of the buffalo on the wall. The ones Ethel and Zippo both insisted they hadn't named, just called by name. "Aunt Ethel, that isn't…"

Smiling, she stepped out the door.

It was those next, fleeting moments Daniel would remember, years later, at Lisa's three years-clean checkup, and again at her five years, when the doctors told her she didn't need to come back every six months anymore, she just had to stay vigilant, always. Or at least, it was those moments he would focus on. Not what came afterward. From then on, when he let himself think about this night, he would picture his aunt's bare, gnarled feet in the grass. Her lumbering gait as she approached the cheetah, which hunched, coiled, its purr—or growl—audible even from the house. The pink bonnet on her head, the yellow overcoat on her shoulders, and the swing of her hand off her hip that told him she was dancing.

Part Two
Tales from the Rolling Dark

Shomer

> "Melancholy can smile. Sorrow cannot. And smiling is the legacy of my tribe."
> —Friedrich Torberg, *Tante Jolesch*

"So you'll do it?" Aunt Jessica asked, holding Marty's hand, as they stood in a ring around Uncle El's body.

"Of course I will," Marty murmured. He couldn't tear his eyes away from his uncle's face. He'd never seen an unprepared corpse before, and what amazed him was how little like Uncle El the body already looked. His eyes had come open, right at the end, but crossed and out of alignment, like balloons that had drifted separately to the ceiling. His top lip, too, had slid sideways, and looked frozen halfway toward one of those twisted-mouth expressions Uncle El had used to crack up first his nephews, then his children.

On the other side of the hospital bed, El's son Leo glanced up at Marty. Through his tears, a wicked smile spread. El's smile. "Want any of us to tell you what it is you're doing first?"

An hour later, over blintzes in the deli where El used to sneak Marty and then, in succession, the rest of his nieces and nephews and finally his own children off to midnight meals, Leo told him.

"*Shomer*," Marty repeated through a mouth full of sweet cheese and sour cream. Outside, the drizzle drifted down through the dark and shrouded passing cars, the bus stop across the street, a pedestrian hurrying up his row-house stoop, so that everything looked wavy, wrapped in plastic.

"It means guard," said Leo, who'd taken one bite of his blintz and then sat staring into his plate.

"What am I guarding?"

"Dad," Leo said, and Marty stopped eating. "My dad."

Marty stared at his cousin, then at his cousin's reflection superimposed in the dark window, wavering like everything else.

"I hadn't really heard of *Shomer*s either," Leo said. "The synagogue asked, and Mom thought it sounded nice."

The fact that Leo also hadn't known about it was a little reassuring. Every time Marty came east, he left aware of yet another blessing or ritual he didn't know, which made him feel yet again like a pretend Jew and, more surprisingly, made him care. But this word he'd never even heard.

In the diner light, Leo looked more hollow-cheeked than usual, his dark, curly hair even greasier against his dress-shirt collar. Of course, at 24, already a featured Salon.com columnist, Leo could still claim the look as a style and mean it. Whereas Marty—now 35, with his freelance technical drawing accounts drying up in the recession and the gallery that had shown and occasionally even sold his paintings shuttering its doors, and with his last relationship long enough ago that his mother had started asking if there were any "cute baristas" at his local coffee shop—Marty's ongoing inability to hit each belt loop or get a tie knot all the way up under his neck just gave him away. At least, that's how it felt to Marty.

"The synagogue has a guy they pay to do it," Leo said. "Most synagogues do, did you know that?"

"Don't tell my mom," said Marty. "She might ask about the salary. On my behalf."

Leo glanced up from his plate, his half-smile quick and grateful and his eyes full of tears again. For a moment, Marty felt like the cousin he'd always meant to be to El's children, and hadn't quite become, somehow. *That* cousin. Because El had certainly been *that* uncle. At least for a while.

"Professional *Shomer*," Leo said. "It'd be a conversation starter."

"What do you mean, guard your dad?"

"His body. Someone's supposed to sit with his body every second until it's in the ground."

Shomer

"Like, in the embalming room?"

"Jews don't embalm, moron."

"Oh, yeah." Marty blushed and scooped up another forkful of blintz but didn't lift it. "I knew that, actually."

"Remember Grandpa in his coffin? With all that makeup on him?"

"The Grandpa Action-Figure," said Marty, and this time, Leo smiled all the way.

"I forgot about that."

At his death, their grandfather had weighed well over 350 pounds, and his prepared body had looked so little like him, the face so rosy-cheeked but devoid of even one of his thousand trademark expressions, that Marty's father had said he looked like a G.I. Joe. And for the rest of the *shiva* week, as mourners brought soup and *kugel* and sat on Grandpa's couches under the soaped-over mirrors and told Grandpa stories, the cousins had holed up in bedrooms or basement corners, imagining Grandpa Action Figure adventures. Grandpa Action Figure leaps from the fifteen-foot upstairs balcony, creating a crater in the floor and a tsunami in Chesapeake Bay. Grandpa Action Figure climbs the Shot Tower. Grandpa Action Figure waits until all the mourners have left, and then comes home.

"We're not even supposed to have visitations like that, are we?" Marty asked. "Open coffins?"

"Nope. I have no idea whose idea it was. My dad hated it."

Abruptly, Leo put his face in his hands. Leo didn't generally leave even his laughter unguarded, and Marty wasn't sure how to react. Raindrops rilled down the window. It was possible, Marty realized, that he would never eat another blintz. He'd never really liked them. Or, he'd only liked them sitting across from Uncle El, in Baltimore, in the middle of the night.

"So where do we sit?" he finally asked. "Your dad and I?"

"At the funeral home." With a visible effort, Leo lifted his head, steadied himself. "It's just because it's Shabbat. The *Shomer* Pro was already on his way to Virginia for the weekend. He'll be back tomorrow. And the Blank says he'll come early in the morning and spell you."

"Robbie the Blank?"

"You know any other Blanks we're related to?"

That jabbing tone was an inheritance from Uncle El. How old had Marty been before realizing he didn't actually like it?

"So I go to the funeral home once the body gets there, and I just sit?"

"I think you're technically supposed to recite Psalms. Obviously, you don't have to do that. You just…guard him."

"From what? Embalming?"

"I don't know, Marty, I've never done it, alright? I've never heard of doing it. It's just my dead dad, and apparently someone's supposed to guard him, and immediate family aren't allowed, and my mom thought of you. Do it or don't."

Taken aback—again, by the nakedness of the emotion more than the emotion itself—Marty shifted in his seat, waved a hand in the air. "Of course I'll do it, Leo. I already said I would. I'm honored."

"It's a *mitzvah*, supposedly."

"I'd do it if it were a mortal sin."

"Thank you, Marty. Just guard him, okay? Stay awake. Be with him. Ferry my dad to the afterlife."

"Do we believe in the afterlife?"

"Since when does Judaism require belief?"

Ninety minutes later, armed with his sketchpad, a *Tanakh*, and a travel Boggle set—"You've got a pretty good shot at beating him, for once," Leo said as he handed it over—Marty let his mother drive him to the Rosenberg Funeral Home. As he opened the passenger side door, she grabbed his hand and said, "My little brother is going in the ground. I'm glad you're going to be with him." And then, when Marty'd kissed her sopping cheek, "I bet someone in there could find you a razor and some shaving cream."

Marty held his mother's hand. "They probably have really good tie tie-ers, too."

"That's just morbid," his mother said, smiled, sobbed, and left him in the rain.

For just a moment, turning to the building, he thought there'd been a mistake. The Rosenberg Home was low and rectangular and long, flanked on both ends by poplar trees and fronted by a wide, circular driveway. Before the front doors, lined up single file, hearses sat silent, their back curtains drawn, reminding Marty disconcertingly of

Shomer

taxis queueing for airport passengers. So, a funeral home, alright. But a deserted one, judging from the utter lightlessness in there. And a Chinese one, if the character-covered, hand-painted signs in the black windows were any indication.

Midnight dim sum? Marty thought vaguely, the weight of the day—of watching his uncle die, his cross-country trip, his mother's tears and his cousins' and his aunt's—all settling over him. That would certainly be a proper way of performing *Shomer—Shomering?*—for Uncle El. Dazed, with chilly water droplets creeping into his collar and down his back, Marty moved up the steps, between the hearses. He half-expected to see drivers snoozing at the wheel, or poring over tomorrow's *Racing Form* for Pimlico. But the hearses were empty. Reaching the front doors, he raised a hand to his eyes and squinted into the blackness. The new face appeared so fast that Marty mistook it at first for his reflection.

Which was kind of funny, given that the tiny man who opened the door wore a white robe, had white hair tied back in a ponytail, and was Chinese. Chinese-American, as it turned out.

"Mister…Burnstein?" the man said, bowing slightly.

"What? Oh. No. But, yes, I'm here for him. For El Burnstein. My name's different. Marty."

The white-haired man just stood in the doorway, still the only visible form in the sea of blankness behind him, studying Marty's face. Even with the door open, Marty heard no sounds from inside the home.

"But you are the *Shomer*, yes?" The white-haired man pronounced the word perfectly, Hebraically. At least, it sounded that way to Marty. Bowing again, the white-haired man said, "I am sorry for your loss. This way." Turning, he moved into the dimness, his robe seeming to float on it like a paper lantern.

Marty followed. Halfway across the long foyer, or whatever it was, his eyes began to adjust, and he started to make out shapes. A circular reception desk. Rooms to the right, one with a door wide open. A single room to the left, with larger double doors, also open. To the left of those doors stood a single, large vase of long-stemmed flowers. Drained of their color by the dimness, they looked like scratches in the dark, gestural impressions of flowers, as in Chinese scroll painting. The rug beneath Marty's feet felt deep and soft and dark. Like earth, he thought.

Which was appropriate enough. Jewish funerals were about returning, as quickly and simply as possible, to the clay from which we were made. Ahead of him, the white robe descended down a staircase draped in even deeper shadow, and Marty hesitated at the edge of it. As usual, he felt ill-prepared, and also, he had to admit, a little nervous. And then ridiculous. If he were indeed a ferryman, well...what had he thought this river would look like? He started down.

Only after he'd reached the bottom did the Chinese man switch on the overhead fluorescents. They didn't twitch or hum, just revealed the long, sterile hallway. No carpet here, no flowers, only hospital-gray linoleum, open doorways spaced quite a ways apart, a couple of empty gurneys tucked neatly against the blank, white walls. One gold-filigreed coffin, empty and unlatched, standing upright.

Not his uncle's coffin, then. If El had had his way, he'd have gone in the ground naked, without any box whatsoever, to speed his return to the earth. It's what Jews did, apparently. But neither his sister nor his wife had been able to stomach that idea, so they'd gone for the simple, pine receptacle.

"This way, please," said the Chinese man, and led him directly into the first room, where again he waited until Marty was beside him to turn on the light. The door swung shut automatically behind him.

All at once, Marty closed his eyes. He wasn't ready to see his uncle's body again, or rather his face. What had been his face and so obviously wasn't anymore. But when he opened his eyes, he saw a square, small, closet-like room. Wedged not quite lengthwise—because it wouldn't fit—against one wall sat someone's old, green couch, the middle pillow squashed down almost level with the frame but the other pillows puffed up and brighter green, as though no one had ever sat on them. In front of the couch sat a low coffee table with a single reading lamp and a scattering of books on it. One of them, at least, was a *Tanakh*. The spine said so in plain, transliterated English.

"Do not please open the door," the Chinese man said. And before Marty realized what was happening, could formulate even one of his half-dozen questions or even ask *which* door, because there were two in there other than the one through which he'd come, the Chinese man left.

Shomer

For the first few minutes, Marty just stood in the center of the room. Before it had become the *Shomer* Pro's office, or whatever it now was, this had clearly been a closet. It was too small, the walls too bare for it to have been anything else. Adjacent to the couch, almost completely blocking the wooden door at the back of the room, sat a squat bookcase, with a few more books lying haphazardly atop each other, halfway leaning out of themselves. On the wall facing the couch, he was surprised to see a square window at eye-level. But whatever it looked out upon—not the parking lot, surely, because there were more rooms in that direction, and because he had to be at least ten feet underground—Marty had no view of it, because on the other side of the glass, heavy blue curtains had been drawn all the way closed. Beside the bookshelves sat another low table upon which sat a single, empty glass and a full pitcher of water. The glass looked pitiful, standing there, and disconcertingly like a vessel in a ritual: the Elijah cup, placed just so, in what Marty was certain was the precise center of the table. Underneath the table stood a small stack of magazines. Slowly, carefully, as though afraid of disturbing something, Marty leaned closer, then blinked in surprise. Almost laughed.

Crossword Master Challenges? Either the Shomer Pro kept a private stash down here for between-Psalm entertainment, or this room really had been prepared specifically with Uncle El in mind.

From somewhere deep in the bowels of the Rosenberg Home, far away from the *Shomer* room, something metallic tapped. And tapped again. Then came a rattling clatter, not loud, but startling in the absolute silence that had preceded it, like bare feet racing down a hall. Marty opened the door through which he'd come, stuck his head out, but the Chinese man had turned off the lights out there again, and he could see nothing. He put out his hand, felt around for the switch, couldn't find it. The stairs were just to the right, he knew. He wasn't as far from the drizzly, dreary outside world as he felt. Nor was he alone in the building, clearly, despite the silence rushing back in around him, filling his ears completely, as if he'd suddenly sunk into water.

Only as he retreated back into the *Shomer* room and the little bubble of light from the single, overhead bulb, did the question he really should have asked occur to him: *Where was Uncle El?*

The answer seemed obvious enough. He was behind the blue curtain. In the room with the door Marty wasn't supposed to open. Unless that was the other door, and he was meant to go straight through this one, sit down next to the coffin, assuming his uncle was in the coffin, and...

No. The tools of the *Shomer's* trade—the *Tanakh*, the couch, the water, the light—were in *this* room. *Pay no attention to the man behind the curtain*, Marty thought inanely. Except that there was no man behind the curtain. Not anymore. And his job was to make sure no one else paid any attention to whatever was left behind.

Abruptly, another thought surfaced, dragging with it emotions Marty had forgotten were down there, or convinced himself he'd buried, and he sat hard on the depressed pillow and gripped his knees with his hands. The irony was not lost on him, was in fact unmistakable. For twenty years—more—he'd longed for just one more night alone with Uncle El. Like when he was a kid, and El had taken the train down from college and spirited Marty away to the diner for blintzes, to some minor league baseball stadium he'd never been able to find since where fans hooted every time their Owls scored or threatened to score, to the Delaware shore in the dark in the middle of winter to swim for thirty seconds in their underwear and then drive straight back home, shivering, singing along to awful country songs on El's old car radio. So much of the code Marty used for processing the world—the numbers and slashes for transcribing baseball games in scorecard boxes, the slanting or adjacent *-ing* and *-ed* and *-er* and *-un* combinations that signaled opportunity on a Boggle board, the squiggles and dots of *trop* in Torah portions in prayer books that indicated changes of pitch or chances to make the secret pretend-farting noise with your lips—he'd learned from El, on those nights. And now his wish had been granted. They were going to spend one more night alone together.

Did you know, he found himself mouthing, almost saying, into the empty room? Straight to the blue curtain, while he imagined his uncle sitting up just on the other side, leaning his ear to the glass. *Did you ever understand, all those years you made fun of me for being resentful when you started bringing Robbie and Leo and my sister along, how hard that was, for me? What a jolt that was? Realizing that those nights, that magic, wasn't between us like I'd always thought, it was all you? That what you were great at—what you loved—wasn't showing the magic to me, just showing it to kids? Any kids?*

It wasn't quite true, Marty knew, wasn't so simple, certainly wasn't fair and never had been. He was weeping anyway. Feeling every bit the selfish brat El had made him feel he was, later, sometimes, without ever saying so. *But it* wasn't *selfishness, Uncle El*, Marty thought, wiping viciously at his face. *Not only. I just don't think you ever understood what it meant to have a companion like you...then realize that that companion wasn't really* for *you...that there aren't anywhere near enough companions in the world to go around...that there aren't enough freezing, free nights to swim in...that you actually didn't have that much to say to me once I was old enough to start wanting to share* my *wonders with you...*

That wasn't fair either, although it was at least a little true. By the time Marty had been old and fully formed enough to want to show his uncle *his* discoveries, El had kids of his own, work responsibilities, dry cleaning and milk to stop for on the way home, his aging parents' endless little illnesses, the thousand tiny obligations of adult life that Marty had learned, much later, stole away all but the most essential friends and interests and nephews simply by eliminating the time for them.

Nevertheless, Marty mouthed, not quite daring to whisper, but speaking directly to the blue curtain. *In the end, you were less interested in me than I was in you, Uncle El. Weren't you?*

Without realizing he was doing it, Marty found himself opening his sketch book, slipping a charcoal pencil out of its case, starting to make quick, gentle strokes across the top of a page. These were softer strokes than his usual, made with twitches of his fingers, as though he were brushing lint off a suit coat rather than drawing. His uncle's bumpy, bald head slowly took shape under his pencil, so that Marty's hands seemed to be cradling it as they created it. The tears he was crying were grateful ones, now. Not angry. Not sad. Not anymore. *Thank you Uncle El*, he was thinking. *Thank you. For so many things.*

The tapping started again, startling him, even though it still sounded far away. And then—from even farther—he heard a long, high-pitched, unmistakably human sigh. And another. Except it wasn't a sigh. Only the distance made it seem like one. Marty could tell by the hitch in the voice, the way it wavered, soared upward, choked off. Somewhere in the Rosenberg Home, someone was wailing.

"*Baruch ata adonai,*" he found himself saying, setting the sketch pad on the table. He started singing, softly but out loud, now. He sang the blessing all the way to the end. "*Shehechianoo, v-keymanoo, veheegianoo...*" Only as he finished did he realize how wrong his choice of blessing was. *Thank you, God, for letting us reach this day?* Well. Maybe it wasn't completely wrong. He *was* grateful. Or at least, there was nowhere else he'd rather have been.

Another wail. Two taps. Then a thunderous rattle, much closer, that launched Marty off the couch, toward the door next to the blue curtain, then out into the hall. Which was still dark. Silent, the second he emerged.

Or, almost silent. Not quite. Somewhere, not too far, something— a bunch of somethings—were rustling. Low and steady. Like closeted clothes in hanging bags, with a hand moving through them.

"Hello?" Marty said. Naturally, he'd forgotten his cellphone. He had no idea what time it was.

The wailing, when it came, was clearer out here. A woman's voice, saw-edged and exhausted, rushing at him through the dark. He ducked back into the *Shomer* room, pushing the door closed rather than waiting for it, and stood a moment with tears drying on his face while the wail faded, slowly, to an echo. Only several long seconds later, when the wail had faded completely, did Marty realize the rustling was in the room with him.

If there had been light in the hall, he might have bolted, right then. He almost did anyway. But something held him rigid, absolutely still. A weight, a *grip* on both his arms. Carefully, he swung his head around to look.

What he saw was the couch with its sunken middle pillow. The bare walls. His sketch pad with his uncle's head just taking shape there, featureless, yet already unmistakably El's. At least, it was unmistakable to Marty.

Nothing else. The grip on his arms lessened a little. Slipped away, and Marty heard himself say, "No. Wait."

It's just my dead dad, Leo had said. *Someone's supposed to guard him.*

Shomer

In one step, Marty moved to the window and pressed his face to the glass, trying to locate a slit in the curtains. He wanted to see, to perform his assigned task for Uncle El. But whoever had arranged those curtains had done so with purpose. They weren't just pinned together but sewn shut down the center, then tacked in place at the corners. No light from this room spilled into that one. And no hint of what was in there filtered through to Marty.

He hesitated one moment longer, and only then because the rustling started again. It wasn't in the *Shomer* room. It was in the walls. Or else it was behind the blue curtain. With El. The resumption of the rattling clatter drowned it out, even though the clatter came from farther away, and when it ceased, the rustling did, too. Marty heard the tailing, sobbing end of a wail. *Just what sort of training*, he wondered, did a professional *Shomer* receive? Then he reached out, grabbed the knob on the door next to the window, and turned it.

Locked.

More rustling.

It's in there, Marty thought. *It's with El*. With a snarl, he threw himself at the door, twisting the knob, which wasn't locked after all, just a little stuck. The realization flooded him with simultaneous relief and horror as the door swung open. Air rushed out, stale and old. Too late, he wondered if he should maybe have grabbed a *Tanakh* or something, *did he know any Psalms? 'Yea, though I walk through the valley of the shadow,' wait, did Jews say that one?*

The light switch, this time, was where it should have been, on the wall right next to the door. Marty fumbled, flipped it. He stared. Then, through his tears and the heart-hammering that threatened to splinter his ribcage, he started to laugh. He couldn't help it.

Marty Action Figure braves the closed door, flings it free...and liberates the bathroom.

When his breathing had calmed and his tears had stopped for the time being and the uneasy, spasm-like laughter had quieted in his throat, Marty washed his face in cool water, dried his hands on the neatly hung towel. No mirror. But then, there wouldn't be in a *Shomer*'s room. Or else the glass would be soaped over. Leaving the bathroom door open but switching off the light, he returned to the couch.

For a long time, he sat and sketched. He didn't think more about Uncle El, or at least didn't think anything specific. In his heart was a weight. But the weight came from accumulated memories, 35 years of everyday, bedrock love, not loss. Or rather, bedrock love and loss had become synonymous, now, maybe more than synonymous: different words for the same feeling. Maybe that's why Jews almost seemed to celebrate this experience. Mark it with food and ritual storytelling. Clutch it to their breasts.

Intermittently, like wind through window-cracks, wailing floated down the hall and through the door. The clatter came almost regularly, every five or six minutes. Every time, it startled Marty, made him look up, but mostly because whenever it stopped, he thought he heard rustling again, just for a second. Then Marty would glance at the dark bathroom, or over to the door he hadn't opened, the one almost completely blocked by the bookcase. But he made himself stay put. This was his post. He was sure of it. Almost sure.

Much later, the drawing not done but shaped, Marty put his pad aside, considered doing a solo Boggle round in El's honor. The idea, though, of clattering the lettered dice-cubes in their little cage in the suffocating near-silence unnerved him. He reached for a *Tanakh*, opened to the Psalms. But those proved less than soothing, strangely savage. Almost none were about grief or even comfort. Mostly, they were brutal, or heartbroken. *'You break the teeth of the wicked.' 'I am a stranger to my brothers, an alien to my kin.' 'It is for your sake that we are slain all day long.'*

But after a while, the words did seem to knit themselves together before his eyes, form a sort of blanket or gauze that Marty could feel wrapping him. Maybe the Psalms really did have power, to keep too much of himself from bleeding away, or else to hold at an almost-safe distance his dawning understanding of what other people's deaths, even more than one's own, really mean to the living. *'You are my help and my rescuer; do not delay…'*

He had no idea how he fell asleep, or for how long. But the screaming woke him up.

Heart thundering, he lurched up, swaying, clenching his fists as the screams silenced themselves. His eyes shot to the blue curtains, then to

Shomer

the door behind the bookcase. *He'd failed. Let his guard down. And now Uncle El…*

With a cry, he moved toward the bookcase, intending to shove it aside so he could get through that second door. But a new round of rattling stopped him in his tracks. He held still, listening not to the rattle, but for the moment just after it, the rustling. And there it was. *Or was it? Was that even a sound?*

Abruptly, he turned and walked out into the hall. A wail greeted him, piercing, shot through with breath. Again, he felt behind and all around him for the light switch, couldn't find it. Only after a few seconds did he realize there were more sounds. Not rattling, exactly, but clicking. Sliding sounds. And murmurs. He was almost sure he could hear murmurs, now. Exhaling long and low, and with a single, uncertain glance back into the *Shomer* room, Marty started down the hall into the dark.

He could sense—*smell*—the open doorways when he passed them. Antiseptic, pine-scented wax, metal. His knee bumped a gurney, sending it squeaking a few feet ahead until it bumped something—the open coffin—and causing Marty to freeze, his own hairs crawling up his back, shoulders hunching as though he expected to be grabbed. Edging more toward what he assumed was the center of the hall, he continued on.

Only when he'd reached the T at the very end did Marty start to see light. Only a little, and far to his left. A strip of flicker-less yellow under the bottom of a closed door. He waited until the next round of rattling. The murmuring that accompanied it. It was coming from right there. Breathing through pursed lips as though that might slow his heart, Marty moved toward the light. He stopped outside the door.

The sounds weren't actually intermittent. Not here. There were constant sliding noises, clicks and taps. Very occasional muttering. Marty flung the door open.

As one, the three Chinese men leapt to their feet, Mah Jongg tiles spilling off their holders and scattering across the table. All these men were older, *old* in fact, two in jeans and neatly tucked button-up shirts, plus the white-robed man who'd let Marty into the funeral home. The surprise on that man's face looked completely incongruous, brand new, and almost lost, as if it had wandered onto the wrong face by accident.

"Mister Burn..." the man started, then corrected himself. "Marty. Mr. Marty. Did you need something?"

Behind and above them, another wail bloomed. Much closer. Much harder to listen to, from here. Operatic in its anguish.

Marty waited until it finished. The men still stood, staring. All he could think to ask was, "What are you guys doing?"

Though he couldn't have been sure, Marty thought the look they all exchanged had amusement in it. Certainly, it was kind.

"The same as you, I think," said the white-haired man. "In our way."

"*Shomer*-ing?"

"That is not what we call it. But..."

"It's not what we call it either," Marty said, slipping into an exhausted, lonely smile. "I don't think."

The wail again. Again, Marty waited until it passed.

"She's with you, isn't she?" he asked.

The old guy on the left nodded. He had a red ribbon pinned to his shirt, and some sort of outlandishly large belt buckle. "She is performing her part. We perform ours."

"I'm sorry for your loss," said Marty.

"We are sorry for yours."

"Need a fourth?" he asked, earning himself a set of strangely satisfying startled glances. The only way the moment might have been better would be if El had taught Marty the game. But that had been his grandfather, years and years ago.

The white-haired man smiled. "You know how to play?"

"I'd need a card."

"Card?" Then understanding dawned on the white-haired man's face. He shook his head. Again, he looked kind. "Ah. Of course. Jew Mah Jongg. Entirely different game."

His companions were nodding, too. The guy with the belt buckle said, "Completely different. Very frustrating. So few ways to win. So many to lose."

Yet again, Marty felt tears well in his eyes. His uncle's absence seeping in. "Yep," he said. "Sounds like a Jewish game, alright."

He left them to it. Not until he reached the T and turned into the dark corridor did he hear the rustling. Much louder, now, even though it

Shomer

was coming from way down at the end of the hall. From the closed room where he should have been sitting. Where El lay helpless. Ignoring the dark, the coffin on the wall, the warnings shooting off in his brain, that *grip* again seizing both his arms, Marty shot down the corridor.

When he reached the door to the *Shomer* room, he paused for a split second. Long enough to make sure. To hope he'd been wrong again. But there was no mistaking it, this time. The rustling. He pushed open the door, half-expecting full dark, but the light was as he'd left it. So was the couch, the open *Tanakh*, the Elijah glass on its table, his sketchpad with El's half-formed face. Of course it was. Because El wasn't in here. He was *back there*. Unguarded, where Marty had abandoned him.

Marty strode straight to the other side of the room, reached over the bookcase, twisted the doorknob—which was *cold*, like a fistful of ice—and shoved at the door, scrambling atop and over the bookcase as he pushed. Then he really did freeze. Stopped scrambling, blinking, breathing. He held absolutely still.

Or…let himself *be* held. Later, when he had time to think about it, he decided that was more accurate. Because he really could feel that grip on his arms. And around his waist. Even more, he *knew* that grip. But he couldn't let himself process it yet.

On a gurney, in the center of a blank, tiled, windowless, featureless room, under a single white sheet that covered neither his face nor his feet, lay Uncle El. Frigid air poured down over him, a fall of faintly glowing blue, like an iceberg calving. The blue swept and swirled around him, nuzzled along his chest, as though cuddling up, or sniffing for signs of life. Constantly, it washed away, but then reformed in the air. Marty hovered in that doorway for barely a blink, less than a second, just long enough to realize that air, no matter how cold, doesn't glow, or have any sort of head, let alone that long, wolf-like, sniffing thing atop El's chest. And that whatever lights there were in this room, they weren't on. And that the blueness hunched on El's chest was turning now, right toward Marty.

Then he felt himself yanked backward, falling over the bookcase and landing hard on his ass on the floor of the *Shomer* room, the door swinging shut—*had he done that?*—as he scrambled to his feet, turned to run, turned back, thought of his uncle, nearly collapsed in a flood of guilt and then grabbed for the couch as the guilt drained out of him, as quickly as it had come. He could feel that grip on his shoulders again, turning him toward the hallway, could feel the push in his back, the weight so familiar. El's hands.

Staggering forward, he threw open the door and ran smack into Robbie the Blank, who had just reached it, the Chinese man in white flowing behind him.

"In there," Marty babbled, shaking, pointing, as his overweight and preternaturally becalmed cousin drew him to the couch, sat him down. "It's in there."

"Of course it is," Robbie said, as though he knew.

"Of course he is," said the Chinese man. "You did not go in, did you? It's so cold, to protect the body."

Marty started to argue, wanted to protest, to grab them both, to scream. But the understanding he'd already had was spreading through him, now. No—nothing so grand or certain as understanding. But he knew what he'd seen. He could *hear* it in there, still, though he was sure the Chinese man would say it was simply the sound of the air. He let Robbie pour him a glass of water, and drank it. The liquid tasted tepid, flat, so plain and of *this* world, and warmed him like whiskey.

Robbie even gave Marty his car keys, saying he'd arranged for his own ride home. Moments later, Marty was out in the still-drizzly gray of early morning, watching the wet drip off the poplar trees. He sat for a long time in Robbie's car, thinking of Robbie down there in that room. Of El in the room beside him. *Standing guard.*

Because that was it. Wasn't it? Maybe. It made a sort of sense. How Jewish, really, to provide an opportunity for one last *mitzvah*, performed not for the dead, but *by* them, for the living. During the week of his grandfather's *shiva*, Marty had asked every one of his older relatives why all the mirrors had been soaped over. And he'd gotten a different answer every time. *'Because we should not be thinking of ourselves this week.' 'Because we can no longer see what your grandfather saw.'* It was Robbie's father, Marty realized, who had said, *'Because the Angel of Death was just here. And he might still be close. And you don't want him to see you.'*

He'd said that winking, but not quite as if he were kidding. And if Marty was right, and really had seen what he'd seen in that room, then

Shomer

the blue thing—Angel of Death, or whatever it was—was right where it was supposed to be, because El was keeping it there. And away, therefore, from anyone else whose grief and pain might draw it. No wonder immediate family couldn't be *Shomrim*. Their wounds were too raw, too easily detected. The dead would be too weak to hold the Angel's attention.

But a nephew, perhaps, or a friend. Someone at risk, but not quite as much risk. Someone the dead, or the memory of them, might still be able to help, to push for just a little longer out of harm's way…

Marty's tears were quiet ones, now. Not bothering to wipe his face, he set Robbie's car in motion and drove through the empty streets to El's house, where the first well-wishers had already arrived, and where they'd all spend the next week eating *kugel* on paper plates, gathering in quiet corners, telling El stories all day long, under mirrors carefully soaped to spare his uncle's loved ones, for those first, awful days, their first true glimpse of the world without him in it.

Miss Ill-Kept Runt

> "My mother's anxiety would not allow her to remain where she was…What was it that she feared? Some disaster impended over her husband or herself. He had predicted evils, but professed himself ignorant of what nature they were. When were they to come?"
> —Charles Brockden Brown, *Weiland*

Chloe comes clinking out the front door into the twilight, pudding pop in one hand and a dragon in the other. The summer wind sets her frizzy brown hair flying around her, and she says, "Whoa," tilting up on one foot as though anything less than an F5 twister, a tag team of grizzly bears, a fighter jet could drag her *and* the fifteen pounds or so of bead necklace around her neck off the ground. The plastic baubles and seashell fragments and recently ejected baby teeth bump along her chest as she tilts, then straightens.

"I told you to get in pajamas," says her father from the side of the station wagon, where he's still trying to wedge the last book and pan boxes into the wall of suitcases and cartons separating the front seat from the way-back, where Chloe and her brother the Miracle will be riding, as always.

"These *are* pajamas," Chloe says, lifting the mass of beads so her father can see underneath.

Sweating, exhausted before the drive even starts, her father smiles. Better still, the Miracle, who is already stretched in the way-back with his big-kid feet dangling out the open back door and his Pokemon cards spread all over the space Chloe is supposed to occupy, laughs aloud and shakes his head at her. In Chloe's world, there are only a few things better than pudding pops and beads. One of them is her older brother noticing, laughing. The baby teeth on her newest necklace are mostly for him; she actually thinks they look blah, too plain, also a little bitey. But she'd known he would like them.

"Miss Ill-Kept Runt," her brother says, and goes back to his cards.

She's just climbing into the back, enjoying the Miracle's feverish sweeping up of cards, his snapping, "*Wait*" and *"Don't!"* at her, when her mother emerges from the empty house. Freezing, Chloe watches her mother tighten the ugly gray scarf—it looks more like a dishrag—around her beautiful dark hair, linger a last, long moment in the doorway, and finally aim a single glance in the direction of her children. Chloe starts to lift her hand, but her mother is hurrying around the side of the station wagon, eyes down, and Chloe hears her drop into the passenger seat just before her father wedges the Miracle's feet inside the car and shuts the way-back door.

"Stan," her mother says, in her new, bumpy voice, like a road with all the road peeled off. "Let's just *go*."

It's the move, Chlo. That's what her father's been saying. For months, now.

Her father's already in the driver's seat and the station wagon has shuddered to life under Chloe's butt and is making her necklaces rattle when her mother's door pops open, and all of a sudden she's there, pulling the back door up, blue-eyed gaze pouring down on Chloe like a waterfall. Chloe is surprised, elated, she wants to duck her head and close her eyes and bathe in it.

"Happy birthday," her mother says, bumpy-voiced, and reaches to touch her leg, then touches the Miracle's instead. He doesn't look up from his cards, but he waves at her with his sneaker.

"It's not my birthday yet," Chloe says, wanting to keep her mother there, prolong the moment.

Miss Ill-Kept Runt

Her mother gestures toward the wall of boxes in the back seat. "We'll be driving most of the night. By the time I see your face again, it will be." And there it is—faint as a fossil in rock, but there all the same. Her mother's smile. A trace, anyway.

It really has *been the move*, Chloe thinks, as her mother slams the door down like a lid.

"Say goodbye to the house," her father says from up front, on the other side of the boxes. Chloe can't see him, and she realizes he sounds different, too. Far away, as though he's calling to her across a frothed-up river. But right on cue, she feels the rev, *rrruummm, rruummm;* it's reassuring, the thing he always does before he goes anywhere. She bets he's even turned around to give her his *go!* face, forgetting there's a wall of cardboard there.

Then they are going, and Chloe is surprised to find tears welling in her eyes. They're not because she's sad. Why should she be, they're moving back to Minnesota to be by Grammy and Grumpy's, where they can water-ski every day, Grumpy says, and when Chloe says, "You can't water-ski in *winter*," Grumpy says, "Maybe *you* can't."

But just for a moment, pulling out of the drive, she's crying, and the Miracle sits up, bumping his big-kid head against the roof and squishing her as he turns for a last look.

"Bye, house," she says.

"Pencil mouse," says the Miracle, and Chloe beams through her tears. It's her own game, silly-rhyme-pencil game, she made it up when she was three to annoy her brother into looking at her, and it mostly worked. But she couldn't ever remember him *playing* it.

"Want to do speed?" she says, and the Miracle laughs. He always laughs now when she says that, but only because their father does. Her father has never said what's funny about it, and she doesn't think the Miracle knows, either.

"*Play* speed," he answers, grinning, maybe to himself but because of her, so that doesn't matter. "In a minute." And he glances fast over his shoulder toward the wall of boxes and then turns away from her again temporarily.

But Chloe has noticed that his grin is gone. And when she settles onto her shoulder blades and stretches out her legs to touch the door while her head brushes the back of the back seat, she realizes she can hear her mother over the rumbling engine, over the road bumping by.

"*Oh, freeze,*" her mother is whispering, over and over. Or else, "*cheese.*" Or "*please.*"

It isn't the words, it's the whispering, and Chloe realizes she knows what her mother's doing, too: she's hunched forward, picking at the hem of her skirt on her knees, her pale, knobby knees.

Knees? Is that what she's saying? No. *Please.*

"Bye, trees," Chloe whispers, watching the familiar branches pop up in her window to wave her away. The blue pine, the birch, the oak where her father *thinks* the woodpecker always knocks, the black-branched, leafless fire-trees the crows pour out of every morning like spiders from a sac. After the fire-trees comes the open stretch of road with no trees. The trees after that are ones she doesn't know, at least not by name, not to say hello or wave goodbye. Then come brand new trees.

"*Please,*" comes her mother's voice from the front seat.

"Dad, Gordyfoot," the Miracle all but shouts.

"Right," comes her father's answer, not as shiny as usual but just as fast. Seconds later, the CD's on, and Chloe can't hear her mother anymore.

Fire-trees, Chloe is thinking, dreaming. *Fire on a hillside with no grass, in a ring of stones, but not warm enough. No matter how close she wriggles, she can't get close enough, she's been out on this mountainside with the gray rocks and gray snakes for too long, and this cold is old, so old, older than daylight, older than she is, she could jump* into *the fire and never be warm...*

Jerking, Chloe struggles up onto her elbows, almost laughing. She has never been camping, not that she can remember, the snakes she knows are green and slippy-shiny except when they're dead and the crows have been at them, and the only cold she's felt the last few months is the lily-pond water from the Berry's backyard.

On the CD, Gordyfoot is singing about the Pony Man, who'll come at night to take her for a ride, and out the window, the sky's going dark fast with the sun gone. Chloe thinks it's funny that the Miracle asked for this CD, since he says he *hates* Gordon Lightfoot now. But she also understands, or thinks she does. It's hard to imagine being in the way-back, in the car with her parents, and listening to anything else. They

Miss Ill-Kept Runt

keep the entire Gordon Lightfoot collection up there. Also, if the CD wasn't on, they'd have to listen to their mother. *Freeze. Please. Pencil-bees.*

For a while—long enough to get out of their neighborhood and maybe even out of Missouri, half a CD or more—Chloe watches the wires in her window swing down, shoot up, swing down, shoot up. It's like starting and erasing an Etch a Sketch drawing, the window fills with trees and darkening sky and the thick, black lines of wire, then *boop*— telephone pole—and everything's blank for a second and then fills up again. Gets erased. Fills up again. Gets erased. Abruptly, it's all the way dark, and the wires vanish, and Venus pounces out of the sky. It's too bright, has been all summer, as though it's been lurking all day just on the other side of the sunlight.

With the Miracle coiled away from her and his head tilted down, she can see the semi-circle scar at the base of his neck, like an extra mouth, almost smiling. Chloe has always thought of that spot as the place where the miracle actually happened, though she's been told that's just where the clip to stop blood flow went. The real scar is higher, under the hair, where part of her brother's skull got cut open when he was five years old. Of course, she'd been all of a week old at the time and doesn't remember any of it. But she loves the story. Her mother curled on the waiting room couch where she'd been ever since she'd given birth to Chloe, expecting the doctors to come at any moment and tell her that her son was dead. Her mother erupting from that couch one morning and somehow convincing the surgeons who'd said the surgery couldn't work that it *would* work, just by the way she said it. By the way she seemed to *know*. And it had worked. The pressure that had been building in the Miracle's brain bled away. Two days later, he woke up himself again.

"What?" he says now, turning around to glower at her.

"Speed, speed, speed," she chants.

He glowers some more. But after a few seconds, he nods.

"Yay," says Chloe.

They can barely see the playing cards, which makes the game even more fun. Plus, the piles won't stay straight because of all the vibrations, which frustrates the Miracle but makes Chloe laugh even more as their hands dart between each other's for cards and tangle up and slap and snatch, and finally the Miracle's laughing, too, tickling her, Chloe's shrieking and they're both laughing until their father snarls, "*Kids, Goddamnit,*" and both of them stop dead. Her father sounds growly, furious, nothing like he usually sounds.

Because he's trapped up there with Mom, Chloe thinks, and then she's horrified to have thought that, feels guilty, almost starts crying again.

"Sorry," she whimpers.

"Just...sssh," her father says.

It's the move, Chloe thinks, chants to herself. She lies back flat, and the Miracle stretches as much as he can stretch beside her.

"The Pony Man" is on again, so the same CD has played through twice, but only Chloe seems to have noticed. She's listening very closely, like the song says, so she'll hear the Pony Man if he comes. But all she hears is their station wagon's tires *shushing* on the nighttime road, which she imagines to be black and wet, like one of those oil puddles birds get stuck in on nature shows. She's fairly sure she can hear her father's thumbs, too, drumming the beat on the steering wheel, and if she closes her eyes, she can see his stain-y *Show Me!* shirt and the wonderful, white prickles around his happy mouth. He has told Chloe he's secretly a cat, and the prickles are whiskers he keeps trimmed so Mom won't know.

He's been shaving more closely lately, though. Smiling less.

Then she realizes she can hear her mother, crying now. Even the cry is new, a low-down bear-grunt, and Chloe turns toward the Miracle's back and pokes it.

"Tomorrow I'll be half as old as you," she whispers. The Miracle doesn't respond. So she adds, "The next day, I'll be *more* than half."

The Miracle still doesn't respond, and she wonders if he's sleeping. His back is hard and curved like an armadillo shell.

"Catching up," she tries, a very little bit louder, and as she speaks she glances into the seatback above her head, as though she could see through it, through the cartons to her parents. As though they could see her.

"You'll never catch up," the Miracle murmurs, just as quiet, and Chloe thinks she sees his head tilt toward the front, too.

"I can if you wait."

"Will you just go to *sleep*?" he hisses, and Chloe startles, squirms back. The Miracle's whole body drums to the road or the steady beat of

Miss Ill-Kept Runt

her father's thumbs. But when he speaks again, he's using his nice voice. "It'll make the drive go faster."

Chloe almost tells him she doesn't want it to go faster. She likes the way-back, always has. Shut in with her brother, Gordyfoot's voice floating over and among them, her parents close but not with them, the stars igniting and the hours stretched longer and thinner than hours should be able to go. Silly Putty hours.

Chloe doesn't remember falling asleep, has no idea how long she sleeps. But she dreams of bird-feet hands. Hands, but the fingers too thin, yellow-hard. *Her* hands? *Reaching through the bars toward the frantic, fluttering thing, all red and beating its pathetic little wings...*

A bump jolts her awake, or else the *cold*, that *old* cold, she almost cries out, wraps herself in her own arms, blinks, holds on, drags her brain back to itself. *Air-conditioning, it's just her father blasting the air-conditioning to stay awake, it's not in her chest, there are no hands in her chest.* Chloe's eyes fly all the way open, and just like that, she knows.

She *knows*.

They're not my parents.

She knows because "The Pony Man" is on again, the CD repeating, *how many times, now?* She knows because her father's *isn't* tapping the steering wheel, which he always does, always always *always*, especially to Gordyfoot. She knows because her mother would never let it get this cold, her mother can't stand the cold, they always wind up fighting about it on night-drives and then swatting each other off the temperature controls and laughing and sometimes, when they think Chloe and the Miracle are sleeping, talking love-talk, very quietly.

They are talking now, but not that way. And in their changed voices. Her mother's bumpy, grunty and low. Her father's a snarl. Someone else's snarl.

Most of all, she knows because her mother's eyes—her *real* mother's eyes—are *green*, not blue. She very nearly screams, but jams her fist in her mouth, holds dead still. But the realization won't go away.

They aren't my parents.

It's ridiculous, a bird-feet hands dream. She wiggles furiously, trying to shake the realization loose.

But in the front seat, the new people—the ones that were her parents—are grunting. Snarl-whispering. And Chloe's mother's eyes are green.

At least "The Pony Man" finally goes off. But the next song is the "Minstrel of the Dawn" one. Another song about someone coming.

Stupid, Chloe insists her to herself. *This is stupid.* She feels around for the snack bag her father has let the Miracle stow back here, even though they've already brushed their teeth. The spiny, sticky carpet of the way-back scratches against her palms, and the engine shudders underneath her. Her hand smacks down on the paper bag, which makes a little *pop*. Chloe quivers, holds her breath, and up front, the grunting and the whispering stop.

Chloe doesn't move, doesn't breathe. Neither does anyone else in the car. They are four frozen people hurtling through the empty black. Even the CD has gone silent—because her parents have shut it off, Chloe realizes. It is so quiet inside the car that she half-thinks she can hear the cornfields passing, the late-summer stalks looming over the road like an army of aliens, an invasion that didn't come but grew, their bodies grasshopper-thin, leaves heavy, fruit swollen fat and dangling.

"Chlo?" says her not-father, in his almost-snarl.

Nearly faint from holding her breath, Chloe says nothing. After a second, she hears rustling, but whether from the corn or up front, she can't tell.

"See?" her mother whispers. "I told you. I told you, I told you, I—"

"Oh, for Christ's sake," says her father. "Five years of this. *Five years.* You can't really bel—"

"But I can. And so do you. You always have."

"Just shut up, Carol."

"He's coming."

"Carol—"

"He's coming. Face it. Face it. He's—"

"*Shut up!*"

The CD blares to life, and Chloe almost bangs her head against the seatback in surprise. Her breathing comes in spasms, and she can't get it calm. "The Pony Man" is playing again. *Why,* she wonders? *And why is she minding, anyway? According to her mom and dad, this is the first song she ever knew. The one they sang her to sleep with when she woke up screaming when she was a baby.*

Miss Ill-Kept Runt

Then Chloe thinks, *Shut up?* Her fingers grab so hard at the carpet that she pulls some out, little quills like a porcupine's. *When has her father ever said that, to anyone?*

And why is her mother laughing?

If that is laughing. It's mostly grunt. Panic breathing.

What Chloe wants to do, right now, is wake the Miracle. She can't believe he isn't awake already, but he hasn't stirred, still lies there with his back curved away and his scar smiling at her. If she wakes him, she knows, she'll have to tell him. Explain, somehow. And she's worried they'll hear.

Instead, she lifts herself—so slowly, as silently as she can, matching her movements to the *shush* of the tires—onto her elbows again. Turns over onto her stomach. Raises her head, then raises it more. Until she's above the seatback.

She's hoping she can see. *One good glimpse*, she thinks. *Then she'll know. Then she can decide what to do.*

But her father has packed the boxes too tight. There aren't even cracks between them. The only empty space is at the very tiptop. Pushing all the way up, Chloe straightens, and her beads *clank*.

This time, she very nearly throws herself out the back window. She's ready to. If they turn…if they pull to the shoulder and stop…she'll grab the Miracle and yank him awake, and they'll *run*.

But the car neither stops nor slows. The CD player continues to blare. The "Minstrel of the Dawn," who'll say your fortune when he comes. If her parents are talking, they're whispering so low that Chloe can't hear them. Apparently, they haven't realized she's moving around. Not yet.

Stretching, gripping her beads to keep them still, Chloe tries to get her eyes level with the opening at the top of the boxes. The little crack. But all she can see is the dark inside dome-light, the tiniest sliver of windshield, at least until a truck passes going the other way, its lights flooding the car and shooting shadows across the ceiling, but the shadows could be corn, seatbacks, surely her parents aren't that thin or that long. It's all Chloe can do to keep from burying her head between her knees in the tornado-position they taught her in kindergarten.

The words are out of her mouth almost before she's thought them or had time to plan.

"I have to go to the bathroom."

For a second, she just sits, horrified, clutching her beads.

But she had to. She needs to see. She's smushing her beads against her chest and holding her breath again, as though any of that matters now.

There is no response. Nothing at all. The car plunges on into the dark, and out her window the corn stalks twist their grasshopper-shoulders to squirm even more tightly together, denying any glimpse of field or farmhouse behind them, so that Chloe's vision is blocked on three sides. The only way she can see is behind, the road that leads back to the home they've left.

"I have to go to the bathroom," she says again, meaning to be louder but sounding smaller.

This time, though, the CD shuts off, and that silence wells up from the floorboards. Chloe has begun to cry again, and this makes her angry. *It's stupid*, she thinks, *this is stupid. Or the world is a nightmare.* Either way makes her angry.

Then comes the sigh, long and explosive, from the front seat.

"I thought I told you to *go*," growls not-Dad.

"Sorry," Chloe says. "I did."

All too soon—sooner than she thought possible, and she's seen no exit sign or prick of gas station light penetrating the leafy, squirmy blackness of the fields around her—Chloe feels the car start to slow, hears the *CLICK-click, CLICK-click* of the station wagon's blinker. In her mind, she can see it so clearly, that little green triangle-eye winking at her from the dashboard. *"It's where I keep the frog,"* her father has always said, patting a spot right above the blinking turn-signal, and they'd watch it blink together, and he'd say, *"Ribbit"* in time with the clicking. Until now.

It happens all at once, the corn parting like a curtain and the station appearing, its light so bright that Chloe's eyes water and she has to look away. The Miracle mumbles and rolls over. The light sweeps across the old-mannish wrinkle on his forehead as he dreams. Chloe knows that wrinkle like she knows the frog in the dashboard, her father's cat-whiskers, "The Pony Man." A wave of affection so wide and deep rushes through her that it is all she can do not to throw her arms around her brother's neck and bury her face there.

Miss Ill-Kept Runt

Then, all at once, she goes rigid again. She hasn't heard any doors opening, they've barely stopped moving. But the silence has gone just that imperceptible bit more still. Her parents—*both of them*—are out of the car.

Chloe whirls just in time to see the face fill the back window, black and scarfed, too big, the doors yawn open and she can't help it, she scurries back, pinning herself against the seat and the boxes with her hands raised and her mouth open to scream.

But her mother is already gone, stalking across the blacktop toward the light, the mini-mart inside the station. She doesn't look back, doesn't wave Chloe on or call to her. But for one moment, the set of those shoulders—the stoop and shake of them—is almost enough.

That is *my mother*, Chloe thinks. *That is my mother crying.*

She is half out of the car before she realizes she has no idea where her father is. Whirling, she bangs her head hard against the top of the door, expecting him to be right on top of her, with new long arms that open like wings and bird-feet hands. At first, she still doesn't see him, and then she does.

He's at the edge of the lot, right on the lip of the road where the cornfield devours the light. Like her mother, he has his back to her, and abruptly Chloe wants nothing more than to call out, lure him here. *He and Mom have been fighting,* she thinks, rubbing the back of her head, making herself breathe. *That's all it is. It's the move, Chlo. Ribbit.*

Something red flickers in his fingers. Chloe has leapt from the station wagon and is backing across the tarmac after her mother before she realizes it's a cigarette. Fast on the heels of that realization comes another. *She has never seen her father with a cigarette before. But he's been smoking lately. That's what that smell has been.*

Stopping by one of the silent pumps, Chloe bathes in the bright light, willing herself to cut it out. Beyond her father, the cornstalks, barely visible, wiggle their leafy antennae in the not-breeze, rattle their bulgy, distended husks. By tomorrow—maybe by the next time she wakes—her family will be at their new house. By tomorrow afternoon, she will be on Grumpy's boat, the rubber boots on the red kid-skis gripping her ankles and the Donald Duck lifejacket wrapping her in its sloppy, damp embrace.

Inside the station, she spots her mother crouching by the peanut butter cheese crackers. She is in profile, but the scarf hides just enough so that Chloe can't see her eyes.

"Going to the bathroom," she says. Her mother doesn't turn.

She dawdles a moment in the candy aisle, running a finger across the silvery *Chunky* wrappers, the boxes of 10-cent Kisses along the bottom shelf. She has almost reached the bathroom when her mother says, "Need help, sweetie?"

Chloe wants to dance, turn around and race at her mother and jump into her arms. Then she does turn, and something prickly and *old*-cold rolls over under her ribs.

Her mother's face, smiling softly down. Tears streaming from her blue eyes.

"No, thank you," Chloe whispers, and shuts herself in.

The toilet has poop in it, and a mound of tissue. Chloe doesn't actually have to go. Sinking into a huddle by the door in the ugly yellow light, she tries to hold her breath, but her chest prickles and she bursts out coughing. Crying again.

She can't stay here, the smell is too much. But she doesn't want to go back out. She's terrified to think what else might have changed by the time she opens the door. Each new breath of putrid air triggers a cough, each blink fresh tears.

Run, she thinks. *Sneak past the Kisses, bolt out the door, find a way to Grumpy's.*

Except that the only place to run is into the corn. In the dark. Chloe can't imagine doing that.

And then she realizes she doesn't want to. She already knows the safest place. The only place that hasn't changed, that's still hers. She needs to get back to the way-back, where the Miracle is.

She has just gotten the heavy door partway open when she hears them. Bumpy-voiced Mom, growly Dad, whispering just out of sight in the next aisle.

"You see?" her father is saying. Halfway snarling.

Her mother sobs.

"I told you."

"You did. It's true."

Miss Ill-Kept Runt

"You dreamed it, Carol. And no wonder. I mean, those nights. When we both really thought we were going to lose him…"

"But we didn't," Chloe's mother whispers, her voice seeming to twitch back and forth now. Chloe's mother/changed-mother/Chloe's mother.

"Because of you," her father whispers. "Because of your unshakable hope."

"Because of *him*. Because he came. Because he—"

"Because of *you*. You saved him, Carol. You saved your son. You do see that now. Right?"

Soft sob. Silence.

Then footsteps. Chloe pushes hard at the door, but by the time she gets out and hurries down the candy aisle after them, they are already at the pumps, arms around each other, halfway to the car. Her father goes straight to the driver's side, dropping his cigarette to the tarmac. It is her mother who waits by the way-back doors and touches Chloe's hair as she climbs in beside her brother.

"Is it my birthday yet?" Chloe asks, not quite looking at her mother's eyes. She doesn't want to see anymore. Doesn't want to think.

She hears her mother gasp, glance at her watch. "Not yet," she whispers. "Oh, shit, not yet."

The door drops down, and the car starts, and up front her parents are snarling and whispering again. Chloe crouches low, curls into a ball with her knees just touching her brother's back. If he wakes and feels that, he'll be furious. But if she's sleeping when he does, he won't mind. *Sleep*, she commands herself. Pleads with herself. *Sleep*.

She dreams cold. Old-cold. Green eyes. Bird-feet hands that aren't her hands—weren't—aren't—reaching for the beating-wing bird. Straw into gold, hillsides of stone. Old stone. Grasshopper-cornstalk squeezing in the window, slithering through it, crouching over her in the empty dark with its antennae brushing her face, and its husks, its dozens of husks hard and bumping against her chest, her legs. Those hands prying into the cage, reaching through the bars. Ribs. Toward the red and beating thing.

Chloe wakes to a silent car, bright sunlight. She is flat on her back, but she can feel the Miracle's heat against her forearm. He is moving now, stretching. Out the window, there are trees overflowing with green, shading her from the brilliant blue overhead. Minnesota lake trees. Somewhere close, there's a hum. Motorboat hum. Chloe is halfway sitting up when she hears them.

"You'll see," says her father, sounding tired. But only tired. And happy, almost. Sure, in the way he somehow still hasn't learned not to be, that the worst is behind him.

He pulls open the back door, arms wide, and it's him, her CatDad with his whisker-face, and she sits all the way up—just to revel in it, just to watch it all land—and he staggers back. Staring.

Revel? That's what *it's* doing, anyway, Chloe knows. The cold one inside her. The one moving her arms, blinking her eyes. Making her watch.

Vaguely, glancing toward her brother, Chloe wonders whether she really did figure it all out, or if the knowledge just came with the intruder. The cold one with the bird-feet hands, practically dancing down her ribs under her skin in his glee. Now she really does know. She knows how this happened. She knows when the cold one first appeared in her mother's hospital room. Her mother, whose eyes have always been blue, it's this *other's* mother that confused her.

Anyway, she knows what the cold one promised. She knows what he got her mother to offer in exchange.

"Where is she?" Chloe's father is murmuring, hovering right outside the way-back door and waving his hands as though trying to clear a fogged windshield, while out the side window, her mother stands rooted, hands over her mouth, shuddering and weeping. There is something almost comforting about it, about both her parents' reaction. At least they can tell. At least she really was *her*. There really was a something named Chloe.

I'm right here, she wants to scream. *Right here*. But of course, the cold one won't let her. He's having way too much fun.

Her father is on his knees, now, just the way the cold one likes him. Murmuring through his tears. Through his disbelief, which isn't really disbelief anymore. *So delicious when they understand,* the cold one tells her, in his inside ice-voice. *When they can't stop denying. Can't stop pleading. Even when they already know.*

So pathetic, her father looks down there. Hands going still. Head flung back in desperation. Or resignation. "Please," he says. "What have you done with my daughter?"

MILLWELL

"We stumbled upon the skeleton of a chamois, which had probably met its death by falling into a chasm, and had been disgorged lower down. But a thousand chamois between these cavernous jaws would not make a mouthful."

—John Tyndall,
A Day Among the Seracs of the Glacier du Geant

So the first thing you're going to ask is what we were doing up there, right? It's a stupid question, because you already know, but you want to hear me say it. Alright, I'll say it. We were looking for him.

See? Not even worth an eye-roll, is it? So come on, Mr. Sgt. Preston Mountie, what else you want to know? Wait, let's see if I can guess.

Were we stoned, want to know that? No we weren't, at least I wasn't, and even if the Indian was, by the time we came down…by the time I came down…

Just…hold on. Okay? Go feed King or something. Just hold on.

Aren't you hot in that? *No*, Jesus, I don't want another blanket, I don't even want this one. You look hot in that uniform. And no, I don't mean you look *hot*. Although the way you're staring, you seem to think I do. Come on, all these years patrolling the foot of the ice fall, you're telling me I'm the *first* teen you've seen stupid enough to climb the glacier in a mini-skirt? People do it all the time, half the summer tourists who go up there do it with their shirts off. Course, I'm not exactly a summer tourist, I mean not like that, and yes, I've heard the warnings, and…

Godgodgodgoddammnit. Okay. Okay. Wait. Okay.

From the top, yeah?

First of all, right, I know better. Even though I'm American. My family's been coming here every summer since I was seven. I've been on the glacier half a hundred times. I was here the year that kid—what was he, German?—walked five feet out onto the toe, in full view of the parking lot, and dropped down that crevasse. Remember? Remember just standing there and listening to him scream until he froze to death, because he was so far down you guys couldn't even find him, let alone figure how to get him out in time? Were you here then? God, I've never forgotten. At the end he didn't even sound like a kid anymore, remember? That growl? Like a bear in a trap.

Okay, fine, stare some more. When did everybody get so stare-y around here?

Like I said. We've been coming for years, and I've got lots of friends here, including the Indian. You know the Indian? Yeah, I thought you might. But tonight…let's just say I've never seen him like that.

You actually met the Indian? Well, whatever they've told you, they're wrong. He's really smart. And he's like the world's happiest kid. When the Eskimo was around, the two of them used to play warring tribes. Have canoe races on land, stupid stuff. The whole idea of having "enemies" just cracks him up. Everything does. That's such a dumb philosophy? I don't think so.

But he wasn't laughing tonight. None of them were. They were just sitting around the fire-circle pounding Molsons and staring at the trees. And no, by the way, we didn't have the fire lit, 'cause when you guys say there's fire danger we pay attention, even though you think we don't, and also, it's blazing outside, who needs one? More like the Okanagan than North Jasper.

Those kids…we used to have a lot more fun. Land canoes and ice-blocking. Hi-ball, back before they took it away, jumping in lakes from trees and rafts we made, playing tag in the abandoned railway tunnels. God, I used to love how *not* uptight you all were. Remember? When cops were for criminals and insurance companies were for car crashes and everything else was for playing on?

Millwell

Before the Eskimo disappeared. Now the rest of them pretty much do what you want us to. Sit around. Except for the drinking part. It's true, they drink. A *lot*. *They* do. They don't even mack on each other.

Don't check your fancy Mountie watch on me, alright? Amazingly enough, I don't actually *want* to think about it yet, I know that must just seem astonishing to you. I still don't even understand…Can you at least pass the Kleenex? Thanks.

Like I said. The Indian was like my last holdout. Last summer he took me owling all the time. Just prowling around the woods, going, *hoohoo-hoooo*. He was damn good at it. We saw owls like half the time. Barn owls. Snowy owls. The rest of the time we'd just go way the hell deep in the trees. So weird. I mean, it's not like the ocean or the desert or even the glacier, is it? Everyone talks about all the bird cries and the insects and all that. Must be some other woods. Yours are dead flat silent.

So here we are, first party of summer, and it's a hundred-five degrees—in *Canada*—and I want to float the river or owl the woods or whatever. And even the Indian's just sitting on a rock, glugging a Molson. Chucking stones in the water, not even skipping them. I'm about to leave, and the Indian catches my eye and mouths, "Wait."

And I know right away he's faking, making fun of everyone else's mood and they don't even realize it. There's this twitch around his mouth. It's really sexy and it always means…meant…anyway, right then, he just dropped his beer in the dirt and bellowed, "*BEAR!*"

Well, they turned around. Most of them. No one got up or anything. I think somebody probably said, "Good one, Indian" on the way to sticking a bottle back in his mouth.

Then he and I got out of there.

First thing he said when we got back to the road was, "Let's go to town. Let's go jump up and down in front of the gas station where the hi-ball used to be until they bring the hi-ball back. Why'd they take it, anyway?"

"Uh, because half the people who played wound up breaking their ankles or falling off the edge of the trampoline?"

"Yeah, but the other half went *really high*." Then, all of a sudden, he says, "To the woods." And he grabs my arm and we go running through the trees. He was in full Indian mode now, talking to the forest and yanking me behind him and not slowing for anything. Saying stuff like, "Ho-ho, elk. Surprised you, didn't I? Indian and Barrett, coming through. Hello, timberwolf, long time no see. Meet Barrett. She's a hottie, eh?"

Then he stopped in his tracks and grabbed me and mashed his mouth against mine.

He was crazed. Hopping everywhere, all that shine to him. Like a firefly in a jar. I didn't mind him kissing me, I just couldn't get him to stand still. I couldn't figure out his mood. Then he says, "My uncle's dying," and then, "I *really* miss the Eskimo." And he just sits down in the dirt.

Honestly, I was kind of stunned, at first. Mostly because he went so still. Just sitting there. I crouched down, and I guess my sucky insect repellent was wearing off, because there were bugs crawling up my legs. "What made you think of the Eskimo?" I asked.

He slapped a mosquito dead on my neck. "I always think of the Eskimo. Especially lately. He was the only one who...He was my best friend. And he *never* went up there unprepared. He was always careful, he knew the ice, it's been three years and I still don't understand it."

"You know understanding doesn't mean anything on the glacier. You taught me that, remem—"

He stood up and yanked me to my feet, and I mean *hard*. And there was this look on him. No twitching mouth, now. He looked like he was going to punch me.

"Let's go back," he said.

Well, I was pretty bewildered by now. And hot, and sweaty. And the whole night just...I let him pull me along. I tried one *hoo-hoo-hooo*. No owls came, and the Indian didn't even turn around. We were halfway back to the others when I grabbed his hand and made him stop.

"If that's how you feel," I said, "let's go find him."

The Indian stared at me. When he spoke, he was mostly talking to himself. "I haven't been up there since...*why haven't I?*"

Why hadn't any of us? We'd loved it up there. Even after the Eskimo, that first year. That's when the game started. The looking-for-him game. It was our excuse. Plus we really *were* looking for him. I think the Indian even thought we'd find him. For a while.

Millwell

Twenty minutes later, we were standing at the edge of the tourist center parking lot, a soft stone's throw from the toe of the glacier.

She doesn't look so good, you know. Your glacier. I mean, she was never exactly the most *picturesque* twenty thousand year-old ice floe, was she, always reminded me of a giant, bumpy, white tongue. Only now it's not so white anymore, and it's a *lot* more bumpy. A giant, twenty thousand year-old *diseased* tongue.

It's also quieter than it used to be. At least before you're on it. God, I remember standing in that parking lot when I was a kid, and it freaked me so badly. That rushing sound, with absolutely nothing moving. Like breathing, but in no rhythm. Plus all the snorting and smacking.

"It looks sleepy," I told the Indian. "Or dead."

"It's not daytime," he murmured, and started hunting around at his feet. "Help me find a stick."

We were looking for something long and thick, you know, to poke for crevasses. I told you, he wasn't stupid, not even reckless. Unless you count being up there at all, which I guess you probably do.

Oh, *shit*. Oh, Indian.

Go ahead, stare, I don't care.

Nnnnnnhhh...

I'd never been up it at night before. Never even at dusk. And when the Indian found a stick he thought was long enough, and shot me his new, tough-guy face, and I realized we really were about to head up the moraine...hell yeah, I was scared.

But it was a hundred degrees. At eleven o'clock at night. And it was my idea, remember. I wasn't pulling back now.

Before we even hit the ice, the Indian turned his ankle all the way around on some loose rock, and he swore and hopped all over the place. When he managed to put both feet down again, there were tears on his cheeks.

"Maybe this is a bad plan," I said.

"It's the only plan," he told me, and the moon just *appeared* over the peaks, like someone stuck a knife through the sky and slit it. We got a single shiver of wind, too. One deliciously chilly breath. That was our warning.

"Wait here," the Indian told me, and stumbled back to the parking lot.

I thought he was headed to improvise a wrap for his ankle. I stared a while at that moon-slit cat-eye hole in the sky for a while. But when I turned around, the Indian had the lid off one of those park service trash cans, and the bag already out. Then he leaned over and tipped himself halfway upside down inside the can.

"Indian, what the..." I shouted, and he popped back up with a couple black plastic squares in his hands. He waved them at me, and I realized they were garbage bags. He dropped the one with garbage in it back in the can, replaced the lid, and limped back to me.

And by the way, no, they weren't for body bags. It's like I keep telling you, not that you seem to hear a single word. *We didn't know.* Understand?

"Might need these, if we can find a long enough icy patch," the Indian said.

"How'd you know they were stored there?"

"What, you didn't?" When I shrugged, he did, too. "Ancient First Nations lore, I guess. Where mysterious white man park service hide-um spare bags."

He stuck his stick in the first scrap of snow at the toe of the ice floe, and it went right through, but not far. Two inches, maybe, then *clunk*. Rock. More like a melting mini-drift from some freak summer storm than the bottom of that glacier. Up we went.

The Indian kept poking around just to be extra safe, even though he could barely find enough snow to get the stick tip wet, let alone hide a crevasse. But the night got brighter. And bluer. It was like the moraine still had a shine on it, or a frost. Also, we could at least hear sounds, now. That rushing, way down underneath us. Which doesn't make sense, does it, I mean, it can't be colder *inside* the planet, right? Also there were these weird *shushes*. I couldn't even tell you where those were coming from.

The point is, we were watching the ground. Listening to the ground. I'd started to get this tickling in my feet and the backs of my knees. Like when you're standing at one of those summit viewpoints with no railing? We'd finally gotten to where there's still more ice than rock—maybe a hundred feet from the lot?—and I don't know why, I just *looked up*.

I'm not the screaming kind. But I'll admit it, I made a noise, and that's why the Indian jumped straight ahead and landed on what looked

Millwell

like a little white smear of dust and then *dropped* all the way to his thighs in ice. Just *bang*.

The funniest part—I mean, it wasn't funny, *believe* me, it so already wasn't funny—was that *he* didn't even react until like five seconds later. He just stood in the hole, gaping like a ground squirrel, and then he started barking, "Crap, crap, crap, crap, crap," scrabbling with his hands and scattering rock and ice clods all over the place, and I kind of panicked, it was like watching a movie of someone in quicksand. I dropped down and crawled forward and grabbed his wrist and helped draw him out.

As soon as he was lying beside me, he rolled over and stared in my face with that punch-something look again. And the ground…I've felt it before, but it's the weirdest sensation. That surface-layer of heat from being in the sun, but you know it's fake. Or, fragile. A warm that won't last, a cold you *know* is under there. Like fried ice cream. Or something that was living five seconds ago.

"Why did you *do* that?" the Indian shouted.

I waved my hands, trying to quiet him, then pointed up. There were actually tears in my eyes, I have no idea why. "I saw that," I said. "For this retarded second I thought it was a grizzly bear."

He looked where I'd indicated. His face didn't change, exactly. But his tone did.

"One of those rare *yellow* grizzlies?" he said quietly.

"With really big tires. Yeah."

Neither one of us exactly smiled. But he let me pull him up.

When did they start parking those crazy buses up there, anyway? I guess the tour company's not as nervous about the glacier anymore either, huh? God, the first time I went down on the ice was in one of those. I was maybe eight, and it scared me so bad. Driving halfway up the mountain along the side of the glacier, first of all. The way the guide was talking, and the way they drove—maybe two miles an hour, I could have handwalked faster—made it seem like we were skirting something, alright. Then the turn, and those *huge* tires just grabbing the land. Like they didn't want to go. And the inching down. Inching. Inching. So, so slow. I think they said it was the steepest incline traversed by a four-wheel vehicle in the whole hemisphere, is that right? And they did it that way because it was the only place they were sure the glacier wouldn't open up and swallow them.

By now, the Indian had the garbage bags shaken out, and he was cutting head-sized holes in them with his pocketknife. This is probably offensive to say, but he did it so skillfully. It really was like watching someone skin a buffalo. He didn't tell me what he was doing, and I didn't ask, and a few minutes later he re-folded the bags, started poking again with the stick, and we went up again.

The rocks disappeared. And even though you could barely hear that whooshing sound, it was there. And this…*breeze* isn't really the word… *chill*, I guess, started rising around our ankles. It was like wading way out to the ocean. And back ten thousand years.

Anyway. We were moving slow, now, inching just like those buses. Putting our feet down extra-light, as if that would help if we happened to hit a spot with no ground. I kept glancing up at the peaks above and the black cliffs to the sides. All that dead, hot rock. Once I turned around, and it was kind of amazing. We hadn't gone very far. The parking lot was maybe a hundred yards away. And yet on a whole other planet. It was like looking at the earth from space.

I kept almost tripping, because I kept forgetting the glacier isn't flat. It humps up, drops down, smacks up against itself in little ridges.

Where are all your birds, by the way? Didn't there used to be eagles?

The Indian hadn't said a word in quite a while. Way, way below, I heard a truck pass. The loudest sound in half an hour. I was keeping my eyes on the ice, now, and even so, I couldn't have said when we hit the weeping.

I realize that's not a scientific term. It's what I've always called it, though. You know what I'm talking about? How all of a sudden there's runoff just *pouring* down the ice? Streaks here, gushes there, not a continuous flow, more like a hundred thousand transparent little ant colonies racing all over the place. Channeling through grooves they've made themselves, diving a thousand feet down holes they've drilled in the ice, what do they call those, millwells? The flow is silent, all the glacier sounds are coming from underneath, but the *movement*. And the color. Even in the dark, in almost no moon. That *blue*, like the blood in your veins you can't ever see because it turns red in the air. You ever think about being blue inside?

Millwell

Finally, it occurred to me that even at the pace we were going, we'd climbed a long way. Not only that, but we'd consistently angled to the right. As if the Indian had a destination in mind after all. And he did, it turns out, just not the one you're thinking.

"Hey, Indian," I called, and was startled to see him fifteen feet ahead, climbing faster and faster. Stepping over rises. Still limping. "Wait up."

Instead of slowing, he pointed. At least now I knew what the bags were for.

"No way," I told him.

He turned around, and there was his Indian grin, in all its glory. "Way," he said.

He was pointing at this long, flat plain of ice that dropped at a steeper angle than the slope we'd climbed. It skimmed halfway back down to the parking lot and emptied into a jumble of piled moraine. The Indian flipped me a garbage bag. "Put this on."

"But...how do you know it's safe? How do you know there's not some gaping hole under there that's going to eat us when we slide by?"

"Look at the flags."

I looked. All the way down the pitch, the park service had planted little green flags.

"How do you know those aren't the *Keep Off: Ten Thousand Foot Plunge* flags?"

"'Cause those ones aren't green," the Indian said, and grinned even wider.

Before I could think what else to say, he was on his ass, sliding back and forth on the ice. Testing out the bag. Like he was getting ready to luge, you know? Bending at the waist, bending back. I knew he was right; I remembered the flags from my bus trip. They meant that the rangers had checked this stretch within the last 48 hours, so the buses could let tourists off to walk there.

One more time, I looked up, and this is almost funny, now, but I was kind of disappointed. We'd gotten, I don't know, maybe a fifth of the way to the top? I figured it might take us eight seconds to slide down the Indian's ice patch, then another five minutes of moraine-stomping to return to ordinary old paved land. It seemed like we'd gone farther. Talking to you now, I'd have to say yes, it was blacker than it had been a few moments before. A lot blacker. That moon-slit in the sky had sealed up, for one thing. And yes, I think I even caught the first real gust in my teeth. But I just thought it was the glacier. Or I didn't think about it at all. I glanced down and saw the Indian knifing away from me across the ice, howling like a timberwolf.

"You bastard," I called after him, dropped on my own ass, and kicked off.

The ice bumped underneath me, because of course it wasn't anywhere close to flat, and also, it was *wet*. Even through the bag I could feel it. I started to spin sideways, like I was on one of those flying saucers, so I decided I'd be better off the Indian's way and started to lie back, and then the Indian said, "Oops."

That was it. *Oops.*

Obviously, I tried to stop right away, flipped over on my stomach and grabbed the ice, and a whole clod of it came up in my fingers, like I'd raked its face. My own face bobbed up and down with the jouncing I was getting, and I must have hit my forehead at least once, which is how I got the shiner you still haven't bothered getting me anything for. But I was too panicked to notice. It took forever—as in, probably two seconds, but it felt like forever—to claw myself still.

When I did, I shook my head to clear it. I was blinking furiously, too, trying to see through the wetness all over my eyes, some of which was tears and some glacier melt.

All around me, I saw dirty, lumpy blue ice. No Indian.

By now, my fingers had figured out they were joint-deep in really serious cold, because they started aching so bad that I jerked them out of the ground. That set me skidding again, so I jammed my feet down and pushed hard and stood up.

"Ind…" I started to yell. But I'd seen him by then.

Somehow, he'd plummeted down an ice-waterfall that hadn't been there when we'd started. At least, it hadn't been visible. A big one, like twelve feet. He was lying on his stomach, completely still, with his head mashed down in the blue wet.

I thought he'd broken his neck. I think I was chanting, "Shit, oh shit," as I scrambled sideways toward him. His head came up, and his *skin*, God, the glacier had already turned it white, white and blue, and there was ice-water just *streaming* down it.

"Hold on—" I started to call.

Then the idiot jammed his face *back down.* And I realized he wasn't moving like anyone hurt. He looked like a goddamn snorkeler.

"Indian…" I murmured, and skidded the rest of the way.

Without lifting his head or turning toward me, the Indian slapped the ice beside him. Slapped it again. On the third slap, I saw it.

I know what you're going to say. I also know it's true, okay? The glacier *moves*, I get it. Constantly, all the time. Not just up or down, but side to side, in and out. That's how mammoths roll out of the earth ten thousand years after they've vanished. And why whole skeletons aren't ever found, even of people who died just a few days or months ago. The glacier rips them to pieces.

But I'm telling you…this was *planted there*. And it was whole. And on purpose. The most perfect little *inukshuk* I've ever seen in my life.

"You know what that means," the Indian snarled, still without lifting his head. His voice came out hissy and echoey, as though one of those little rivulets had drilled into his throat.

Ripping the garbage bag off my head, and also aware, finally, of the ache and swelling over my right eye, I dropped to my knees. That little thing. So…*pitiful*, somehow. Like an abandoned kitten. I almost scooped it up.

Except I didn't quite want to touch it, either.

It wasn't only the way the stones fit together. Those things always seem so perfectly balanced, you know? As if the top of the earth really were a broken whole, not a bunch of randomly spewed or churned up crusty bits. But this one…the rocks looked almost locked in place, and they formed this totally human shape. Little round legs, little round chest, littler, pinker round head. And two twiggy sticks drooping out of the sides, like miniature snowman arms.

I just stared at it. It didn't stare back or anything. It just sat in the ice in its little hole. Ever seen the picture of those English guys that lost the race to the South Pole? After they were dead? That photo with the flags just barely sticking out of the snow? That's what this thing looked like.

"It's so…" I murmured, dazed. And cold. Which I still thought was because I was kneeling on a glacier.

"It marks places of death," the Indian said. Without looking at me, he wriggled around and jammed one of his eyes even deeper into the ice.

"What the hell are you *doing*?" I asked.

"It also marks places you shouldn't try to cross."

"So it's either a warning or a tombstone."

"Which means that either way," the Indian said quietly, "he's here."

I was still gaping at him when the sleet hit us.

I know the glacier makes its own weather. I know the time of year and the temperature on the rocks right beside it in the regular world has nothing to do with what happens on the ice. But we didn't even hear this storm coming. It's like it was hiding up top, peeking over the ridge to see when we had our backs turned. Then it flung itself over.

Sleet. Hail. Whatever was in that wind banged so hard off my skull that I swear it set off echoes inside me. I ducked, cussing all over the place, and the Indian twitched where he was lying and started to curl into a ball, but he didn't get up. The wind crashed down next, this gurgling, thrashing wave that boiled over us like whitewater but didn't suck back. I tried getting a look at the top of the glacier, but I couldn't even see the rocks fifteen feet to our right anymore. Shivering and swearing, I started to stand, my foot accidentally kicking the *inukshuk*, which tipped over and vanished, and just as I started straightening out of my crouch, the Indian grabbed my wrist and yanked me face first into the ice beside him.

"*Hey!*" I screamed. "*Get off!*"

Instead, he popped up on his knees and grabbed the back of my head with both hands.

"*What are you…*" I started, and he mashed me into the snow.

"Look," he snarled.

I was squirming, flinging one pathetic fist into his ribs, half-thinking he was going to murder me right there. But his tone stopped me. He wasn't angry, or murderous. He was panicking.

"Barrett, please. Holy shit."

And he pulled me, by my hair, to the lip of the millwell he'd been staring into. It couldn't have been more than three inches in diameter, but all that water hurtling across the surface of the glacier was plunging

Millwell

into it. So much water. As though the ice were trying to sweep us into itself through that little hole, and not just us. The mountains all around, the lakes at the bottom. The whole world it had carved and made.

The sleet was driving needles into my back, and the shivers sweeping up my spine were smashing my jaws together. I could feel my bare legs and my ears and my fingers and the tip of my nose screaming. But I hardly noticed. I was too busy jamming my eyes shut, because no matter what, *I did not want to look where the Indian was forcing me.*

"Indian," I whimpered, and he positioned my face directly over the millwell and shoved down, and the shock of it rattled my eyes open. Then I went slack. Staring.

"Tell me what you see," he hissed.

But I couldn't see anything. Just blue, gushing water. My lids started blinking frantically—can eyes drown?—and I tried lifting my head and the Indian just shoved down harder, and then I saw it. Thought I did. Thought I saw...

"I see its eye," I babbled. I can't even tell you what I meant. I was staring down a thousand year-old channel into the ten-thousand year-old ice that made the world. And seeing an eye. All pupil, totally black. And blinking. The Eskimo's eye? The *glacier's*?

Rearing back, screaming, I broke free and scrambled away, not even thinking about the flags, the sleet, anything except that blinking *whatever* below. And the thing is...you'll say I dreamed it, and maybe I did... but I could feel movement underneath. Not just the streaming water. Something heavy. I shoved off my hands and knees and staggered to my feet and finally, finally whirled around.

No Indian. No anything, except sheeting, frozen rain, streaming ice, empty space.

"*FUCKER!*" I shrieked, and the wind ate my voice, and nothing answered. I started looking around frantically, trying to figure out where the flags were, which way I was facing. And then I just lit out, straight down. I knew I could drop through at any second. I knew how dumb it was. I knew I should have stayed right there at least a little longer. Until the Indian found me, or I could see.

But I'm telling you, I could still feel it. And when I moved, it moved, too. Just gliding along under there. You ever seen a killer whale stalk a seal from under an ice cap? Also, the glacier was deafening. Even over the wind, I could hear it *shushing*, gnashing away at itself. Twice I went down flat on my face, which is how I got the rest of the bruises you still haven't bothered bringing me anything for. Every time I went down, I kept expecting the ice to open up, or something to explode through it. I have no memory whatsoever of the moment I hit moraine. All I do remember is this weird, beady feeling on my arms—like I was falling through a curtain—and just like that, it was a hundred degrees again. And absolutely silent.

It was a long time before I could make myself turn around. When I did, I saw the storm still raging up there, whirling around on itself. After a few minutes, it just kind of *collapsed*, like an imploding building. Clouds and sleet and wind and all. And it was just the rocks, the pathetic scrap of glacier. The parked bus. And no one and nothing else.

And that is exactly as much as I can tell you about what happened to the Indian, and how the Eskimo wandered into the glacier parking lot and right into the arms of your boys in the cruiser.

As for why he's just sitting in that chair in the lobby like that, how the hell should I know? Maybe that's what happens when you're frozen alive, or swallowed by a dying glacier, or whatever the hell happened to him. As far as I'm concerned, he fits right in, looks pretty much like everyone else around here these days. It's like when the glacier melted, and all that white, wonderful wildness went out of the world, all that *cold* had to go somewhere, so it just poured off the rocks into town…

Into everyone around here and…

Wait…

Oh.

Man, that really *sucks*…

Like Lick Em Sticks, Like Tina Fey

"Under the heat there's a coldness, and even the coldness can't be pinned down...His fleeting pleasures and undeniable pain aren't so much depthless as unfathomable."
—Robert Christgau on George Jones in
Growing Up All Wrong

"Take the goddamn gun out of your mouth and give me a Juicy Fruit."

Sophie leans back her head with the barrel on her tongue and the sea wind whipping through the trees, through the car-window into her bobbing blonde hair. The road rolls on before them through the Georgia pines, and the headlights play across it like stones they're skipping.

"You can still taste that?" she says. "You like that taste?"

"Take the goddamn gun out of your mouth," says Natalie, and puts a hand to her own windblown hair.

It looks blacker in this light, Sophie thinks. Or it is blacker. She lowers the gun from her lips. "Better?"

"Juicy Fruit," says Natalie.

Sophie pads her hand around the glove-box until she finds the last stick of gum, shriveled into its foil wrapper like a dead caterpillar. She hands it to Natalie.

"Ugh. Even touching it gives me the wallies. How can you eat that?"

"This from the woman last seen sucking a gun barrel."

Natalie glances down to unwrap the gum, and the car swerves onto the gravel shoulder before she catches the wheel with her knees and jerks it back toward the road.

"Watch your driving," Sophie says.

"So can I see the nothing when I hit it?"

"Seriously," says Sophie. "You're going to wreck us."

Wrenching the wheel to the right, Natalie spins the car onto a dirt trail, and they bump along it until the pines clear and they're idling in front of three sand dunes that have humped up out of the ground, side by side, like whales surfacing. The moonlight burns their sand-skin white. Natalie shuts off the car.

"You know," Sophie says, "a gun is just like a Lick Em Stick someone stuck a trigger on."

"What?"

"A gun is just like—"

"And there you have it. The single dumbest thing I have ever heard. And I've been driving around with you all night, every night, for almost a month."

"And sharing Moon Pies and tent-sleepovers and 'Gilmore Girls' and at least two boyfriends for a good twenty years before that."

"I'm trying to block all that out."

"And yet, a gun is like a Lick Em Stick someone—"

"A gun is nothing like a Lick Em Stick anyone stuck anything on. A gun couldn't be less like a Lick Em Stick if it were a…Guns aren't even straight. And even if they were. Saying something's like something else because they have sort of the same shape—or not at all the same shape,

Like Lick Em Sticks, Like Tina Fey

in this case—is just stupid. It's like saying a brain is just like a sponge-blob someone stuck a thought in."

"Now, see, that's just cynical, that's what that is. It's worse. It's nihilistic."

"*Nihil*. Rhymes with *bile*."

"Oh. I thought it was nil. Rhymes with kill."

Natalie's slap rocks Sophie's head off the seat-rest into the door. "Shit," she says, "I'm sorry."

"Didn't hurt." Sophie sits up. Natalie puts her cold hand on her friend's cold cheek.

"Sorry," she says.

"For what?"

"Three weeks," Natalie murmurs.

"As of tonight," says Sophie. "I know."

"I'm hungry."

"Me, too."

They watch the dunes, waiting for them to sink, but they don't. Unconsciously, Natalie fishes in the pocket of her denim skirt and draws a cigarette from the crumpled pack. The second the cigarette touches her lips, before she has even thought of lighting it, she gags, spits it out the window into the sand.

"Well, hell," she says. "I'm cured."

"One good thing, anyway," Sophie says. "Hey, maybe we could open a business. Let them pick us, instead of our picking them."

"Shut up, Sophie."

"Guaranteed to work. They get their lungs, we get—"

"Shut *up*."

Reedy sand-grass nuzzles against the sides of the car, and the stars dangle like a mobile. Somewhere not too far, an alligator bellows.

"Nat?" Sophie half-whispers. "Let's just go see them. We could just look in the window. Please, let's—"

"Sophie, I swear to God, don't—"

"Just to see. Just once more. Those little faces. Little feet."

Natalie starts the car, grinds into reverse, wrenches the wheel around and sends it bumping back down the trail. When they reach the asphalt, she fishtails onto it, her wheels kicking up a spray of dirt like a Jet-ski throwing wake. They hurtle down the rolling road between the pines.

"You hit some nothing," Sophie says, lifting the gun off the seat and sticking the barrel back between her teeth.

"Baby," says Natalie.

Sometime just after midnight, Natalie surprises Sophie by pulling into the parking lot of a Waffle House. The building is low and brick. Teenagers crowd around two booths near the front, and a couple of solitary truckers sip coffee in the back. Through the grime and the flittering moths on the windows, all of them look yellow.

"Where are we?" Sophie says, and fabricates a yawn. Yawning, of all things, turns out to be something she genuinely misses.

"Waffle House," says Natalie.

Sophie smiles. "Thanks, Sparky. Waffle House where?"

"Waffle House is its own where." Again, Natalie reaches into her pocket for a cigarette. But this time she doesn't even glance at her hands, just tosses the whole pack out the window. "No," she says. "Waffle House is nowhere. Always." And she looks at Sophie.

"Oh, shit," says Sophie, and her tongue sneaks onto her lips. "Here? Now? It's time?"

Natalie puts a hand to her own chin. The hand doesn't shake, but she wants it to. Wishes it would. "I don't know. How do we know? The bastard didn't say. I don't know, I don't know, I don't know."

"I'm going to call them," Sophie says, catching Natalie off-guard, and before she can grab an arm and stop her, she's out of the car, walking fast into the shadows of the pines.

Natalie considers giving chase, opens the door to do just that. Then she just sits with her legs swung onto the pavement, feeling the sticky night air rush up her skirt. So warm. How did they stand it all those years? From this distance, all she can see is her friend's silhouette. The stocky, bouncy frame—like a gym-bag full of volleyballs, Sophie's fiancé Willie used to say happily, stroking her thigh—the blond head bobbing. Phone against her ear.

Against her ear. With her baby boy's voice filling it.

Unless she's talking to Natalie's baby boy.

Like Lick Em Sticks, Like Tina Fey

At the last second, Sophie senses her coming, whirls around as her friend swoops out of the light and rips at the phone. "They're not home," she squeals, but Natalie's long nails are raking the inside of her wrist and the phone has flown from her hands. "Ow," she says.

"What do you mean they're not home?" Natalie drops to her knees, padding around in the shadows for the phone. "It's after midnight, where would they be?"

"Maybe your mom did what you said. Maybe she took them. Maybe they're gone, and we won't ever—"

Silencing her with a growl, Natalie stands with the phone in her hand, staring like it's a heart she's ripped out. Then she slams it to the pavement and stomps it to pieces.

When she looks up a few seconds later, meaning to apologize, wanting to clutch her oldest friend to her and scream, Sophie is gazing over her shoulder. Natalie turns slowly and sees the trucker.

Just a boy, really. Long, lanky southern boy, skin like a slicked summer peach and an alligator smile he hasn't mastered and doesn't mean.

"Well, damn," he says, and then his smile goes slack, and Natalie feels a twinge, a real one. *You're not so far over your head*, she wants to tell him. *Don't stop now.*

Or else, *Stop right now. Turn around. Run.*

"Thelma and Louise," Sophie whispers, and Natalie jerks back to herself. "What?"

"Thelma and Louise. Taking back the night. Look at him. He's perfect."

"Sophie…"

"Who'd miss him?"

I would, Natalie thinks, knows that makes no sense and probably isn't true, and steps into the light. Even from ten feet away, she can feel him vibrate like a string she's struck.

"Well, damn," the boy says again, swaying in place. He takes a woozy step forward.

"Don't," Natalie murmurs, and he takes another step. Still five feet between them, but she can already taste his breath, bubble-gummed and maple syrupped and hot with him. It's as though she's developed a new shark-sensitivity to every twitching, fumbling, ridiculous movement living things make.

"Don't," she says again, and he steps closer still.

"But I really want to," he murmurs. So close, now. His mouth so near. His cheeks no longer yellow but sweetly tan and red.

"So do I," she says.

"Thelma and Louise," chants Sophie. "Thelma and Louise."

Grabbing her wrist, Natalie yanks her past the kid toward the Waffle House. She really has to pull because Sophie is jamming her feet down like anchors, and from her mouth comes a brand-new, mewing sound. The kid shudders, desire unfurling from him like a sail. *They weren't home*, Natalie thinks. *They're gone. Oh, Mom. Thank you.* She practically has to hurl Sophie into the restaurant while holding the door with her hip.

For a second, she thinks Sophie's going to turn on her, that they're going to have it out once and for all. But there's something instantly soothing in here, familiar in a way almost nothing else has been these past few weeks. The fluorescents are bright, the music on the radio is Buck Owens, and the dead-eyed, red-haired counterwoman halfway smiles as she nods them toward a booth. All they have to do is…act naturally.

But there's a mother and daughter at the counter. The mother is wrapped in bright-colored scarves, and the daughter, who can't be more than twelve, is feeding her French fries. Maps lay spread in front of them between the ketchup bottles. The woman tucks a stray strand of hair behind her daughter's ear and laughs. Natalie's mouth has formed an O. Her heart isn't really hammering, she knows.

"Well, hi, y'all," Sophie says to the teens in the front booth.

They're staring, of course. The girls, too, though the too-thin redhead in the back is forcing her eyes down to the table, playing pitifully with her napkin. She looks like a French fry dipped in ketchup, barely noticeable even when she's right in front of you, and she knows it. God, Natalie remembers that sensation. Remembers whole Saturdays traipsing around the Goodwills with her mother, trying to find clothes to bring out the blue in her eyes. The only feature she was sure she could do anything with. Once, not more than a year ago, when they were sitting half-drunk on the lawn chairs in the dirt, Natalie's mother had told her, "It's so sad, really. One more proof of just how much God hates women. You only really start to radiate sexuality—the confident kind, the kind

Like Lick Em Sticks, Like Tina Fey

that's you and that you really intend—long after you have any use for it. Also long after it's probably healthy for you to have it."

A wise woman, Natalie's mother. Wise today, anyway, now that she's a grandmother at 37 with a double-wide and two new babies to look after, only one of them blood-related, neither of them hers. *Is she that wise, though? Has she really gone?* Natalie doesn't think so. And even if she has gone, she's left a trail. In the hopes that Natalie will come one day and find her.

Veering away from the booth, she tugs Sophie to the counter and orders a double patty melt to go.

"Hey," Sophie says. "That sounds so good." She orders one, too. Behind them, the teenagers return uneasily to themselves.

"Be just a minute," the counterwoman says.

Natalie fumbles in her pockets for the cigarette pack. Patsy comes on the radio, "Walking After Midnight," and Sophie makes clip-clops to the beat with the salt and pepper shakers.

"You know," she says, in the chirping-bird voice Natalie has loved since they were kindergarteners. "A patty melt's just like a dead thing someone slapped cheese and onions on."

Smiling, grateful, Natalie turns. "That doesn't work at all."

"Why not?"

"It's not a metaphor. It's not even a comparison. It's just what it is."

"Well, that there's the difference between you and me, Nat. I call things what they are."

"I think I'll go throw up, now."

"Got to eat something first," Sophie says, grinning, and Natalie feels sick but starts to smile back anyway, and then the woman in the scarves touches her hand.

"Oh, honey," says the woman. "You're just like me."

Stunned, Natalie almost collapses right there. She turns shakily, but all she can see is black and gray hair sneaking from under the scarves on top of the woman's head.

"What do you mean?" Natalie whispers.

"Cold all the time," the woman says. "Bad circulation. I can't ever get warm. Want your fortune read?"

"What?"

"Come on, she needs the practice," says the woman's daughter. "No paying customers for a week. I'm going to the bathroom, Mom." Hopping off the stool, the girl wanders away.

The counterwoman returns with the burgers in a bag, and Natalie turns to go, but Sophie pushes her down onto the stool.

"Give her good news," Sophie says to the woman. "She could use some." She keeps her hands on Natalie's shoulders while the woman produces a deck of cards and shuffles them. Natalie's mother was better at shuffling. Bad at winning, though.

Humming a melody Natalie assumes is meant to be gypsy but sounds like Patsy out of tune, the woman shuffles again, then fans the cards on top of the map.

"Touch two," she says, and Natalie does.

The woman sets aside Natalie's choices, reshuffles the deck, fans it open again.

"And two more."

Natalie touches two more. The woman smiles. Her teeth are grainy and brown, but her black eyes are bright.

"Good. Let's see what we can know." The woman turns over a card. A black ace, Natalie thinks, from the brief glimpse she gets, then a second one. The woman's hands slow, and her smile twitches.

"That's not funny," says Natalie, her voice a bobcat-murmur, her whole body tensing. "You have no idea how not funny—"

"I'm sorry," the woman says. "I did this wrong. Out of practice, as my daughter told you. I'll just reshuffle, and we'll..." Suddenly, her smile vanishes completely, and she looks up. "Oh," she says. "Oh, I'm so sorry. Goddamn it."

From the direction of the bathroom comes a giggle which explodes abruptly into full-blown laughter. The daughter is still laughing as she hurtles past the stools, past the teenagers in the front booths, and out of the restaurant.

Staring after her, the woman in the scarves stands and begins to collect her things and fold the maps. She flips over the deck so Natalie and Sophie can see it. Every single card is a black ace.

"She thinks she's hilarious," the woman says. "Thinks she's Tina fucking Fey. I'm sorry. I hope I didn't scare you." On impulse, she reaches

Like Lick Em Sticks, Like Tina Fey

into her purse and lays down an extra ten dollars on top of her check. "For your patty melts." She leaves.

A few moments later, after Sophie has slathered her burger in ketchup, she and Natalie follow. Back in the car, Natalie switches on the radio and dials through the stations until she finds the one from the Waffle House. It's Loretta, this time, sending 'em all to Fist City.

"This is the best DJ on earth," she says, tears streaming down her face. Real tears. How did those get there?

"Wow," Sophie says.

"Shut up," says Natalie, and pulls them out of the lot into the dark.

"You know," Sophie says, after they've driven another long while, the pines far behind them and in their place peach trees squatting in rows on their stubby trunks like old women under hair-dryers at the beauty salon, "she's got it all wrong."

George Jones on the radio this time, the static sewn into his voice like a smoker's rasp. Singing flat and sad, no drama at all. "Just a Girl I Used to Know."

"Who?" Natalie murmurs.

"Tina Fey."

"Has got it wrong?"

Sophie swats her on the arm. But carefully. Or at least softly. Not like Natalie swats, these days.

"Tina Fey wouldn't be the daughter loading the deck. She'd be the customer getting mistakenly told she was going to die."

"You think so?"

"Complications would ensue."

"Complications."

"Hello? Ground control to Natalie Robot? Switch brain back to on position. Over."

"We have to get rid of these burgers," Natalie says, and Sophie looses an explosive sigh.

"My God, yes, even the smell is giving me the wallies."

"The willies, goddamnit."

"I know."

"Well, what's wrong with the willies?"

"I liked my Willy," Sophie says.

Natalie almost rockets them off the road. One good kick to the pedal, a quick swerve, and they'd be launched through the peach trees. Maybe if they got going fast enough, they'd just fizz away into the dark like an Alka Seltzer tablet. Which is a Sophie comparison if ever there was one.

She glances toward her friend. Sophie's the one crying, now. The sight makes Natalie furious, but she has no idea at what.

"Nat, I'm so hungry," Sophie says. "We have to choose."

"I know," says Natalie.

"Anyone you want, Nat. Any way you want to do it. Anything you think is fair. We can't shirk it. We can't pretend we can avoid it. It's just—"

"What do you suggest, Sophie?" Natalie doesn't mean to start shouting, barely notices that she is. "Next breakdown victim? Next guy in bad pants? Oh, I know, how about next black dude, you always had a thing for black dudes."

"That's just mean."

"Damn right."

"Natalie, I'm serious. It's killing me."

"Maybe we should let it kill us."

"You know it won't work. You know what he said. It'll be like trying to kill yourself holding your breath. In the end, instinct will take over. Then we'll just act. We won't have any choice. That's what he said. Is that what you want?"

"He said a lot of things. Maybe we're stronger than he is."

"Maybe you are, Nat."

Natalie can't even remember his face. Can't remember whether it hurt. Can't even remember how she and Sophie wound up with him that night. But she can see him straightening over her, mouth already dripping with her. The pull of him overwhelming, sucking up every little passing ball of magically cohering, animated dust like a black hole. She'd wanted him to kiss her some more.

No. She'd wanted to feed herself to him.

What will it be like? she'd asked, not really caring.

Like Lick Em Sticks, Like Tina Fey

And he'd actually paused for a second, as though between courses, or maybe he was thinking about it for the first time. Eventually, he shrugged.

Like coming loose. Like letting go of all those stupid, prickling, hurtful sensations you were always told are what matters. Like a slow slipping away. Same thing that happens to everyone before they die. Only it won't be slow. And you won't die.

As he'd finished her, Natalie had thought of her mother. And now, she thought of her mother's resigned, almost dispassionate reaction later that same night when Natalie banged on the door, handed her her grandson and also Sophie's son, and told her she should disappear. Leave no trace. And never come back.

He'd been right, of course. What's happening isn't slow. Just not quite fast enough.

"Natalie," Sophie whimpers.

"Shush." Natalie leans her head back, closes her eyes, feels them roaring into the blankness. Watch out, nothing. Bad moon rising.

"Natalie, what if we went home?"

"Shut the fuck up."

She opens her eyes just in time to see the deer's flank as they slam into it. The animal's head snaps sideways and the antlers bang down on the hood so hard that the back wheels come off the asphalt momentarily, and when Natalie jams on the brake, the thing doesn't fly off, it stays stuck a second and then just slides down the grille, the bones booming as they splinter underneath like 4th of July firecrackers. Even as they skid to a stop, Natalie knows there's part of it still trapped in the rear tires, its weight like a trailer pull dragging them back.

"Oh my God," Sophie whines. "Oh my God."

Natalie is gripping the wheel so hard, her knuckles are threatening to explode through her skin. With a grunt, she makes herself let go, draws her hands into her lap.

"You hit it," Sophie says.

"You think?"

"Is it dead?"

Opening her mouth to give that the response it deserves, Natalie freezes. Then she turns. Sophie shrinks back. It takes an absurdly, almost endearingly long time before understanding dawns.

Neither of them has any idea whose throat is making that sound as they spin to their doors, wrench them open, and leap from the car. The animal is a splayed, shredded ruin locked to the bumper, its head bent up under the rear axle and its antlers shattered all over the road. Natalie and Sophie dive together into the pumping gore in its crumpled ribs like little kids diving for candy in a burst piñata. Blood saturates Natalie's skirt, pools around her thighs when she kneels atop a rib and snaps it as she plunges her face down, almost banging her forehead against Sophie's. The sound Sophie is making might be laughter. Natalie reaches out as she buries her lips in the foam, spitting aside the hairy skin, and strokes her friend's hair.

Sophie is the first to straighten, moments later. Natalie follows, settling back on her haunches, her fingers still twisted in Sophie's hair. Gently, she disentangles them and lets go. Sophie's face has twisted up, and she's spitting over and over, trying to clear the taste from her teeth and her lips. Natalie just wipes a disgusted hand repeatedly across her own mouth. Still kneeling in the mangled deer, they stare at one another.

"So..." Sophie finally murmurs, glancing down one more time at the animal, then back at Natalie. "We're vegetarians?"

Natalie closes her eyes, shudders just once, opens her eyes.

"Humanitarians?" Sophie says.

They stand together, their arms around each other, bits of cartilage clinging to their skin, their legs and skirts dripping. Natalie is about to return to the car when Sophie's hands tighten on her arms.

"Nat," she says. "I'm going home."

"What?"

"Just listen, okay? Stop looking at me like that and pretending you're better and be my friend and listen."

"Okay," Natalie whispers. Merle on the radio, sweeping gently out the open driver's side door. "Mama Tried."

"I've been thinking about this. A lot. And what I've been thinking is—seriously, now, just wait, just hear me out—what better gift could a mother give her children?"

"Sophie..."

"Think about it, Nat. I am. I can't stop. He's all I think about. His little feet. God, his little feet. We could be back there in three hours.

Like Lick Em Sticks, Like Tina Fey

We could be with our children three hours from now, and never have to leave them again."

"Sophie, please, you've got to—"

"What did you hope for when Eddie was born, Nat? What did you think you could do for him? What did you want for him? How about no worries, ever? How about no pain? Ever."

"Sophie, you need to—"

"How about living forever?"

It was like a cobra strike, Natalie thinks seconds later, her teeth still buried in the softness under her best friend's chin, Sophie's dead, twitchless body flat beneath her. Like a goddamn bolt of lightning, Natalie thinks as she gulps and drinks. The only concern she'd had at the instant she'd acted was that it wouldn't taste good. Would make her retch and gag like the deer had.

And it was cold, alright. A little sour, not quite right. But it tastes fine. She's still lapping away, burying her face deeper in Sophie's throat, hips rocking side to side to Merle's rhythm. It tastes fine.

The Nimble Men

"But the air, out there, so wild, so white…"
—Thomas St. John Bartlett,
in a letter to Robert Louis Stevenson
from the Orkney Islands in the winter of 1901

Ever notice how Satie, played in the dark at just the right volume, can tilt the whole world? That night, I had *Je te Veux* on the tinny cockpit stereo, and even before the snow, the pines at the edge of the great north woods just beyond the taxiway appeared to dip and lean, and the white lines disappearing beneath the wheels of our little commuter seemed to weave around and between each other like children at a wedding dance as we made our way to the de-icing station. Then the snow started, white and winking, a drizzle of starlight, and even the air traffic control tower looked ready to lift its arms and step off its foundations and sway.

And then Alex, my junior co-pilot of four months, opened his thermal lunch box. The reek flooded the cabin and set the panel lights wavering in my watering eyes. I swear to God, the iPod gagged. Alex just sat in the steam, eyes half-closed and grinning, as if he were taking a sauna.

"God, you Gorby, tell me that isn't poutine."

"Want some, Old Dude?" said Alex, and lifted the container from the cooler.

Out the front of the plane, the world went on dancing, and the snow whirled through it. But I couldn't stop staring at the mess in Alex's container. A few limp, bloated French fries stuck out of the lava flow of industrial-colored sludge like petrified slugs. Congealed, gray lumps clung to their sides and leaked white pus.

"Is that meat?" I asked. "Cheese?"

Alex grinned wider. "It's your country. You tell me."

"Where'd you even find it? We had, what, three hours? Where does one even find poutine on a three-hour layover in Prince Willows Town, Ontario?"

"If you turn over control of the stereo, I'll put it away for a while."

We'd reached the de-icing station, and I pushed on the brakes and brought the coasting plane to a rolling stop. No matter how many times I did this, I was always surprised by the dark out here. At every other point within two miles of this tiny airport, manmade light flooded and mapped the world. But not here.

I peered through the windscreen and the wavering skeins of snow. It took a few moments, but eventually, my eyes adjusted to the point where I could just make out the de-icer truck parked a few meters off the taxiway in the flat, dead grass. Weirdly, it had its boom already hoisted, as though we were meant to make our way into the fields to get sprayed. I couldn't see either the driver of the truck or the guy on the enclosed platform at the top of the boom, because both were blanketed in shadow. But the platform looked tilted to me, almost chin-to-chest with the rotating metal stand that supported it. It reminded me of one of the dead Martians from *War of the Worlds*.

We sat and we waited. The truck didn't move.

"Peculiar," I murmured, and Alex passed his poutine container right under my nostrils. My eyes watered, and I turned on him. "What was that for?"

"You were muttering, Old Dude. Just making sure you were conscious. Now about control of that stereo. You ready to deal?"

For answer, I clicked on the intercom. "Ladies and gentlemen, this is your captain speaking. We hope all six of you have settled comfortably in

The Nimble Men

your seats, that your luggage is crammed effectively between your knees and the seat in front of you—" Alex snorted at that— "and we look forward to having virtually no time to serve you during our brief skip-hop to Toronto. We will be cleared for takeoff shortly. In the meantime, sit back, relax, be happy this flight is *not* bound for Winterpeg, and please pay no attention to the gigantic, alien-shaped creature about to swoop down upon us. It comes in peace, to de-ice the wings. Also, we do apologize for the odor escaping into the cabin under the doors of our cockpit. It came with my co-pilot, and I'm afraid there's little we can do about it. If you need assistance of any kind, please don't hesitate to call on Jamie, our charismatic, experienced, and resourceful in-flight technician, at any time. We should be in the air shortly."

Alex laughed. "Come out with me tonight," he said. "Let's do Hogtown."

"Do it?"

"Paint it. Rock it. Suck it dry. Come on, Old Dude. You keep saying you'll let me show you *my* Toronto. I say it's time. You told me it's been three years, right? It's—*whoa*. What was that?"

He had his cap turned backward on his head, the container in his lap, and a gravy-soaked French fry halfway to his lips. For the thousandth time in the past four months—but the first tonight—I remembered how much I liked him.

"I think we just painted Prince Willows Town, Young Polyp. Milked it, licked it, whole works."

"You're babbling again, Old Dude."

"Northern lights, Alex. You've heard of them, maybe."

He shook his head. "Wrong time, right? Also too low."

As usual, he was correct on both counts. I turned back to the windscreen, peering down the tarmac toward the tops of the trees, where we'd both seen a spiraling flash of green, then aquamarine.

But there was nothing now except the snowflakes, settling in their millions onto the branches of the pines as though completing some massive, unmarked winter migration. We watched that a while, and then I glanced again toward the de-icing truck. It sat silent, and the snow shrouded the high platform's window glass.

"The Nimble Men," said Alex, savoring the words.

"What?"

"Is that the coolest name you've ever heard for the aurora, or what?"

"The Nimble Men?"

"It's catchy, no?"

"How many other names do you know, Alex?"

"Well, there's *chasmata*. That's from Ancient Rome. They thought the lights were cave mouths. For sky caves. Come on, Old Dude. Trump me. What you got?"

I would have smiled if not for the de-icer, hunkered in the dead grass like a junked car on a lawn.

"Well, there's one story…" I said.

"That's the Old Dude I know. Lay it on me."

"There are several versions. Usually, it goes that sometime during the Depression, a poor woodsman went out in those woods—"

"Those woods right there?"

"Whichever Ontario woods you happen to be closest to. Didn't anyone ever tell you a ghost story?"

Alex nodded. "Carry on."

"So the woodsman was out." This time I did smile. "Rockin' the forest."

That earned me a salute with a sludgy fry.

"And while he was out, he saw the lights."

"The Nimble Men," said Alex.

I held up a finger. "But not in the sky. In the trees. The woodsman had an inkling. He raced home. When he got there, his wife said their old, sick dog had got out, and their daughter had gotten frantic and gone after him. The dog came back. But the daughter didn't. She was never seen again. The woodsman went looking with his lantern every night for the rest of his life, but he never found so much as a trace. According to some, he's still looking, and those are his lights. Hey, Alex, I don't like this."

He'd been nodding and chewing, but now lowered the cardboard fry-boat back into his lunch box and wiped his hands on his uniform pants. "You're right, Old Dude. Why are we just sitting here?"

I flicked on the radio and called the tower. "This is Northwoods Air 2-8-4."

The response was immediate, the voice so clear it might have come from inside the cabin. "Northwoods 2-8-4, go ahead."

The Nimble Men

"Bill, that you?"

"What is it, Wayne?"

"We're at the de-icer. The de-icer isn't moving."

I don't know what I expected. *We'll wake him up*, maybe. Or, *How's that*? Or, since Bill had a little of Alex's puckishness, *Moon him*.

Instead, there was a long silence. I was about to repeat myself when Bill's voice came back.

"Sit tight," he said. "Don't move."

"What—" I started, and the link closed. Went off. I tried talking into the communicator again, but it was like yelling into a fist.

"Hey, another one," Alex said, but by the time I turned, there was just the faintest blue streak, a smear on the snow-curtain.

On normal nights, the de-icer springs awake the second a plane rolls to a stop. The truck maneuvers close, and the driver makes contact over the com-link. The pilot shuts down all systems and closes the vents so no fluid gets inside the cabin. Then the platform jockey swoops in with his pod, unfolds its nozzle-arms, and engulfs the wings in a blast of bright purple antifreeze. The whole process takes less than five minutes. Sometimes less than two.

But we'd already been here quite a while. I could make out the platform jockey now, or at least his shadow. He was hunched or slumped in his pod, fifteen meters off the ground. I couldn't see his face, because he had nothing illuminated. I couldn't hear his voice, because the truck hadn't plugged into us and made contact. As far as I could tell, the truck still wasn't running its engine. This time, the glimmer in the trees flashed red, and the redness hung a moment at the very edge of the forest before winking out.

"See, I don't get it," Alex said. "It doesn't make sense."

"That's what I'm—"

"Your story. I mean, what's the deal, Old Dude? The lights came to warn him? Or they're his daughter's soul at the moment of her death? Or a presentiment of his future as the Wood-Wandering Lantern Guy? You've got to get more specific, here."

The lack of movement on the taxiway was really starting to get to me. I almost clicked on the intercom and called Jamie in to take a look. But that would only have triggered a new round of Alex-hits-on-Jamie. Not that Jamie seemed to mind.

"It's not my story. And the lights were probably all of those things, depending on the telling," I said. "You know how those stories work."

"I know that one could work better."

"What does he mean, *sit tight, don't move*?"

"Let's go see," Alex said, unhooked himself from his belts and stood.

That at least drew my gaze from the taxiway to his face. "Go where?"

"Out. Tell me you've never wanted to go out there. You ever done it? We've got a perfect excuse."

"We can't go out there."

"Why not?"

I thought about that. "Aren't there regulations? There've got to be regulations."

"And yet there you are, already unhooking your belt." His grin was an eight year-old's, and lit him all the way to his moppy curls. And there I was, unhooking my belt. "Old Dude," he said approvingly. Then he threw open the cockpit door and marched into the tiny cabin of our commuter plane, chanting, "Oh, Jamie…"

By the time I emerged, he was standing as if onstage with his arm around our blond, too-thin flight attendant, who was without doubt closer to my age than his, and facing our six passengers. All of them were apparently traveling alone, since they'd each claimed their own row— we called them rows, though they were really only sets of single seats on either side of a narrow aisle—leaving only the front empty.

"What's going on?" called an exhausted-looking grad-school type in a green McGill sweatshirt from a couple rows back.

"Who's up for hide and seek? Come on, I'll count ten," Alex said, and Jamie dropped her head and shook it and laughed.

"Excuse him, ladies and gentlemen," I said. "He's American, he's just eaten his first poutine, and it's made him punchy."

"*Avez-vous poutine?*" said a white-haired woman three rows back, perking up as though she thought we might offer her a plateful with her complimentary ice water.

"*Je l'ai fini,*" Alex said, patting his non-existent gut. I couldn't see his face, but I was sure he'd winked.

I moved to the door, unlocked it, and Jamie swung toward me in surprise.

The Nimble Men

"Wayne?"

I made a waving gesture, casual as I could make it. "We're just…"

"Checking something," Alex said. "Right back, y'all."

"Checking," I said quietly to Jamie. "It's not the plane. Not to worry."

Before she could ask, and before I had time to reconsider, Alex pushed the door outward. Frigid, resin-scented air gushed into the cabin, sweeping tendrils of snow around our ankles as the folding stair lowered itself to the ground.

Jamie took an immediate step back. Because of the cold, I realized, only the cold. But Alex hesitated, too, just momentarily. In thirty-one years as a pilot, I'd never once left my plane except at a gate. Certainly not on a taxiway or runway. I stared into the blackness, the snow cocooning the world. A high, industrial whine rode the air-currents, seeming to burrow uncomfortably into my ear canals.

I glanced over my shoulder. The only passenger not watching was the chubby, middle-aged guy in the seat closest to the open door. He had his head against the window, his tie still knotted tight at this throat, his eyes closed too tightly to be sleeping. At least, that's how it seemed to me. His skin looked pale and wet as the window-glass.

"He okay?" I murmured to Jamie.

She shrugged. "He's been like that since we boarded. I don't think he's having a heart attack or anything, if that's what you're asking. Are *you* okay, Wayne? This doesn't seem…"

"You're right," I said. "Hey, Alex, why don't we just go check in with Bill again."

"Because, Old Dude," he said. "We're the Nimble Men." And with his hands artfully tucked in the pockets of his ridiculous thrift-store bomber jacket, he strolled out of the plane, down the steps to the tarmac.

Why did I go? I've wondered that ever since. Because the lifeless de-icer bothered me, sure. Because Alex's enthusiasm for everything had stirred the embers of my own, dead not so long then. But there was something else. A *need*. Sudden. Overpowering. Was it mine? I still don't know.

I went down the steps. Behind me, I heard a single, saw-edged gasp or sigh from the not-sleeping guy. I heard another sound, too, or thought I did. That high, electrical whine, though we were the only plane out here.

When I reached Alex's side, he smiled. "One small step for Nimble Men..."

To my surprise, I smiled back. "See, now you're doing it."

"Doing what?"

"Are the lights the Nimble Men? Are we?"

"You know you're the coolest pilot I'm ever going to work with in my life, right, Old Dude? You know you've ruined cockpit chatter for me forever."

"Why, thank you, Alex. Sometimes, I feel the same."

"When we get back inside, could we at least put on a *Gymnopedie*? One of the *Gnossiennes*?"

Now I stared at him. "You know Satie, too?"

"I know *Je te Veux* makes you morose."

"For a punk kid, you know a hell of a lot of things, Alex."

"That's what things are for. Right?"

"Some things," I said, and immediately wished I hadn't.

"Hey, man," Alex said.

Ignoring him, trying to ignore myself, I looked across the tarmac at the de-icer. There really didn't seem to be anybody in the truck. There was someone on the platform up there, alright, but as far as I could make out, he still hadn't even noticed us. Unless the driver had left his keys in the ignition, or we could find a good stone to throw, we were going to have a hard time getting the platform jockey's attention. The whining was louder out here, too. Or, not louder. Closer. More shrill. If it hadn't been January, I'd have thought there were gnats in my ears.

Jamie's low-heeled shoes clicked on the folding staircase, and she appeared between us. Alex put his arm around her. Lights blossomed in the closest treetops, a scatter of turquoise and Kelly green and deep pink, as though someone had scattered a handful of marbles up there. The branches rippled with the color, then swallowed it.

"Jesus," said Jamie.

Alex put an arm around her waist. "Wacky north woods beautifulness. My favorite kind."

"Is that ice, do you think? Airport lights reflecting in the branches?"

Of course, that was right. Why hadn't I thought of it? I gestured

The Nimble Men

back toward the plane. "Seriously, is that guy alright?" I asked. "The passenger in 2B?"

"I think mostly he's crying," said Jamie. "I've got my eye on him."

"I know you do."

"We shouldn't be out here, Wayne." She touched my hand.

"Go inside. We'll be right back."

More lights. A royal-blue flurry this time, concentrated in the pines nearest the taxiway, maybe thirty meters away. Up in the platform pod, I could see the jockey's shadow just a little more clearly through the snow. He was turned toward the forest. I still didn't think he'd seen us.

Unease flickered through me again. It felt almost good. It filled the emptiness, or at least colored it.

As if sensing that thought, Jamie squeezed my hand. I'd worked with her a long time. I squeezed back. "Go on inside. We're coming."

"You can offer White-hair in there the rest of my poutine," Alex said. "I didn't actually finish it all. Although it's kind of cold, now."

"Bleah," said Jamie, and turned for the plane. I saw her look backward at the woods as she climbed up. Maybe she was hoping for another light show. But I had the idea she was hoping the opposite. Maybe that was just me.

The whining swelled still more. Underneath the shrillness, I could hear another sound, now. A sort of low grinding. Then that faded. I lifted my hands over my head, waved them at the de-icer platform. Next, I tried jumping up and down.

"See?" said Alex. "You're still nimble. You know she digs you, right?"

I stopped jumping. "What?"

"Jamie. She's just waiting for you to say the word. She's been waiting a long time."

"What are you talking about? She told you this?"

"She didn't have to tell me. I know. It's one of those things Alex knows."

"Let's get that guy's attention and get out of here," I said.

"I'm just telling you. She's waiting for you to say you're ready. I say it's been three years, Old Dude. And no disrespect. But I say three years is plenty. I say you're ready. *Shit*."

It came from nowhere, wasn't anything, vanished just as quickly. A flash of green-yellow right over our heads, like lightning stabbing into the ground. Or eyes blinking.

"Did you hear that?"

"Hear it? You have ears in your eyes, Old Dude?"

"Hey," I said. Our breath plumed in front of us. "He moved."

Both of us craned our necks back, trying to see. The guy up there *had* moved. I was sure of it. But he'd stopped now. And he was still staring straight at the woods. The whining was creeping deeper into my ears again. And there was yet another sound, this one more familiar. But several blank seconds passed before I realized what it was.

"That truck *is* on," I said.

"Well," said Alex, and for the first time, I heard doubt in his voice, too. Just a flicker. But that rattled more than anything else out here. "If it won't come to us…I guess we just go get it."

He started that way, and I followed, and the driver in the cab finally sat up. He looked astonished to see us. Then he started flinging his hands wildly in front of his face, as though he had bees in there.

"What the fuck?" Alex mumbled, still moving, and I grabbed his wrist.

The driver was waving more wildly. But not at anything in the cabin. He was also shouting, but he had the windows rolled up tight, and all I could hear was that he *was* shouting. Not what he was saying.

And overhead, that sound had returned, not so much louder as higher, almost a shriek. The grinding was back, too. Alex and I were halfway between the de-icer truck and our open plane, right at the edge of the tarmac.

It didn't actually sound like grinding, I realized. It seemed too deeply lodged inside my own head for that. It sounded like teeth gnashing.

The lights didn't exactly erupt from the trees. They just slid from behind them, as though they'd been hiding there all along. They hovered at the edge of the forest, coagulating like snow-melt on a windowpane. Forming.

I didn't have to warn Alex. He was already running.

Of course he was decades younger, much faster. Maybe he didn't even see what the lights became, the thing with wings. Or the million smaller things, all of them shining.

The Nimble Men

They came like a blizzard on a glacier, all at once and from everywhere. I was flat-out sprinting, but knew I wouldn't make it. They were in my hair, ears, eyes, and they *ached*. It was useless to swipe at or fight them, but I was still running anyway, until the first blast from the de-icer blew me straight off my feet. The de-icer didn't stop. It went on pummeling me with fluid, and I started to scream, then shut my mouth tight for fear of what I'd swallow, liquid or light, and tried scrambling back upright. Then I gave that up and crawled.

The lights were screaming. Or I was. Or Alex and Jamie were from the doorway of the plane, both of them soaked, dripping, waving, shouting. I reached the steps, and the gnashing got louder, seemed to clamp down on my spine and chew straight through it, and I sagged bonelessly sideways, feeling light, so light. Then Alex yanked me inside and slammed the door tight.

For one long moment, there was only darkness and silence. Because I hadn't opened my eyes, I realized. Because I was too terrified to open my mouth. I felt a towel on my face, Jamie's gentle hand against the back of my neck. I opened my eyes to find Alex, dripping purple droplets everywhere like a freshly bathed poodle.

"Okay?" he said.

I nodded, trembling. "I think. You?"

He started to laugh. "Holy shit," he said. "Holy crazy Canadian shit."

It wasn't funny. But with Alex there, you couldn't help smiling anyway. Jamie was doing it, too, while pointlessly patting over and over at my face. I took her hand to stop her. Then I just held onto that.

We were back in our seats, our heads wrapped in scratchy airline towels, ears still ringing, hands still shaking but settled firmly on the controls that would guide us either safely back to the terminal or up in the air and as far from Prince Willows Town as this plane's pathetic fuel tanks could carry us, when the cockpit door opened. Alex was the one who turned. Then he said, "Wayne."

I turned, too. Jamie stood in the doorway, face waxy, eyes blank. "He's gone," she said.

"What?" I asked.

"The guy in 2B. The crying guy. He's not on the plane. He didn't go out past me either. He's nowhere."

I stood up, shaking my head. "That's ridiculous. He must have—"

"Wayne," Jamie said, and her eyes filled with tears. "He's gone."

It happened only occasionally, Bill told me once, years later, over one final round of Molsons, before both of us left the flying game for good. Only in the dead of winter, on the coldest nights. Mostly not even then. No one really knew when or how the realization had been made about the de-icing fluid. But that seemed to help. Sometimes. To keep them back. Sometimes.

"Always so sad," Bill had said. "Always, always, always."

At least, that's what I thought he'd said. It wasn't until that night, back in my hotel, pouring a drink, that my hands started to shake, and I realized I'd heard him wrong. Not *so* sad. *The* sad. Always the sad.

Was it grief that drew them? Or reacted with something else in that air, in those woods, and created them? Had *my* grief drawn or created them? If so, it wasn't the anti-freeze that saved me. It was the sobbing man. His was fresher.

Had they swallowed him? I like to think he was one of them, now, instead. Reunited, maybe, with what he'd lost. Or at least in company, with the Nimble Men. Sometimes, that thought comforts me.

You can't fly to Prince Willows Town, any more. Not long after that night, they closed the facility, redirecting all traffic to the bigger, better-serviced airport at Sudbury, where the light-towers are numerous and brighter, and the trees keep their distance.

PART THREE:
Book Depository Stories

Esmeralda

The First Book Depository Story

"I care not how humble your bookshelf may be, nor how lowly the room which it adorns. Close the door of that room behind you, shut off with it all the cares of the outer world, plunge back into the soothing company of the great dead..."
—Arthur Conan Doyle, *Through the Magic Door*

PROLOGUE

We first heard about them the way one hears about everything these days: on the web. Some self-styled "urban explorer," wired on whatever and driven by transgressive urges most people claim they get over in high school, snuck into his 532nd abandoned building in the Detroit metropolitan area. Fortunately, he brought his digital camera and an extra memory card.

Within hours, the first Flickr page went up. Within weeks, the first wiki/blogspot/Facebook groups appeared. The histories of that initial depository were always stitched together out of tall tales and myths. Someone could have found some Roosevelt School District official and asked, but no one did. Soon, the first Crawlers—no one seems to know where that name came from—began braving the empty streets to start exploring and mapping the place. Not long after that came the first trespassing arrests, and the first disappearances. Before too long, the various strands of lore surrounding the Roosevelt Book Depository had coalesced into a story composed of enough truth to become the truth, as far as anyone who studies such things in centuries to come—and publishes them in whatever digital or ethereal or cerebral format one publishes in those times—will ever be able to tell:

A public school district, emptying of students as the last desperate families flee the neighborhoods, its buildings collapsing and its funding gutted, quietly takes over an abandoned tire warehouse on one of those Detroit streets that hasn't seen a functioning streetlamp since the Riots. There, school functionaries—or, more likely, the gang thugs and drunken ex-Teamsters they pay with the last of the district's cash—begin delivering truckloads of used or never used textbooks, supplies, notepads, posters, maps, writing implements, and whole libraries full of outdated, donated boys' and girls' novels and biographies of presidents and sports stars to what they have already christened the Depository. The plan, originally, is to sell it all, in the hopes of renovating the last functioning elementary school in the area.

Then the elementary school closes. The funding is zeroed. The officials disperse back to their homes, which have never been nearby. The ex-Teamsters return to their barstools, the thugs to their gangs.

And in their warehouse with its smashed-in windows and gaping doorframes and ruthlessly tagged cement walls, the books and notebooks and maps and visual aids of the former Roosevelt District Schools lie where they've been tossed, in tottering dunes or great lakes of paper. They huddle like penguins in the Michigan winter snows. They curl and molt in the sucking humidity of mid-summer. They are shredded for nests to house raccoons, rats, pigeons, the homeless. They begin to decompose. To sprout weeds and toadstools. To change.

By the time that first unnamed explorer finds them, they have lain in that space for more than thirty years.

After that, less than six months passed before the discovery—or creation—of the second depository, in the mildew-ravaged, fogbound port hangars near Fisherman's Wharf. That one drew an entirely different breed of explorer. There were boho college kids drifting up the coast through the Youth Hostels. Then a team of college professors from Berkeley who wrote the first academic papers and held the first

Esmerelda

symposium on the subject, which they dubbed The End. If they were aware of any irony in naming a brand new phenomenon that, they kept it to themselves.

By the end of 2010, there were depositories in Chicago, St. Louis, Ft. Lauderdale. They were always urban at first, their foundations usually the refuse from bankrupt school systems. But then the owners of the last used bookstore in Dallas—a giant conglomerate formed by the desperate owners of the twenty-five largest remaining open shops in Texas—announced that they were closing. And instead of holding a final sale, or throwing everything up for auction on eBay or listing it on ABE, they rented twenty-five U-Haul trailers, filled them at random, and dispersed across the country to seed the depositories.

Other shop owners followed suit. It became an ethical stance, a point of pride, a last great act of self-defeating defiance. They would not scrape the last, dreadful pennies from the bottom of the book well. Instead, they would spread their wares like spores, bury them like acorns in the rich, loamy mulch of decomposing language in the depositories, in the hopes that they would sprout there. Grow a new generation, not of readers—people still read, despite what the academicians tell us—but bibliophiles. A healthier, younger subculture.

Then individuals began following the shop owners' lead. Readers who'd spent their whole lives building and tending their personal libraries formulated wills directing their children to wheel whatever they didn't want to the nearest depots and bury them there. Without open shops, and with the online outlets flooded with merchandise that few sought, selling books became a chore, and a fruitless one at that. Easier by far to find a depository and leave everything there, for whoever might want it.

Of course, the depositories didn't mostly attract bibliophiles. They drew squatters, first. Pushers and junkies. Cultists. Fetishists. When the rate of reported disappearances began to climb, the police took to discouraging, then forbidding visiting the depositories. But they never cleaned them out, rarely patrolled them. And people—whatever their reasons—kept coming, though less often and usually after dark.

Meanwhile, the books lay atop each other like bodies in ditches. In breezes, or in a beam of sudden flashlight, they stirred, seeming not so much to have come to life but retained it, somehow. Occasionally, a page even lifted like a waving hand, extending itself toward whatever had disturbed it, or else waving goodbye.

ESMERALDA

I'm already in bed when the knock comes. Sitting up, shivering as the twist of sheet and heavy blanket slides from me, I stare at the misshapen shadows stretched over the hardwood floor. It's the snow outside that has given them their head-like humps, their ice-claws. They look like illustrations in a book of fairy tales. Ezzie would have loved them.

I'm musing on that, wondering whether the bottle of rye on the bedside table is as empty as it looks and also whether I've stored another in the bathroom medicine chest five steps from my cot, when the knock comes again. So there really is someone out there, and that means one of two things: the police have finally found something, or Ezzie's relentless sister Sarah has finally found me.

"Just a…" I start, but my voice comes out even thicker than its current usual, and I suck rye-residue and sleep-fur off my teeth and try again. "Hold on."

My feather-robe and fuzzy slippers were both gifts from Ezzie, of course. For the feather-robe and fuzzy slipper birthday party she threw me during our first year in the downtown Detroit loft. Not so long ago, really. Christ, barely three years.

It's my lucky night, turns out; there is indeed a fresh rye in the medicine cabinet, right between the ibuprofen and Ezzie's razor case, which is my only keepsake. She would have approved, if she'd approved of anything I do anymore. The thing she'd held most dear, after all. Unlike most cutters, from what I gather, for Ezzie it was less about the wounds than the weapon.

Uncorking the rye, I take a swig, then replace the bottle and slide the razor case under my robe into my pajama shirt pocket. I turn toward the door, pull the robe as closed as it will go against the constant chill, and as an afterthought decide to take the rye along. In eight steps, I've

Esmerelda

crossed my lake-rot, one-room efficiency to the front door so I can peer through the fish-eye.

"Knock knock," I say.

The guy out there is big, maybe six-five, in a black coat that looks warmer than all the clothes I own combined, plus black gloves and a black Derby, even. Not a cop. Also not Sarah, unless she's grown a foot and a half and cut off all her hair. Sarah and Ezzie and their dark waterfalls of black curls...

"What?" the guy asks.

"Knock knock."

He stares at the door, and the Lake Superior wind whips up and blows snow on him. It's kind of great, really. A strapping young Oedipus befuddled by the Sphynx. Me. Finally, he takes the plunge.

"Who's there?"

"Exactly," I say.

Pause. Befuddlement.

"Exactly who?"

"Exactly my question."

Poor Oedipus. Big wind. I gulp rye from the bottle I have every intention of sharing with my caller, providing he convinces me to let him in.

"Please," he says, and he sounds nothing like a cop or a vengeful relative or anyone else I know anymore. I open the door. He hurries past me and stands shivering in the center of my all but empty room. Then he starts to unbutton his coat.

"I wouldn't suggest it," I tell him. "It's not much better in here."

Experimentally, he loosens another button. His head almost brushes the bulbous, bug-filled light-fixture that provides the efficiency's only illumination when I bother to switch it on, which isn't often. He removes his hat, and I can't help but smile at the hair, which is black and flat as road tar, with little flattened spikes jagging down his forehead. Little-kid-after-sledding hair.

He takes in my cot, the nightstand, the remaining 365 or so square feet of empty space.

"No...no books," he says, and I understand, abruptly. I consider showing him my iRead, which is the only thing I use now, just to see his face. There's nothing quite like confronting a Crawler with an iRead.

Except I can't quite bring myself to do it. Every time my heart beats, it bangs against the razor case in my pocket. Cold and plastic and empty of Ezzie.

"How'd you find me?" I ask.

"Will," he says. "I'm Will."

"That's nice."

"Can I sit?"

The question cracks me up. I gesture around the couchless, chairless, rugless room. "Pick a wall."

Instead, he sits where he is, folding his long legs under him and his arms across his chest. Then he looks expectantly at me with wide, shiny eyes. I hold out the rye bottle.

"You're going to need it," I say.

"Not as much as you do," says Will, without guile.

I laugh again, glancing down at myself. Feather robe with the feathers molting. Slippers with the toes poking through. I can't see my hair, of course, but I can feel it trying to flap off my head in a thousand different directions every time the draft pours through the windows.

I take a gulp, extend the bottle again, and he says, "Look. I'm sorry. I don't mean to intrude. I just…I have to know what you saw."

The laughter evaporates in my throat, and the rye on my tongue.

"Please. I have to know."

"I'm not sure I know what you mean," I lie. My hands start to shake, and I slip the one not holding the bottle into my pocket.

But he's all too eager to explain. "Oh. I see. You probably…I mean, since you don't…since I'm guessing you don't go to the depots anymore, you probably aren't keeping up with what's happening."

"Probably not." Ezzie's lens case beats, and I sit down opposite my guest.

"I just need to ask you one thing, okay? Then I'll leave you alone. At the moment your wife—"

"She wasn't my wife."

"Sorry. Lover—"

I start to squelch that, too, but how to explain? The simple truth was that we'd almost never been physical with each other, and even if we'd

Esmerelda

wanted to be, the overgrown bramble-hedge of scabs and scarring up both of Ezzie's thighs would have been a serious turn-off for me. I hate pain. The funny thing about Ezzie—it took years of our friendship for me to learn this—was that she did, too.

My visitor hesitates a moment longer. Then he tries again. "At the moment she…vanished…"

Again, he waits for me to chime in. I can't, and don't.

"I just need to know," says Will. "Did you see anyone?"

Careful, now. Careful. How is this supposed to work? How does the story they all tell themselves go? "How do you mean?" I say eventually. "Are you asking were there others with us in the Depository that night? There were." That was true enough, although they'd all been on the ground floor. None of them had even heard Ezzie scream.

My visitor stares at me, and I realize I've played too dumb. And this is no journalist, no private investigator. He's a fellow Crawler. Maybe even fellow ex-Crawler. And he's paid for the privilege, same as me.

Or, not quite the same.

"Sorry," I say. "Habit."

"So," says Will. "Did you?"

I blow out a long breath. My heart bangs, and my skin prickles in the cold. Ghost-touch of Ezzie's hair across my forearms. "The thing is, I don't really know when it happened. I mean, not the exact moment. Do you?"

Abruptly, Will begins to weep. He wipes the tears away once with the heel of one huge hand, but otherwise he remains motionless. His voice comes out hoarse, as though ice has lodged in it. "Now I do."

In spite of myself—in spite of everything—I lean forward, clutching the rye bottle. "How?"

He tells me.

"It was going to be our last one, at least for a long time. The St. Paul. Have you heard about that one? It's massive. It's in six abandoned warehouses right on the Mississippi. It stinks. Some local told us the river itself catches fire a couple times a year near there. And there aren't any windows, so the wind blows all the filth from the barges and all the snow and ice in the winter right into the depot. So the books are in awful shape, even by depot standards.

"But God, there are so many. So, so many.

"And they're not even textbooks, mostly. Not shit stuff. This one started just like Dallas. The last used shop owners in the Twin Cities all closed on the same date, in the middle of a snowstorm in the middle of January in the middle of the night. They brought everything they had left to the warehouses. I've heard Crawlers say that for that first year or so, there were even sections. *Local History. True Crime. Classics.*

"Sections. Can you imagine?

"Anyway. This was our honeymoon. It was Bri's idea, even though I'm the Crawler. I don't even think she'd been to a depot before she met me. But she loved the adventure. Dressing up in black, going to those neighborhoods, getting dirty. Hiking between twenty-foot mounds of books with our flashlight beams on each other's faces and all that moldy paper whispering all over the place. Bri used to say it was like sneaking into an old-age home and finding all the residents sitting up in their beds gossiping all night.

"You know how it is, I guess. I don't know why I'm telling you.

"This was summer before last. Our St. Paul night. It was so humid. The river wasn't on fire, but it smelled oily. There's a park on the Minneapolis side where I guess people with no sense of smell can picnic and watch barges, but on the St. Paul side, there's just warehouses and landfills and five hundred million mosquitoes. That whining never leaves your ears. I swear, it's like the world has sprung a leak, and everything is just spilling out of it somewhere.

"For our honeymoon, we'd hit five depots in four cities in four days. St. Louis, Topeka, Lincoln, Wall. You been to Wall? South Dakota? It's right on the prairie, maybe a hundred yards from that famous drug store. It's just a big barn. There's almost nothing in it but maps and dried-out pens and thousands of copies of some old biology textbook about evolution. But we saw a buffalo. It strolled right past the doors while we were inside. One buffalo. Bri loved it."

He stops, and I think he's going to weep again. He seems to think so, too, and keeps one hand hovering near his eyes. But then he drops the hand and goes on.

Esmerelda

"At the first four depots—every night until the last night—Bri covered herself completely before we went. Black tights, long black skirt, black sweater, black wool hat. She said it was for germs, and I teased her so hard. My little suburban rich girl. Hardly held a book in her life. Not a real one, and definitely not one anyone else had read first. She always said she'd be sure to send the ambulance when I got diphtheria and collapsed, and I told her I wasn't planning on drinking the books, just touching them, maybe taking a few, and she'd say, 'Diphtheria. Don't say I never told you so.' She had this way of saying things like that. And this laugh. She could make 'Hello' into a running joke. She had so many fucking friends…"

Will is weeping again, and this time he takes the bottle when I offer it. If he sees my hand shaking, he's polite enough not to say so or smart enough not to ask.

Diphtheria. Bri might have had many friends, but Ezzie wouldn't have been one of them. *Diphtheria—virulent and fatal disease causing permanent and irreversible dippiness. No known cure.* That's what Ezzie would have said.

But Will's story has brought it all back. Our first depot night, at the very first depot. The Roosevelt, Michigan warehouse, where the books sprout mushrooms from their ruined pages and the hills of still-shrink-wrapped texts and composition notebooks rise shoulder high and higher, a mountain range of waste paper complete with alpine meadows of pink and green binders and waterfalls of paperclips and liquid paper bottles. Miles and miles of them. There's even weather; the rot and damp create a haze that rises from the ground on warmer nights and drifts about the giant, echoing space, as though the words themselves have lifted right off the pages like little Loraxes and floated toward the window sockets to dissipate over the abandoned thoroughfares of the Motor City.

We were there for hours, sifting things, picking toadstools, staring at the giant graffiti phoenix on the second story wall, massive and orange and angry, rising out of the mural of a broken hardback. I didn't find anything worth having, and Ezzie brought home just one book. The Scott Michelin 4th Grade Guide to Native America, Eighth Edition.

That very night, though we got back to our loft after four in the morning, Ezzie began to work. For weeks, night after night, all night long, she kept at it, barely speaking, rarely even retreating into the bathroom for her razor blades. Finally, I came home from work one evening to find the table bedecked with roses, a plate of the Hungarian goulash she never made anymore steaming on the table, and Ezzie's first real masterpiece laid beside the vase for my perusal.

What she'd done was so simple, really. So quiet. At first, I wasn't even sure she'd done anything. Then, as I flipped the pages, past sketches of Sacajawea and photographs of wigwams, I began to notice little smudges that might have been accidental fingerprints from tiny nine year-old hands, except there were too many, and sometimes they were strewn across the page in unlikely or impossible patterns: half a forefinger here, a thumb all the way down next to the number, a red pen splash in the middle of a chart. As though a spider had stepped in an inkwell and then danced over the text. Then I started noticing the words missing. Some whited away, some stitched closed. Then there were the blotches, bug-shaped, pressed between lines. Some of them, I think, really were bugs. And then the little razor cuts. Thousands of them. If I removed the binding, I half-suspected, and unfolded the whole, I'd find a snowflake pattern in the pages. Or something else entirely.

There was more. I can't explain the effect. It wasn't any one thing, but the cumulative impact. An invented history of a history book no one had read, or would ever read.

That night, while I was asleep, Ezzie went back to the Roosevelt Depot without me. I couldn't believe it when I woke, told her how crazy that had been and how dangerous that place was, as if she needed me to tell her. But she was already back at her work table, hunched over her next project.

I close my eyes, and just like every time I close my eyes, now, I see her there. Crouched in her chair in the middle of the night, cross-hatched thighs drawn up under her nightshirt, unbound hair hooding her, blocking the light of her face from my sight like a blackout shade.

"I don't know why Bri didn't take her gloves to St. Paul," Will says. "Other than that it was crazy hot. Just putting on my hat felt like

Esmerelda

dumping a bucket of sweat on my head. We caught a bus across the river. There weren't any stops near the depot, and the guy didn't want to let us off, but Bri chatted him up and got him whistling Janet Jackson songs, and finally he agreed to drop us. He even said he'd come back in three hours, and that we'd better be there, for our own sakes.

"We walked the warehouses, and the sun went down. At first, we were trying everything we could think of to fend off mosquitoes, but eventually we gave up and let the little fuckers feast. We watched the trash barges floating in the middle of the big, brown river. They weren't even moving. They could have been swim rafts, except no one in their right mind would stick a toe in that water, let alone swim it. In that park I told you about—the one on the Minneapolis side?—there was some kind of military band. We could barely hear it. Not the tune or anything, just that there was one.

"The St. Paul side was completely empty, though. There were a couple abandoned cars, one working streetlight, some pigeons hopping around, and that's about it. But there wasn't anything threatening. Not like St. Louis or Detroit or anything. It was just empty.

"We weren't even the only ones at the depot. Not even close. We came around the corner of this huge ship-container building, and there was this old woman sitting in what I guess must have been the parking lot on a little pile of tires. She had a parasol over her head and everything, and a thermos full of lemonade. She gave us some. She had this whole stack of tatty Dickens novels with her. I have no idea whether she brought them or found them. They were just crappy school editions, nothing valuable, but intact. Totally readable. Nice.

"'It's like summer camp in there tonight,'" she told us.

"It was more like a library, though. Isn't it weird how books do that? I mean, who established the whispering rule for depots?

"There were certainly plenty of other Crawlers in the warehouse. Probably fifteen, maybe even twenty. It seemed like most of them knew each other. We figured they came in a group, maybe some community college urban archaeology class or something. We kept seeing them in little bunches, picking apart a book pile or kneeling near some torn-up notepads or just standing in one of the makeshift rows, taking it all in. It almost felt like we were wandering in a downtown Japanese garden, not a depot, with all those flashlights everywhere and the moonlight outside and the snatches of music from over the river.

"For the first hour or so, Bri stayed by me. I think the place had been a canning factory, once; there were these little curls of rusty metal all over the place. I picked Bri a bouquet of toadstools, and she slid one through the top buttonhole of her sweater. That's when I noticed she wasn't wearing her gloves, and I almost said something. For a while afterwards, I thought maybe that's what had happened, or why it had happened then. Until I started hearing about all the others.

"Do you think there's some reason it's mostly happening to women?"

He stops again, as though he actually thinks I can enlighten him. As though he and I have anything whatsoever in common, except loss. As if anyone does. There's a bleak joke here, somewhere. Something about there always having been more women readers. Instead of making it, I jam the rye bottle in my mouth. In the draft, in the Lake Superior wind, I hear Ezzie's laughter.

"Well," he says. "What happened is, I found a book. *Adventures For the Young and Adventurous.* I only picked it up because it was still sealed in a wrinkly plastic baggy. The spine almost fell apart when I eased the covers open. But the first story was 'The Man with the Cream Tarts.' You know it? I didn't. I didn't even know it was Stevenson until…until months later. When everything was over. The title page had so much mold, even I wished I had Bri's gloves. I used my sleeve to turn it. But the inside pages were relatively clean. And right off, I hit one of those sentences: *'He was a remarkable man even by what was known of him; and that was but a small part of what he actually did.'* God."

Will makes a whistling sound. Then he shudders.

"There was a little window way up the wall behind where we were, and I just sat down right there. I started to read aloud to Bri, but it was too echoey. Every 's' sounded like a rattlesnake.

"Bri finally grinned and pointed at the mold on my book. She mouthed, 'Diphtheria' at me. Then she wandered off around a mound of staplers with their tops pried up. As soon as she was out of sight, I went back to reading.

"I read the whole story. By then, the moon had risen past the window, and most of the light was gone. But my eyes had adjusted. At some

Esmerelda

point, I realized it had been a long time since I'd heard any music from across the river or muffled conversations from our companions in the depot. I closed the book, and the cover came away in my hands like an old scab.

"As soon as I stood up, I finally started to understand how vast this place was. It might be the biggest one of all. When we came in, there'd been shadows, at least, and most of them were moving. But now nothing was distinct, everything was just dark, and I couldn't hear a thing. I felt like I'd fallen asleep in school and gotten locked in overnight. I opened my mouth to call for Bri, then thought better of it and moved off in the direction she'd gone.

"I wasn't going to shout. Not in there. Not yet. But looking for someone in a depot is kind of like looking for land in the middle of the ocean, you know? There aren't any aisles. There's no reason for anybody to have gone one way or another. There's no food court. There's only deeper into the depot, or out the doors.

"My first thought was that Bri had gone out. That old woman with the lemonade would have drawn her. She liked people the same way you and I like books.

"So I went what I thought was back the way we'd come. Only there weren't flashlight beams around anymore, and it's not as though we'd dropped a breadcrumb trail or paid any attention to where we were or anything. I walked what felt like a quarter mile in as straight a line as I could judge, and all I saw were huge piles of paperbacks and towers of old cardboard boxes. I didn't hear anything except my own feet. There was a little light, and it didn't seem far away, just indirect. I couldn't get a fix on the source. Twice, I thought I heard the river to my right and turned down the first passage I came to, only to find another endless depot row.

"By now, I was calling Bri's name. Not too loud. But I was definitely making myself heard. Even to myself, I sounded strange, like some croaking bird in the eaves. I had a flashlight, but I wasn't using it. I kept hoping I'd spot hers. Or anyone's.

"In my mind—I know this can't be true, but I swear I remember every step I took—I walked for an hour. Either it had gotten darker or I'd gone deeper into the depot or my eyes had stopped adjusting, because I could barely even see my hands. A couple times, I put my foot down on a shifting pile of papers and slipped. The first time, I cut my hand bad on a little semi-circular metal scrap. The next, the paper I fell into was all wet, and it stank. It was like lying on lilies in a dead pond. I'd had enough. I opened my mouth to start yelling Bri's name, and then…

"Then…"

For a second, I think Will has stopped because my face has given me away. Of course it must have. I can't seem to get my mouth to close, and the goddamn draft has cemented me where I am, crystallized me like an icicle. He probably thinks it's because I'm anticipating what comes next. Really, I'm just fixating on the scrap of metal, the cut it must have opened in his hand. Little razor cut.

All at once, he's on his feet, looming. I still can't make myself move, but the survival instincts that got me out of Detroit three years ago, that have kept me moving to new places ever since, that launch me out of bed and to the grocery store for rye but also carrots and cereal and winter gloves, has awoken at last. I'm trying to remember where I left the snow-shovel, just in case I need to murder my way out of this room.

But Will, it seems, just wants to weep some more. And why not? What's happened to him has nothing to do with me. Even less than he thinks.

"Look, Dude. The woman I saw…This is why I'm here. This is what I'm telling you, the thing I've learned. It's a breakthrough. Maybe the first one. It might help you, too; if you go find some of the others, I can even give you some addresses and—"

"You're babbling," I snap. Now I'm on my feet, too, waving my feathered arms and squawking in my ridiculous voice, hoarse from disuse. "What do you want here? Why are you bothering me? What could I possibly tell you about what happ—"

"I learned her name," he says.

My jaw smacks shut. My arms are still out, as though I'm going to take flight. But I'm frozen again.

"The one I saw. Her name was Anna." He wipes his tears with his long, bony hand. Despite his size, he looks even younger, now. The tiny bit of me that doesn't want to hurl him through my window wants to make him hot chocolate.

Esmerelda

"Her name was Anna."

"Tell me," I hear myself say.

"Like I said. There was nothing. Just blackness, and I was bleeding all over myself. I couldn't even find the doors, let alone Bri. I started to get up, and for some reason, I looked to my left. And there she was.

"She was just standing there. Dark hair, kind of bushy, pulled back in a ponytail. Glasses. Pale cheeks, penny loafers, flashlight. Clutching a composition notebook against her chest, as though she'd stepped right off the cover of a Nancy Drew novel. She looked at me for about three seconds, maybe even less. This is the strangest part, except it won't sound strange to you; everyone who's experienced it says the same thing. It was the most peaceful three seconds of my life.

"'Hey,' I started to say, and that was it. Poof. No penny loafer girl. No light. Nothing but depot junk. '*Hey*!' I shouted, and once I'd started shouting, I couldn't stop.

"I have no idea how long I was in there. Not much longer, I don't think. Suddenly, I was at the doors, different doors than the ones we'd entered through, maybe half a block farther down the street. I ran back to the lot where we'd seen the old woman, but she was gone, too. I ran to the first set of doors, and I screamed Bri's name over and over and over, but I couldn't make myself go back in there, and my voice didn't even seem to penetrate. It was like screaming into a mattress.

"Finally, I ran back to where the bus driver had let us off, and the bus came, and the driver radioed for the cops. They got there pretty fast, too, for all the good it did. For all the good they ever do.

"For weeks afterward—months—I kept waking up every night thinking I'd heard the key in the lock. Even now, I sometimes think I smell her. Hear her whispering 'diphtheria' in my ear. I went to a grief counselor, and he said losing a loved one like that, when you don't completely *know*, is like losing a limb. There's a part of you that won't ever accept that she's not there.

"I don't know what made me go back to the depot forum websites. I didn't ever want to go to a depot again. But one night I surfed by, and I started clicking around, and I kept following links, and somehow I wound up in a discussion thread marked 'HAVE YOU SEEN...' which I assumed was about book-hunting. The first post read:

"'*Jamie. Twenty-four. Straight blonde hair, beach sandals, pink button-up shirt, gypsum pendant necklace, plastic cereal-box rings on fingers. Vanished Long Beach Depot, 7/22/10.*' At the end was a photo of her.

"There were 488 follow-up posts. The 432nd read:

"'*Laughing, dark-haired Anna. Twenty-eight. Penny loafers. Glasses. Always looks at you sideways. Vanished San Antonio Depot, 2/14/11.*' There wasn't any picture. But I knew.

"Now, you see, right? Now you understand why I'm here. I just want to know she's…somewhere. I just want to know someone's seen her. So please. I'm begging."

He's begging, alright. Weeping again.

But I'm panicking. Trying to dredge up some face from my high school yearbook, someone I can pretend I glimpsed, so he can say *Gee, no, that's not Bri*, and get out of my apartment and let me start throwing my things in a duffel so I can disappear again. He thinks this is news to me, that so many Crawlers have had the same experience. And it is, in a way. The fact that they're seeing each other's ghosts, that the lost ones are somehow finding their way back, but to the wrong places, or else they've become pressed permanently into some new universe of fictional characters who live (or don't live) like dried butterflies in the pages of discarded books, forever who they were at the last moment they were anyone, still accessible to us but at random, a collective cultural memory instead of a personal one…

I'd be fascinated, really. If it had anything whatsoever to do with me.

"Dude," says Will, and now, finally, he's grabbed me. I knew he would. I have that effect, these days, on people like Will. "Please. I don't mean to dredge up bad memories. Maybe there's even hope, have you thought of that? If we're all seeing them, maybe we can get them back? Or at least see our own again. Wouldn't you like to? Wouldn't it be worth anything—*anything*—just to see her one more time?"

I almost break, then. I almost give him exactly what he wants. The whole, pathetic story. Me getting mugged and beaten bloody by some cranked-up street thug who'd been using the Roosevelt Depot as a warm, dark place to freebase. The laughing Crawlers who found me an hour or so later and shoved cigarettes in my mouth and fed me beer and got me on my feet again. Going up that rotted, collapsing staircase in the dark

Esmerelda

to find Ezzie and show her my new bruises and bring her down to meet my new friends.

Finding her.

How much of it did she intend? That's the only thing that haunts me. Most of it, clearly. Almost all of it. It was the logical extension, after all, of everything she'd done as an artist, but also as a person. That desperate, driving hunger to get inside other people's stories. To leave traces. To cut deep enough below the surface of absolutely everything to determine, once and for all, whether there was anything in there. Or to prove that there wasn't.

It must have taken her hours.

All around her, arrayed in a perfect square just longer and wider than her body, she'd laid paper. Some of it blank and white, some of it torn from whatever texts were near, or maybe she'd picked them specifically. Probably, she did. I'll never know. Even if I saw, I wouldn't remember.

The only thing I will ever remember about that moment is Ezzie lying atop the paper, stark naked in the icy February dark, head tilted almost onto her right shoulder, the spray of her blood fanning onto all that whiteness like great, red wings she'd finally unfolded. Her arms and legs a relief map of tiny and less tiny cuts, each of them flowing into the next, pouring like long, red tributaries toward the great, spurting geyser on her right thigh, where she'd pressed too hard—or exactly hard enough—and severed the femoral artery.

For too long, maybe the critical few seconds, I couldn't move. I couldn't do anything but stare. I thought she was already dead, which was so stupid, I mean, I could see the blood still pumping. That new, red ocean bubbling out of the crack Ezzie had opened in herself and spreading across the paper continents she'd created. But she wasn't moving, didn't seem to be breathing. The color had gone completely out of her; she was whiter than the paper. And she looked…not happy, not even at rest, just…still. I'd never known Ezzie still.

Then she woke up, for the last time. That's when she screamed. She even got out a sentence as I lunged forward. *"Stop it!"*

Did she mean staunch the wound? Or get away from her? I didn't care. Slipping and sticking, I dropped onto my knees and plunged my hands onto the open spot, but they went straight through, her skin was like spring ice stretched too thin. It wasn't even warm inside her, just sticky-wet. I could feel the severed strands of artery, or I felt artery, anyway, gristly bits, but trying to grab anything and hold it closed was like trying to tie silly string. I ripped off my coat and started sliding it under her to make a tourniquet, but that just made her scream louder. I'm pretty sure I was screaming, too, and then—God knows how, maybe it was reflex—one of her hands shot up and grabbed my arm.

"Lawrence," she snarled. "It hurts."

And I understood. I still think I really did. It was already too late to save her. If I was going to do anything for her, I had to do it then. I grabbed the first thing handy, and it was as though it had been laid there for me. *The World Book Encyclopedia, 1978.* Heavy and frozen hard as a stone.

Lifting it, I looked once more into Ezzie's eyes. I saw the defiance there. The ruthless, obsessive imagination. The unimaginable pain, and—more surprisingly—the panic. Because she thought I wouldn't do it? Because she suddenly knew I would?

I didn't ask. I slammed the book down and smashed in her skull with one blow.

I don't know how long I stayed there. I remember noticing that the blood against my legs wasn't pumping anymore, and stirred only with my own movements. I remember getting cold.

I have no memory of going downstairs. But the people who'd helped me were still there. What a sight I must have been. Beaten purple from my own encounter an hour or so earlier, shirt and pants saturated with Ezzie's blood, fingertips dripping with her brains. Somehow, I must have communicated that they should go upstairs, because some of them did. When they came down, one of them lifted me out of my crouch and said, "Man, you need a hospital."

Then they took me to one. The next morning, the police were by my bed to take my report. It was a long time before I realized they were asking only about the mugging. That they didn't know about Ezzie. I told them they needed to go back to the depot, check the second floor under the phoenix mural.

They found blood there, gouts of it. But no Ezzie. "You're lucky to be alive," they told me the last time they came. I gave them my address,

Esmerelda

promised I'd let them know where I was, though they didn't ask me to. Then they left me alone.

How did Sarah even find me in the hospital? How did she hear about what had happened? I have no idea. But she's as relentless as her sister was. Also less creative, and less fun. An hour before the doctors discharged me, she called my bedside from her Connecticut home.

"Where's Ezzie?" she said as soon as she heard my voice.

I hung up on her, unplugged the phone, and waited to be released. When I got back to our loft, there were seventeen messages from Sarah. The last one said, "I'm coming."

I packed my duffel. Just clothes and bathroom stuff and a rye bottle. No notebooks, and definitely no books. Ezzie's empty razor case, but none of the artifacts she'd made. I moved to Battle Creek. When I arrived, I let the Detroit police know my new address. The next time I moved, I did the same. If they ever find anything, or they want to do anything about me, I want them to be able to.

But not Sarah. I can't face Sarah.

I look up at Will, who is still staring at me out of his childlike, teary eyes. Childlike, because he still really believes there's more to his story. Maybe there is.

"I'm sorry," I tell him, and I mean it, in my way. "I didn't see anyone."

He just puts on his hat, then. His shoulders have slumped. Shrugging back into his coat, he turns for the door. He's got it open when I grab him, abruptly.

"You didn't answer *my* question," I say.

Now he just looks stupid. Blind, befuddled Oedipus again. Or is that me?

"How did you find me, Will?"

"I...don't remember," he says. "Wait, yes I do. There was an e-mail."

"An e-mail." From a cop, maybe? Someone working the chat rooms and message boards in the hopes of solving something?

"It mentioned you and gave me your address."

"From whom?"

"Didn't say. They rarely do." He takes a step outside in the Marquette wind, turns abruptly back. "I think it came from Arizona, though."

Now it's my turn to stare. "Arizona?"

"I'm just guessing. From the e-mail addy. Phoenixgirl. At gmail, I think."

In my hands, the empty rye bottle seems to throb. Pump. Against my chest, the razor case beats.

"Jesus," Will says, "I'm sorry. I almost forgot. She asked me to give you a message if I saw you."

"A message." Are these tears in my eyes? Is this fear? Am I scared of what Ezzie will do when she finds me? Or heartbroken that her last great effort was a failure, that she couldn't, finally, cut her way in. Or out. Or wherever it was she always wanted so desperately to go.

Am I even sure phoenixgirl is Ezzie? If it's Sarah, then Sarah finally knows.

I'm grabbing the frozen doorframe. It's so cold that it burns my bare fingers. I hang on anyway.

"It wasn't much of a message," Will tells me. "I think it was just… it just said, *'Tell him I'll see him soon.'*"

After-words

The Second Book Depository Story

> "…whilst evil is expected, we fear; but when it is certain, we despair."
> —Robert Burton, *The Anatomy of Melancholy*

PROLOGUE

The first bombing occurred on a fogbound summer Saturday night, on the just-vacated premises of Harbor Lights Books, in the midst of the 7th Annual Naked Bike Ride. The damage proved minimal: a few blown-out windows; a foot-long splinter of wood driven through the windshield of a parked police car; an elderly upstairs neighbor rumbled out of bed and sent shrieking down the stairwell in her nightfrock, convinced of an earthquake, just as the first bikers swarmed past in their goose-pimpled, genital-beribboned glory. Days elapsed before anyone realized there'd actually *been* an explosion.

The second bomb went off near Fisherman's Wharf in the middle of the night, in the exact spot where that half-senile bookwagon man tried to open a Left Bank-style antiquarian stall in the shadows of the shuttered Barnes and Noble. It was during the next day's investigation that someone finally realized that the old card-catalogue notecards scattered amid the refuse in both locations weren't debris. Were, in fact, messages. From the bombers.

The notecards really had come from some long-extinct branch of the San Francisco Public Library. The book titles on the fronts of the cards seemed random, at first—*Insects Do the Strangest Things,* Ferlinghetti's *Love in the Days of Rage*—until police found the one marked *Tom "the Bomb" Tracy and the Play that Shook San Francisco.* Only then did some bright young sergeant think to flip the cards over, take another look at that seemingly innocuous stamp on the back: *Property of the Library.*

We'd heard about the Library before then, of course. Seen their self-proclaimed leader standing on his milk-crate under the Clocktower on weekday evenings. With his goatee and his stick-figure legs and his bleat of a voice, he reminded some of Satan, and some of Pan. We'd seen his followers, too. Most were dropouts from the gutted comp-lit program at San Francisco State, plus some runaways and junkies, all of them sallow, lurking around the book depots near Hunter's Point and Potrero Hill. It was their uniform appearance that first marked them: tan overcoats, the pockets stuffed with moldy hardbacks scavenged from the depots; black, rubber sandals; gaunt faces; most of all, that paper-white skin tone, those eyes blinking fast even against the lights from street-lamps, which drove some online wag to name them Morlocks.

And yet, somehow, it hadn't occurred to us to fear them until that moment. Within hours of the bright young sergeant's discovery, a SWAT team and the entire Homeland Security unit of the Bay Area Police descended upon Library headquarters en masse, arresting everyone in sight and dragging Erick Kinney, who'd taken to calling himself the Librarian, out of the group's warehouse headquarters before rapt television cameras in handcuffs and ankle-chains.

"Do you have any comment?" one reporter yelled as Kinney was hustled past.

And Kinney had somehow dragged himself to a stop. One hand lifted against the glare of the lights, narrow eyes stutter-blinking, satyr-goatee wagging in the misting rain, Manson-smile dancing across his face. "Book 'em, Danno," he'd said. Then he was shoved forward into a squad car.

But despite a furious three-day search involving several dozen officers, the police found nothing more incriminating than a few small baggies of hash scattered amid the dust and food scraps and sleeping-mats and piles of reclaimed, moldering books in the warehouse. Late on a Sunday evening, to none of the fanfare with which he had been arrested, Erick Kinney was returned to his cavernous home and his adoring disciples.

The next bombing, of the rug store that had once housed the legendary Allen Ginsburg/Gary Snyder Six Gallery reading, was bigger. It blew out windows more than a block away and maimed a security guard who'd unexpectedly returned to his post to get his coffee thermos. This time, bomb crews confiscated every mat and scavenged book, testing repeatedly for explosive residue while BATF officials on loan from Washington grilled the whole group. That investigation, too, turned up nothing. There was talk of holding Erick Kinney as an enemy combatant, and also of condemning the so-called Library and driving all of Kinney's followers onto the streets.

Gradually, though, over a period of weeks, the investigation lost momentum. And with virtually all of San Francisco's bookstores now closed, and the libraries long-since eliminated or reduced to weekend hours, the bombings ceased, and the city and Erick Kinney seemed to reach an uneasy peace. Police still kept the building under surveillance. And Kinney still showed up from time to time on his street-corner at dusk, looking more pathetically thin and less threatening with each appearance. He bleated away, regaling tourists and passers-by with his agitprop poems about rotting fruit and dead brain cells. Sometimes people tossed coins at his feet.

Meanwhile, the depots swelled with unwanted books, and the Morlocks from the Library took them over, combing the rows and rows of paperbacks, occasionally spiriting away volumes to their warehouse. And Erick Kinney joined the Naked Bike Paraders and the Beatniks and Emperor Norton on the roll-call of San Francisco's legendary utopian cranks, forever hearkening back to an age few of them actually believed had existed, or else heralding a new dawn even fewer thought would ever come.

AFTER-WORDS

Aaron came back on a damp, foggy night in early June. I'd just shown Mrs. Morton out the clinic's front door. She'd cursed my name, spit on the linoleum in the waiting room, and rebuffed my offer to walk her to the bus. I stood under the dripping overhang anyway and watched her edge down the block, through the swarms of homeless people already emerging out of the mist to perch against the shuttered windows of the shelter next door, even though dinner wasn't for over an hour yet. She didn't actually need the motorized wheelchair I'd offered to make Medicaid provide for her yet. And the drugs she'd begged me for, weeping, gripping my lab-coat in her clawed hands, might actually have helped, if only temporarily.

But she wouldn't have been able to take the drugs anyway. Her dealer-grandson would have ripped them from her hands the second she got back to her one-room apartment. Maybe he wouldn't kill her for not coming home with them. Some of my patients' grandsons let them live.

Retreating inside, I locked the door, making straight for my sanctuary in the back. I did notice, as I turned the knob, that the lights were already on, reprimanded myself for the waste and in the same moment realized I *hadn't* left them on, and the shadow separated from the shelves along the back wall and lurched toward me.

Gasping, I stumbled back, tripping toward the nearest examination room so I could lock myself in. Hands grabbed me around both shoulders and spun me around.

"Aunt A., it's me," he said.

I recognized the voice instantly, of course. But he was backlit by the lamp in my sanctuary. And his presence was so unexpected, and I'd dreamed of it for so hopelessly long, that it still took me a moment to understand what was happening.

"*Aaron?*"

My hands flew up automatically to hug him, pull his face to my shoulder, but he flinched back. I stared at him, silhouetted against my bookcases. There were flakes of what looked like sawdust in his hair, and the grit on his hands and throat had thickened and coagulated into little black spider-shapes. I imagined them scurrying up his sleeves, down his collarbone into the drooping neck of his threadbare sweatshirt. Tears welled in my eyes.

"You look filthy," I said. "Happy birthday."

He flinched again, ran a shaky hand through his mess of dark curls.

"Aaron, my god, are you alright?"

"You still remember my birthday?"

The fury that had also been massing these last four years, ever since he'd walked out of his father's life and mine, erupted from me. "If you were dead a hundred years, I'd remember your birthday, you stupid, selfish—"

"You're not my mother, Aunt A."

"I'm not your aunt, either. So just A. Okay?"

Squinting his eyes, he looked at me, in that wondrous way he'd had even when I'd first met him, when he was three years old. A gaze so quiet it could lure mice from their hiding places, baby oak trees from their acorns. That's how I'd put in the bedtime stories I used to tell him when he was four and five, during the years I'd lived with and almost won the love of his recently widowed, lost, marvelous father. The saddest, best years of my life.

"Go wash your face," I said, and felt myself smile. "Your hands, too. No touching my books with those hands."

I got just a ghost of a smile. He moved off toward the bathroom, limping visibly, and twice he had to put his hands out to steady himself against the wall. *What had they done to him in the goddamn Library?* The home he'd traded his life and my love and his father's love for.

Out of habit, I went to the shelves, trailed my fingers along the spines. The sagas-and-wonders section, Norse gods and *Kwaidan* and Pu Songling. Because they'd always been Aaron's favorites, back when he'd still stopped here on his way home from school and let me read to him. And because this was clearly a night for fox spirits and changelings: fog in summer; my patients spitting curses; Aaron coming back.

Through a fresh swell of tears, I realized I'd better call Oliver, let him know his son was alive. I took a step toward my desk and Aaron reappeared in the doorway.

"Well?" he said.

In truth, he looked better than I'd worried he would. He was gaunt, alright, still grit-encrusted everywhere but his face and hands, pasty in that trademark Library way. But his hair, though filthy, shone its familiar, lustrous black, and his dark eyes still flashed with mischief-specks of hazel and green. Fox-spirit eyes, alright.

"I'm calling your dad."

"What for?"

"To tell him you're alright, what do you think?"

"What makes you think he gives a shit?"

"Aaron, you can't really think—"

"More to the point, what makes you think he wants to hear it from you? God, I've never understood it. Why are you still friends with him. Why did you let him treat you like that?"

"What? Aaron, you don't know anything about it. And it was a long time ago. I still care—"

"I need your help," he said, and one of his legs quivered visibly, and he almost fell down.

Dropping the phone, I moved fast around my desk, put my hand to his cheek, then pulled him against me. "You've got a fever."

He pushed me away, steadied himself. "Not me," he murmured. Then he looked me up and down. "You're looking pretty undernourished yourself, Aunt A." Another ghost-smile.

I couldn't tell if he was concerned or teasing, and I didn't care. "Then let's go eat. Saigon Sandwich Shop. When's the last time? I'll get my coat."

"I need you to come to the Library," he said, and the hope I'd almost allowed myself froze in my chest.

"Aaron," I started, after a few silent moments, "I can't—"

"Oh, don't start, Aunt A. Christ, sometimes you really are like him." The contempt in his voice hit me like spittle. "I'm not asking you to join. Or to do anything that might help the cause. It's not like either you or my father understand about why saving books from extinction might be worth fighting for or anything, how could you?" He flung a single, ironic wave toward my shelves.

"So why are we going there?" I said.

"Because he's sick."

"Who's sick?"

"Erick Kinney."

Whatever else I'd meant to say evaporated from my lips. "The *Librarian,* Erick Kinney?"

After-Words

"Yes, The Librarian Erick Kinney. He's really sick. I mean, a lot of us are sick. Bad flu bug or something. But he's all twisted up. I think he's going to die."

For a long moment, I just looked at him. My long-ago almost-stepson. The closest I was ever likely to get, now, to an actual son. Once upon a time—not so long ago—when he'd still wanted me in his life, that had seemed very nearly enough.

"I'll get my coat and my keys," I said.

"You can't take your car down there. To the Library. It's not safe."

"My Saturn? Too yellow, you think?"

"Jesus Christ, that's still your car? What is it, twenty years old? Aren't you a doctor?"

"Probably still got the dirt from our Sequoia trip."

"The one we took when I was twelve?"

"You'll find it under the dirt from the decade since then."

"We can take that car," Aaron said. This time, his smile was bright and unexpected and gentle. I was so grateful that I almost cried out, but controlled myself.

He leaned his head back, rolled it very slowly around his shoulders, stopped halfway with a wince.

"Are you alright, Aaron?"

"Get your keys."

"I'm getting you antibiotics, too."

"Later."

The homeless had already gone in to dinner, and the smell of burnt tomatoes and chicken grease wafted from the doors of the shelter. From somewhere not far, metal clanged, but we were the only things moving on the entire block. All around us, forever leaning and tilting on its hills, San Francisco rode the waves of marine layer like a fishing trawler.

"Isn't it a little bright yet for Morlocks?" I teased. "Moon might still peek through."

"Funny, Aunt A."

He kept putting his hands in the small of his back, stretching. Once, stumbling on a raised square of sidewalk, he unleashed a violent, unintentional grunt.

"Aaron, what's wrong? Come on, seriously. Are you really sick? Let me help." We'd reached my car, and I watched him ease in, tilting sideways to keep his back straight.

Once settled, he glanced up. "It's just from Crawling. You know, around the book depots. Occupational hazard."

And badge of distinction, apparently. "Bay Bridge Base, right? Somewhere down there?"

Traffic proved predictably dismal. Wisps of fog drifted through the dead ducts of my Saturn's fan, floating between and around us. I couldn't decide whether I was warm or cold, and didn't care. We didn't speak. It felt as though we'd cast ourselves adrift, floated into the bay. I kept my eyes on the road and hoped we'd never arrive.

But all too soon, as we reached the empty warehouses and glass-strewn lots of the wasteland under the Bay Bridge, Aaron began pointing me to the right. Then to the left. I saw the building before he told me to stop, recognizing it from newspaper photographs.

"That's it, isn't it?" I cut the engine, let the car drift to a stop against a curb that in classic Frisco fashion wasn't long enough even for my Saturn. Somehow, I suspected the parking patrol wouldn't be by. I pointed toward the mottled, rectangular gray and green warehouse, hunched between two much larger derelict structures on either side. "That's the Library."

"There's no place like home," Aaron said quietly. Lovingly. "There's no place like home. There's no place like home."

"Stop it," I told him. "You sound—"

"Brainwashed? Isn't that what you think I am? What we all are? SLA'd? Jonestowned?"

"Well? Are you?"

Aaron just pushed open his door, grimacing as he pulled himself from the car. "Come and see."

The fog felt warmer, here, almost fetid. It had been such a strange, damp summer. The street was devoid not only of people but other cars. A few blocks to the right, just visible through the mist, the glassy towers of the latest Rincon Hill revitalization project blazed like great, blue lighthouses. They were mostly empty, too, I knew. Prospective renters had vanished with the housing bust.

After-Words

"I'm going to have to blindfold you so you don't see the secret knock," Aaron said.

"You try it, I'm gone," I told him.

"Kidding, Aunt A. Gullible as ever, I see." He put an arm around my shoulder, squeezed me. "I've missed you," he said.

Through new tears, I watched him scoop a handful of pebbles off the curb and pitch them at the lowered, metal door of the Library. The clatter they made seemed farther away than it should have, like children's footsteps racing around a corner.

Nothing moved or changed. The fog had a stench, here, to go with its disconcerting warmth: cat urine, old tar, mold.

"Maybe they didn't teach *you* the secret knock," I said.

The Library door hoisted itself slowly open.

It was like a cave. No overhead lights. Just a few glimmers floating in what appeared to be a single, cavernous room. No one moving. Fingers of fog began to walk up my back.

"Aaron, why did you bring me here?"

He looked genuinely surprised. "I told you why."

"I just want to make this clear. Whatever rejection you're imagining, it was all on your side, at least as far as I'm concerned, I can't speak for your dad. You hear me? I love you."

"I know you love me, Aunt A. I love you, too."

"But I reject this."

"You don't know anything about this."

"I reject brilliant young people living in rank poverty as some transcendent, subversive statement against the status-quo. I reject malnourishment-by-choice. I reject wasted time. I reject bombing."

"Not one person has been hurt. Not one, except that guard, and he wasn't supposed to be there, and even he only lost a couple fingers."

I turned, mouth agape. He looked away.

"Someone has to fight, Aunt A. Someone has to stand up and say, you can't just take it all. We want it back. We'll *take* it back."

He moved off, shoulders rigid, head rolling again around his neck. The shadows swallowed him. I hurried and caught up.

As I soon as I was through the door, I realized it wasn't actually dark in there. Every twenty feet or so, all the way to the back where some towering red curtains had been suspended from the ceiling, kerosene lanterns balanced precariously on old camera tripods. At the foot of each tripod, arrayed in a sort of daisy-petal shape, lay four or five blue tumbling mats, the kind one finds in elementary school gyms. Stuffing bulged from rents in their vinyl covering, and they seemed to be sagging into the cement. Most were unoccupied.

But not all. As we continued forward, I saw occasional, curled shapes draped in shabby overcoats or humped up under some other improvised covering. I even glimpsed a few faces. Most of those were young. Late teens. Twenty-somethings. The great majority male, almost all of them prostrate. Some were sleeping or staring blank-eyed into the shadows spread like spider webs across the length of the ceiling, their heads sinking into moldy mounds of paperback books, their legs curled up underneath or folded over each other, as if they'd been frozen in the midst of a long-form yoga exercise.

The ones who weren't sleeping were reading, tilting books toward the nearest kerosene lantern. No one spoke. No one looked up at Aaron or accosted me. Shuddering, I realized the place really did feel like a library. Kind of. Certainly, it was nowhere to raise one's voice or shout hello.

"How many of you did you say there were?" I whispered.

"I didn't. I don't even know for sure. People come and go."

I was relieved to hear that, anyway. Also glad that as yet, no one had hoisted himself off his or her mattress and pulled the door down behind us.

"Not a single one of you knows how to dust? Wield a mop? You lie down in this? It's not sanitary."

"Aunt A., have you seen your car?"

Not quite like a library, I thought. All the way back to the curtains, I tried to place the sensation, and then I had it: it was like a Natural History Museum diorama. Something you'd see between the Cro-Magnon room and the Animals of North America hallway. The Reading Chamber. *Look now, children. See those things in their hands? They called those 'books.' See how still they all are? This is what it was like…*

Glancing behind me, I was startled to find that the outside door had been drawn down after all. And yet, the only thing moving in the whole expanse was lantern-light dancing down wicks, spinning shadows

After-Words

through the dust. A few mats away from where I now stood, someone coughed. Someone else whimpered.

The curtains hung in a circular ring suspended fully fifteen feet off the ground. Not until we were right in front of them did I hear the voice.

There really was something goat-like about its quaver, its nagging, monotonous bleat. It wasn't soothing, and it wasn't friendly. And it almost yanked me through the curtains.

"*Then the butterfly stamped…*"

"Aaron, don't," I said suddenly, but too late. He'd already pulled back the curtain.

I don't know what I was expecting. A throne, maybe. A white orgy-couch straight out of *Caligula*. The Wizard, working levers.

The first startling thing was how many of them there were. Twenty, at least, maybe more, all seated in a rude semi-circle, tilting against one another or else stretched lengthwise on the filthy floor mats. None of these people was sleeping, and not a one so much as glanced around. Except the Librarian.

He was hunched almost double on top of a stool. The lantern at his feet cast a reddish glow up the side of his face, which made him look less Satanic than molten. His eyes were small, yellowish-brown, and after lingering on mine for an uncomfortable few seconds, they drifted to Aaron.

"I told you, no doctors," he said, in the same bleat he'd used for reading.

"I brought one anyway," said Aaron. "This is—"

"Your not-Aunt Ariel. Yes."

"You're going to like her, Erick. She's not much for taking shit. Even from people she likes. And I doubt she'll like you much."

There it was again. The ghost of Aaron's smile. I grabbed for his hand, squeezed it, and felt him suck in a sharp breath.

"Sorry," I murmured.

Erick Kinney stared me up and down. Everything about him, from the blades of his shoulders to his drawn-up knees to his hawk's beak of a nose, looked pointy. If he'd had antennae, he could have passed for a grasshopper.

"Aaron, maybe we should go," I said.

Abruptly, the Librarian smiled. Except for the lantern light in his teeth, it was just an ordinary smile. A lopsided and tired one.

"You think you can help? Doctor? Solve the mystery?"

"You mean, How the Morlocks got their limp?"

The Librarian's smile widened. Which made it look more lopsided, something sketched with a crayon by a six year-old. "Well. Alright, then. Make way, boys and girls. The doctor's come to tell us a story."

I shook my head. "Not here."

That gave him pause, briefly, and I wondered when he'd last left the Library. Certainly, there hadn't been any news footage of him recently. His bony fingers trailed over the pages of the chipped, cracked Kipling from which he'd been reading, probing into the crease of the binding and scratching softly at the words on the page, as though he were petting a cat.

"Then Brother Aaron will finish tonight's reading," he said, and held up the book. "Make sure each of you gives it a goodnight kiss."

He didn't so much stand as slump forward off the stool. Very slowly, clearly in pain, he straightened. His right arm dangled, and he dragged his right leg behind him as though he were some Dickens character with a club foot. His ailment was exaggerated, I was certain. Also clearly real.

"Aaron, please tell me you'll come again," I said. "Tomorrow. The next day. Please."

He turned, and in that one moment I forgot where I was, forgot the light and the bombings and everything else except the love I was never going to lose for this boy.

"Soon, Aunt A. You owe me a birthday sandwich."

I don't know why it seemed so important to keep Erick Kinney from seeing me cry. Spinning away fast, I walked straight across the warehouse and out of the Library. Once back in my car, I sat in the driver's seat with the door open to the fetid fog, waiting for the Librarian to make his slow way out of the world he'd created and into mine.

Seated on my examination table in a backless paper gown in the ruthless fluorescent light, Erick Kinney looked no less pointy. His sallow skin seemed stretched too thin, and his dirty blond hair fell in scraggles to his shoulders. His satyr-goatee dangled listlessly off his chin. Except for the

After-Words

angry red rash spreading up his back and curling into his ribs, the man was almost entirely bones and hair. A talking owl-pellet.

Or, not talking, as had been the case since the moment we'd reached the clinic. "Are you in pain?" I asked, arranging implements on my little pull-cart next to the table.

As I moved about the room, I could feel his gaze, but every time I looked up, his eyes were aimed past me, out the door and across the hall. At my bookshelves, I realized.

"You're not answering," I said.

"You're not actually asking," said the Librarian. No smile creased his face, but something flickered in his eyes. Whatever it was, it was hard to look away from.

"Hold still," I told him. "Say aah." I stuck a swab in his throat.

He had his knees open, so I had to stand between them. Up close, he appeared even more grizzled, with little hairs sprouting from virtually every pore. He was also looking right at me, now. There was a *draw* to him, alright. I could feel it in my knees and under the soles of my feet, like an undertow. I held the swab in place a split second longer than I usually do. I think I wanted to see him gag.

He just sat there. Shoulders hunched, eyes dancing.

As soon as I removed the swab, he asked, "Can I look at your books?"

I held up the blood-pressure sleeve. Sighing, he extended his bony arm. In the end, I had to get the child-sleeve to fit him. I was squeezing the bulb, pressing the bell of my stethoscope into the crook of his elbow, when he said, "Is he really that stupid?"

I kept my attention on the pressure gauge as it nudged up, plunged down. "Which 'he' would that be?"

"Aaron's father. For not marrying you."

When I just ripped the Velcro open and removed the sleeve, he laughed. "No mock outrage? No *how-dare-me*? No *how-much-has-Aaron-told-you*? Oh, you're one of mine, alright."

"Hold out your hand," I said, separating the tiny needle from its sterilizing bag. "I'll try to get enough from your finger. I don't need much."

"Blood from a stone."

"A suddenly talkative stone." I jabbed the needle down, watched the blood well vibrant red in the yellow light. He stayed silent as I collected

221

droplets. Somehow, his silence made me more nervous than his chatter did, so I asked, "What else has Aaron said?"

"That you're my kind of doctor."

"Meaning?"

"You serve the people who need serving, not the people who can pay. You read every spare second of your life. You don't judge anyone, except sometimes Aaron."

"I don't judge Aaron. Except about bombing. Want to talk about involving idealistic young people who damn near worship you in bombing, since we're talking?"

"That you keep yourself to yourself, because deep down you know that's not only for the best, it's better."

It was his voice as much as his words, that grated in my ears and all over my skin. That bleat, sharp and quavery, too raw, like notes struck on a ruined piano with the lid thrown open. Or vocal chords with no sheath of skin. I had a momentary but powerful impulse to strap this Morlock, or faux-Weather Undergrounder, or whatever he was, to the examination table, rush back to the warehouse, roust the rest of them, and light the whole place on fire. Bring Aaron home.

"You can look at the books, now," I said, pushing a hard breath through my teeth. "I'll just be a minute. A couple more tests, and I'll run you back."

"So you're going to discover what's wrong with us?" he said, sliding off the table, the gown slipping up his thighs as he landed, too close to me. He wasn't attractive. Just…*present*. In a way I'd almost forgotten people could be.

"I'm concerned that I already know," I said, making myself look away, but not before I saw him startle. "You're going to need a spinal tap to confirm. It's going to hurt."

"What do you know?" he said quietly.

"Your joints hurt, yes?"

"All the time."

"Your back?"

"All the time."

"That rash been there long?"

"A while."

After-Words

"Fever?"

"It comes and goes. Or, it came and it went."

"Diarrhea?"

"Some. Yes."

"Tired a lot?"

He didn't answer that.

"I'll need a stool sample before you go. Bad luck living where you live. By the water, I mean. Especially this particular summer. With all the mosquitoes. This isn't just about you, by the way, and I'm not giving you a choice. I think you've got West Nile, and I'm going to contact the CDC, and they're going to make good and damn sure you get checked."

I was in the process of turning away, and almost missed his grin. My limbs had become heavy, as though Erick Kinney had poured concrete into them in the seconds we'd been standing there.

"West Nile Virus," he said. "Imagine that."

"Bound to happen here sooner or later. And given where you live, and the filthy way you keep yourselves…"

Without bothering with his pants or his socks, he lurched out of the examination room and across the hall into my office.

"There's no cure yet," I called after him, wanting him to turn around. Wanting him not to touch my books. I didn't trust him in there. Which wasn't rational, wasn't like me. I closed my eyes and ground my teeth and held on to the cool metal of my push cart and opened my eyes again. "But there's plenty that can be done to ease the symptoms. Unless it turns into encephalitis or meningitis or something more serious, it's not going to kill you."

"That's what they told my father," Erick Kinney said dreamily, one long finger trailing across the decaying spines of my Hawthornes. Coming to rest for a moment on the fat, green bulk of my Robert Burton. My favorite books. He'd gone right to them. *Contaminated them.*

Which was ridiculous. Juvenile. Stupid.

"Your father had West Nile? What are you talking about? We just discovered it, and by the way, it's not inheritable, and—"

"No, no," he said. "I know. Just chatting. It's rare I find someone worth having a chat with."

"I have to tell you something else, I'm afraid."

"Anything," he bleated. "Lay it on me, Doc."

"The rest of them. Your...whatever you call them. Followers."

"Friends?"

"They're not your friends," I snapped.

He swung his head around. There was that grin again. "No? I suppose not."

"They're going to have be tested, too. Immediately, do you hear? Their lives could depend on it. And this could spread fast."

"Not inheritable, you say," he half-sang, to himself. "In a way, I suppose you're right."

"Hello? Mr. Kinney? I'm telling you you need to help me. You've got to get your people help. This is serious."

He shrugged. "One already died."

I almost dropped the materials I'd been bagging. Stepping into the hall, I felt that new heaviness again in my limbs. On my tongue. It was hard to speak.

"Died? Died how?"

"Couldn't breathe. Clenched up. As far as we could tell."

"You didn't send him for help? You didn't do anything for him?"

"Her. And you seem to have a mistaken impression of the way the Library works, my dear doctor. My personal physician, from here on out. I'm not their emperor. I'm not Jim Jones. I'm certainly not their prison guard. She could have strolled out the front door anytime she liked." For a moment, he stood still, hunched over my desk, the fingers of his right hand straying up and down the spine of *The Anatomy of Melancholy*.

Then he grinned again. "Lurched out, I mean."

My mouth opened. Closed. I wanted to run. Couldn't remember how to move.

"You don't love them," I whispered.

"Good god, of course I don't love them. What's to love? I love the *idea* of them, though. The Avenging Booklovers' Army. An all new branch of the ABA. Isn't that what we do, after all? You and me? We always love the idea of them."

I couldn't speak. Didn't need to. He might as well have been back on his milk crate under the Clocktower, now, except that he was talking only to me. That was part of the secret, I realized. Part of his power. He always seemed to be talking only to the person right in front of him.

"Take an achievement like this," he said, and lifted *The Anatomy of Melancholy* off my shelf, gently, with his crooked hands. It was a 1920s one-volume edition, gilt-lettered, heavy. If it dropped on him, I thought, it would crush him like a cockroach.

"Be careful with that," I said pointlessly.

"Perhaps the greatest act of understanding—no, more than that, of creative insight—no, more than that, too…of *empathy* ever attempted. A complete parsing of the weight every single human being feels, no matter where they're from or what they achieve or whose love they attain, from the moment they draw breath until the moment they cease to do so." He had the book open now, turning his hands this way and that so that every square of inch of his skin brushed the pages, as though he were performing an ablution in holy water.

"Books like this. The greatest tools the supposedly magnificent human animal has ever come up with for transcending its own skin and inhabiting another's…but they can only be used, appreciated, or created when one is alone. There is no literary irony greater than that of the medium itself."

"I'll take that stool sample, now," I said.

He sighed. And then he actually *tsked*. But his fingers lifted away from my book.

"I'll put it back," I told him. *Because I didn't want him touching it anymore.*

"Too late. You've already opened it. Already shown it to your precious…stepson? Ward? Anyway, once that's done, you've left him wide open." He was out of my office now, passing uncomfortably close (*because I couldn't seem to step back*) as he took the collection kit from my limp hands and made for the bathroom.

"Open to what?" I asked. Not wanting to know, helpless to keep quiet.

His smile was different, now. Slow. Self-satisfied. "To every little germ of an idea. Everything we decide we are going to refuse to burn or bury as instructed."

The moment he was out of sight, I forced myself to walk. I went into the examination room, labeled vials, bound everything together, entered notations on the computer. Then I grabbed my keys, shut out the lights, and made for the front door.

"Just leave the kit on the exam table," I called into the silence. "I'll be out front. I'll drive you home."

He wasn't long. And I was relieved to find that on the sidewalk, in the night air, my limbs felt lighter, and they moved when I told them to. Erick Kinney stopped talking until long after we were in the car, down the hill, almost all the way back to the Library. If the radio had worked, I would have turned it up as loud as it would go. I was practically pressed up against the driver's-side door by the time we reached the street of warehouses. He just sat, hunched, pallid, breathing in quick pants like a coyote.

"You know, my father didn't particularly like Hawthorne," he murmured as I pulled my Saturn to the curb. From the pensive way he stared into the fog, he almost seemed to be reading it. "It's just what they sent him. That summer."

"I like Hawthorne," I said.

"Me, too."

"His Veiled Lady."

"His men 'of shabby appearance, met in an obscure part of the street.'" He plucked at his own shabby jeans, turned to me, and through the goatee, under the corpse-like pallor, I glimpsed something. Thought I did. "You should really come in," he said. "Veiled Lady."

And I felt myself stir. Start to unlock my door. For Aaron, I was thinking. Just to get Aaron. Then I was gripping the door handle. Holding on.

"Get them to doctors, Mr. Kinney," I said. "Tomorrow. I'll be back with the police to check."

I wanted him to grin again. His grin scared me. And his shrug made me furious. Fear and fury would keep me nailed where I was. Instead, of course, he sat there reading my face, the way he had the fog. The way he did the whole world. "Goodnight, Personal Physician," he said.

Then he was out of my car, lurching across the street, and Aaron was emerging from the doorway where he'd clearly been waiting, throwing an arm around his mentor's shoulders to help him back to his Library. And I was all but gunning the engine as I turned around, floored the accelerator, and got the hell out of there.

After-Words

I should have gone home. I didn't generally spend much time in my apartment, passed my after-clinic hours eating out or walking the Castro or over to Haight, sometimes seeing concerts or movies but often just haunting the blocks where the used bookshops used to be, and which still retained their traces. I should have done that then.

Instead, I went back to the clinic, figuring I needed to work. Get my brain clear. Get the reek of Erick Kinney out of it. I put *The Anatomy of Melancholy* back in the gaping space it had left on my shelf. I did data entry and paperwork for a while. I ordered out for pad thai and turned on the radio. Eventually, I lay back in my reclining armchair and turned out the lights and let the sounds of my street seep into the room. That far-off clanging, as though something were always being built nearby, just around the next corner, but I could never find it. Occasional stumbling footsteps or slurred shouts from a homeless person or a drunk. That faint echo passing cars leave in fog. My nighttime companions for so long.

Is he really that stupid, the bastard had asked. Damn right, too. Why had Oliver let me go? I'd never understood. Aaron hadn't either, he'd been furious even at five. The last thing I'd ever wanted, to come between the two of them. And I'd never quite gotten past it all either, apparently.

Very early—too early—I'd settled on this image of myself. The creature in the clinic. The Veiled Lady. Alone with her spells, her private regrets. Why had I done that?

I closed my eyes and tried to sleep. But what I saw was the Librarian's wagging beard, his satyr-grin. And what I heard was that bleat, reverberating inside my head. *Burn or bury. That summer.* His panting breath, his crooked hands. *That's what they told my father. That summer.* His followers arrayed around him in the Library, like broken pieces of a model. Kissing the decrepit book he read them. *How the Morlocks got their limp. The germ of an idea. That summer.*

I sat bolt upright, mouth open, grabbing so hard at the chain for the lamp beside my chair that I knocked the whole lamp over, heard the bulb smash on the floor. I stood, the fragments grinding to dust under my soles.

"Jesus Christ," I said aloud. The words small and useless in my useless little room.

Hurrying into the hall, I flipped on every light in the clinic, as though that would help. As though light would make any difference. *It's crazy*, I was thinking. *A night terror. A fog phantom.* I grabbed Erick Kinney's kit out of my drawer anyway, removed the throat swab from its vial, took it upstairs to the little lab I'd built myself, as a hobby, mostly, over the lonely years.

It took me all of three minutes to find it. It was right there for all to see who cared to look. Impossible to miss. I checked the stool sample, too, though I didn't need to. The cells looked different than the ones in my Epidemiology 101 textbook twenty years ago. Had to be different, had to be a brand new strain, after all. But they were unmistakable, all the same. The Scourge of Summer, risen from the dead.

All the way down the hill toward the Bay, I worked it over in my head. Tried to convince myself it was impossible. Then I gave that up and worked on figuring out how it had happened, instead. *How had I even known?*

But I had the answer to that one. I'd figured it out the same way I'd figured out virtually everything I knew: I'd read it somewhere. God knows where. Retained it somehow. Those summers. Those damp, terrifying Julys and Augusts, when families fled the beaches. When parents kept their children indoors, away from their friends, and prayed the killer in the streets would sweep past them. When kindhearted librarians assembled bundles of books from the shelves and sent them in pouches to the already-afflicted, the ones who'd been quarantined, so they'd have something to do to pass the hours while their muscles withered and their lungs froze and they slowly, slowly strangled. The pouches all came with little candies, a card full of get well wishes, and a letter of instruction asking that the books not be returned. That they be burned, or buried, just in case polio really could linger on the pages.

Erick Kinney was seated by himself on the sidewalk outside the Library. The door had been yanked shut. I moved straight past him, kicked repeatedly at the metal. The sound boomed and rolled like thunder. No one came.

"They're gone," the Librarian said, after the echoes from my volley of kicks finally subsided.

After-Words

I looked down. "Gone?"

That grin. Horrible. Lopsided. "Every. Last. One."

My mouth fell open, and I sank to my knees. I would have grabbed the door if there'd been anywhere to grab. I stared straight into the flicker in his eyes. "You *know*," I said.

"Well of course I know."

"How did you know? Weren't you vaccinated?"

"I was indeed. Alarming, no? And that's not even the most fascinating part."

His words, in that goat-voice, buzzed in my ears, seemed to set my brain vibrating so that I couldn't answer, couldn't even remember how to speak.

"The fascinating part—the real poetry, if you'll forgive me—is where I think it came from." And from his lap, he lifted the Kipling book. Held it out to me.

"Your father's," I mumbled.

He nodded. "They thought they were going to have to put him in an iron lung, but they didn't, quite. He just lost the use of his arms. And one leg. He really should have burned this, don't you think? And yet, how wonderful that he didn't."

"It's…" My brain cleared. I sucked fog deep into my lungs. "That's absurd. Impossible. A virus can't live on a page. Not for fifty seconds, let alone fifty years."

"Impossible. Sure. But what other explanation could there be? And just think, Veiled Lady. Personal Physician to the Library. What if it's true? What was our virus doing, all these long years, with no one to hold it, no one to play with? All curled up in a book? What sort of bedtime stories do you think a virus tells itself?"

He was rambling again, off on one of his milkcrate rants. I just sagged against the metal doors, momentarily stunned to helplessness.

"I've been imagining one," he said. "Want to hear it? It's not so different than any of the stories any living thing tells: *'Once upon a time, I got out. I got free. I sailed the summer wind. I met others, and fell in love. I leapt from island to island. I confronted my enemies, and laid them waste. I made more of me. I made more of me. I made more of me.'*"

"Gone," I said. "Meaning, you sent them out?"

He stopped talking, smiled that smile. "Sharing the good word. Like all proper Librarians before me."

My hands flashed out, grabbed his, yanked him sideways toward me. His squeal of pain was awful, pig-like, and satisfying.

"Did you tell them? You murdering, fucked-up son-of-a-bitch, did you tell them what they have?"

"The ones who wanted to hear. Mostly, I just said it was time to go see old friends. Go to the parks and teach the children."

"Jesus. Oh my God."

"Much better than bombing, don't you think? The ironies abound."

Tears blurred my eyes, ran in rivulets down my face. I kept his wrists clutched in mine. "Aaron. He's got it, too. What did you tell Aaron?"

"Well, Aaron's pretty special. As you know."

Absurdly, I felt myself nodding. My breath catching.

"A loving young man. And brave. And very angry. Mostly about what's happened to you."

I jerked his wrists. "Does he *know*?"

"He knows."

"And he went to 'spread the word'? To kill children? I don't believe it."

"Not at all," said Erick Kinney. And he smiled once more. "He said to tell you you were right. That it's long past time he went home to tell his idiot father exactly where he's been."

3/12

DISCARD

East Baton Rouge Parish Library
MAIN LIBRARY

DEMCO